HUNGER

Also by Erica Simone Turnipseed

A LOVE NOIRE

HUNGER

Erica Simone Turnipseed

AMISTAD
An Imprint of HarperCollinsPublishers

HarperCollins books may be purchased for educational, business, or sales promotional use. For information please write: Special Markets Department, HarperCollins Publishers, 10 East 53rd Street, New York, NY 10022.

FIRST EDITION

Designed by Susan Yang

Library of Congress Cataloging-in-Publication Data

Turnipseed, Erica Simone.
    Hunger : a novel / Erica Simone Turnipseed. — 1st ed.
      p. cm.
    ISBN-13: 978-0-06-079730-0
    ISBN-10: 0-06-079730-4
    1. African Americans—Fiction. I. Title.
  PS3620.U767H84 2006
  813'.6—dc22

                                       2006042742

06 07 08 09 10 BVG/RRD 10 9 8 7 6 5 4 3 2 1

For the cheering section—
on earth and in heaven—
and for Kevin

ACKNOWLEDGMENTS

An author gives birth to a book, but once it is born, it lives its own life, touching people the author may never meet. Such is the case with my first novel, *A Love Noire*. There were many wonderful people who brought it to their book clubs, alerted their alumni groups, fraternities, sororities, girlfriends, cousins, and coffee klatches so that they would all support my debut novel. And through my website and travel for the book, I learned that thousands of people felt passionate about the characters of *A Love Noire*. They encouraged me to follow their stories just a little longer. *Hunger* is the culmination of that journey.

Hunger is inspired by the stories we all live: of friends and families left behind in the wake of 9/11, of the women and men who make sense of struggle and loss in the virtual worlds of Web forums like that of the Preeclampsia Foundation as well as singles or grief or parenting sites. Some of those stories dovetail with mine, notably the loss of my daughter, Grace Ayodele Webb, due to the pregnancy-induced illnesses of HELLP syndrome and preeclampsia. And though I have been blessed with an exceptional friend, advocate, confidant, partner, and lover in my husband, Kevin Webb, I sympathize with the heartache of many of my contemporaries who seek lasting love in vain. I thank all of you for your stories, your generous spirits, and your encouragement of me as a writer.

I am very much in the debt of countless book clubs across the country, many more than I can name here. I highlight several that supported my book and e-mailed me often: Mahogany Book Club, Nubia Book Club, Passion 4 Reading Reviewers, RAWSISTAZ, ReadinColor Book Club, R.E.A.L. Reviewers, Sheer Renascence Book Club, SistaGirl Book Club, the Woman in Me Book Club, Sheila Saunders's book club, and Ambre Morley's fabulous group of sistas.

Additionally, I joined Sisters and Brothers of Hotlanta Book Club for an online chat, Kim Wright invited me to join the SABL Readers' meeting, Veronica Speaks of Talking Books, etc. coordinated a joint discussion with Sisters Are Reading, and Theo Perry and Derrill Harris brought me to Just Read the Damn Book, Book Club. I was honored to join Pamela Wilson, Angela Reid, and all of the wonderful women of Imani Literary Group as the featured author for their 2005 anniversary weekend. It was also my privilege to attend the 2003 National Book Club Conference, founded by Curtis Bunn, and meet still other book club members.

Dean Pamela George and everyone at the Afro-American Cultural Center at Yale provided several opportunities for me to present to students and fellow alumni alike. And the cyber communities of Black Ivy and the Yale Black Alumni Network, as well as the Black Ivy Alumni League, were equally supportive.

I am also in the debt of print and broadcast journalists who advocated for *A Love Noire,* from Patrik Henry Bass for *Essence* and Robert Fleming for *Black Issues Book Review* to Debra

Lewis for *People* magazine, Angela Ards for the *Village Voice*, Kimberly Allers for Fortune.com, and Nadira Hira for *Savoy*.

Special thanks to all of the readers of the *Atlanta Daily World* who voted to make me the Atlanta Choice Awards 2004 Author of the Year. And thanks as well to Carol Mackey of Black Expressions Book Club for featuring me in their newsletter.

I offer my heartfelt gratitude to the family and friends who continue to offer prayers and encouragement, notably my parents, Juanita and Alfred Turnipseed; brothers, Alfred Jr. and Tyrone; mother-in-law, Catherine Webb; special auntie-in-law, Doretha Webb; and Evelyn "Big Mama" Turnipseed; and the Women of Zebulun and the Emmanuel Baptist Church Women's Ministry. Hugs to the Gures, the Nelsons, the Bowens, and so many others.

And warmest thanks as well to the team: Dawn Davis, Rockelle Henderson, Gilda Squire, and Morgan Welebir of Amistad/HarperCollins, along with the designers, copy editors, and sales force who pour their expertise into making my books a success.

Hugs to Kelli Martin, Camille Collins, and Stacey Barney, as well as my wonderful agent and friend Nicholas Roman Lewis, for starting me on my way.

A special thank-you to Monique Greenwood and the Akwaaba Writers' Retreat staff at Akwaaba D.C. You provided me with a beautiful room of my own so I could write around the clock just when I needed it most. And thank you to Crystal Bobb-Semple for facilitating the connection.

I was pleased to meet the women of Spelman College as their "Urban Griot" thanks to Heather Ricks Scott. Special thanks to Brenda Greene of Medgar Evers College for her wonderful radio program *Writers on Writing*, the women of Go On Girl! Book Club, the Brooklyn Best Festival, and the *BET Nightly News* for its terrific "Book Bag" feature.

Thank you to the many, many wonderfully supportive authors I've met along the way, including Lori Bryant-Woolridge, Nick Chiles, Cora Daniels, Bridget M. Davis, Edwidge Danticat, Nikki Giovanni, Marita Golden, Lawrence Otis Graham, E. Lynn Harris, Donna Hemans, Travis Hunter, Yolanda Joe, Lisa Jones, Denene Millner, Joan Morgan, Tracy Price-Thompson, Shawn Stewart Ruff, April Sinclair, and Trisha R. Thomas.

A debt of gratitude to the bookstores that hand-sold my book and displayed it for months instead of weeks: Brownstone Books (Brooklyn, New York), Nubian Heritage (Brooklyn and Harlem, New York), Hue-Man Books (Harlem, New York), Karibu Books (Bowie, Maryland), Marcus Books (Oakland, California), Mothaland Books (Chicago, Illinois), Penn Bookstore (Philadelphia, Pennsylvania), Sibanye Inc. (Baltimore, Maryland), Sisterspace (Washington, D.C.), Vertigo Bookstore (College Park, Maryland), and the Yale Bookstore (New Haven, Connecticut), as well as countless staff at Barnes & Noble and Borders bookstores throughout the country.

To all of you who e-mailed from the United States, Côte d'Ivoire, Ghana, Nigeria, England, Ireland, and throughout the Caribbean, I say a most sincere thank you.

And all praise to God, from whom these and all blessings flow.

HUNGER

BEFORE

New York City
September 2000

Noire's gaze bounced between a triangle of activity: Arikè's grass-stained maternity wedding gown being scrubbed furiously by her mother, Arikè herself—clad only in pregnancy thongs—doing her best imitation of a yoga resting pose, her arms and legs spread wide across her bed, and Dennis polishing his brand-new wedding band with his Trinidad and Tobago T-shirt.

She knew it was time for her to leave. She had been happy to serve as Arikè's maid of honor but there was nothing else to do. She picked up her overnight bag, kissed Arikè on the forehead, and walked a mile to the Metro-North train station that would deposit her back in New York City. Thankfully, in less than twenty-four hours she would begin her own journey. Her apartment already sublet, she cringed at the thought of one more night on Jayna's living room floor. She had to leave; she didn't belong anywhere.

"I live alone. That hasn't always been easy to do. For just a single woman. . . ." Noire muttered the song along with Nina Simone, corrupting her melodic reflection into the dirge it was never meant to be. The voices that spoke rapid-fire Haitian Kreyòl around her in the JFK Airport terminal crept into the spaces of her and Nina's song, making it a lament for her current romantic prospects and a foretaste of her year in Haiti.

Noire knew she'd find little sympathy among her peers. Many doctoral candidates would kill for the high-profile fellowships she'd won to Curaçao and now to Haiti, not to mention her enviable position of being Bonita Fuentes's personal protégée. By the force of her own professional reputation, Bonita had thrust Noire into the academic limelight, and had managed to generate enough buzz about Noire to land her a coveted slot at the Comparative Literature Association's annual convention. But even as her professional star rose, her love life crashed and burned, starting with her breakup with Innocent in May—which hurt her as much for its necessity as the knowledge that he had already planned to do the same. So she filled the hole he left with other men's eager penises and her own obsession with her work and Bonita's good opinion of her.

It was a Monday afternoon, the eleventh of September, and Noire was marooned at the end of a three-hundred-person line that snaked in front of the American Airlines counter and nearly out the door. Apparently *everyone* had decided to come early, she noted with a sigh. The first song finished, Noire snickered at the next track coming from her CD player—"Lonesome Cities"—and wondered what Port-au-Prince, Haiti, would bring her.

She used her weight to move her luggage carrier, which represented everything that seemed important to her: the approved predoctoral prospectus that was the reason for her trip, and clothes, books, CDs, empty journals, and a year's supply of tampons, Renaissance Hairtopia hair oil, birth control pill packs, and condoms. The last two were more a matter of being a responsible woman than anything else, she reasoned, but the melancholy that melted over her heart and seeped into her loins assured her that she would indeed put them to use.

Her summer in Curaçao only three weeks behind her, she had been back in the States just long enough to wash her clothes, buy a Kreyòl-English dictionary and new dildo, and grow to hate Jayna's boyfriend of three and a half months with whom she now shared a midtown condo. Despite Noire's best efforts to see very little of him from her corner of the living room floor, she managed to see quite a lot when he "accidentally" walked into the kitchen naked, his physical assets in full view. Seemed that his lucrative career—as private banker to the newly rich and fabulous—hadn't earned him enough money to buy a robe. But Jayna claimed that she had never been happier, so Noire bit her lip. If well hung, nouveau riche, and arrogant were Jayna's criteria, she had found her ideal mate.

Her luggage at last checked, Noire flipped her backpack onto her back and headed for Voulez Vous, the only restaurant that promised a reprieve from the greasy fast food of the terminal. She tucked herself into a booth and placed her order. Once it arrived, she shoved her lukewarm dessert crepe into her mouth quicker than she could taste it and assumed the posture of eating alone: bag on the opposite seat, open magazine on table, gaze nonchalant, and body covering the space of a seat for two. Eating alone was another part of the daily routine that she had mastered and had even come to enjoy, as much for the anonymity as the people-watching and eavesdropping it offered.

The husky French of a woman's voice behind her captured her imagination. She attuned her mind to the language and processed the critical edge in her voice immediately. The respondent's voice, a man's, was lower, and reflected the reverence of one addressing an elder. She listened to his voice but missed his words, their timbre knitting together nausea and arousal at the bottom of her belly.

Noire gagged, then downed her entire glass of water before standing up. She left her meal and her bags in her booth and walked toward the voice she had loved and left. "Innocent." She declared his name as a form of greeting. She clutched the vinyl back of his companion's chair and looked at the face she had not seen since saying good-bye in the same terminal only four months before.

"*Mon Dieu,* Noire!" He sprang out of his seat and kissed her instinctually on both cheeks, tasting a new scent on them, before remembering to switch into English. "How are you? Why are you here? This is my mmu—mother." The last word tripped his tongue and forced his mouth closed. He was happy for the opportunity to gather his thoughts and merely extended his arm toward Maman as if to point her out.

Noire looked at the features that were the antecedent to all that she had come to delight in during her and Innocent's one-and-a-half-year relationship. His mother was a woman with a stern countenance and enduring beauty. Her skin the color and patina of well-aged ebony, she looked like the incarnation of triumph in a hard-won war.

"*Bonjour,* Madame Pokou." She inclined her head and offered her hand for the limp handshake she believed appropriate for the occasion. "*Je suis* Noire," she added, by way of explanation. Noire registered no recognition in his mother's eyes but decided that it must just be a cloak of formality. She pushed the corners of her lips into an obligatory smile and released her hand.

Madame Pokou offered the slightest nod of the head and said nothing.

Innocent read the vacancy in Maman's eyes and traced their gaze back to the confusion in Noire's. He prayed for his mother to feign knowledge of Noire and smile, but when she didn't, he distracted Noire with a lingering hand on her shoulder. "So, what brings you here?" He softened his gaze and remained standing so that Noire would not be alone.

"I won that predoctoral fellowship to go to Haiti."

"Oh, right." He bobbed his head for too long and looked off. "Already? I mean, twice in one year."

"Yeah. Bonita wanted to fast-track me."

"How was Curaçao?"

"Great."

"Great!" Innocent was afraid his grin was pulled too tight. He willed it to look more normal.

"And you? Off somewhere?" Noire heard her voice an octave higher than normal.

"We're going to France to visit my sister. You know, Charlotte." He nodded for Noire. "And Maman came here to see Mireille off. She just started at Howard University this fall."

"Oh yes, she did decide to go, after all." Noire's voice was flat, her remembrance of his anger at his baby sister's indecision about leaving Côte d'Ivoire for college in the States and the irony of his negative reaction to her decision to apply for the fellowship in Haiti.

"She just needed time," Innocent responded to Noire's thoughts.

"Mmm." Noire turned back toward Madame Pokou. "You must be so proud. Of your children." She spoke in the pleasantest, accented French she could and waited for more familiarity to cross her face. It didn't come.

"*Oui*" was Madame Pokou's only response.

"So, we were just getting a bite. We figured, let's arrive early. We had lots of baggage."

Noire missed her cue to speak, her eyes fixed upon Innocent's bottom lip that turned out in a way that always invited her to kiss it. She hated that it still moved her, and hated that Innocent could tell what she was staring at. She looked down.

Innocent felt his pores open up, unleashing perspiration from his forehead, armpits, and crotch. He let a bead of sweat roll down his leg and land in his sock before he said anything more. "When will you be back, Noire?"

"Exactly a year from now." Noire felt her nipples tighten into easily distinguishable points against her T-shirt. She pulled her jacket across her chest.

"Yeah, a whole year?! That's really something." He talked to himself because he didn't know what else to say to Noire. He willed his mind to fashion another question. Anything. "And so, how have things been going? I mean, with everyone."

"Arikè and Dennis got married yesterday. They're expecting in early January."

"Life just moves on. . . ." He clucked his tongue.

"Yeah . . ." Noire felt suddenly depressed, like sandbags were tied around her brain, dragging her thoughts into murky water. "So, I should finish my food."

"Please, can it be my treat?" He regretted his words immediately, but he couldn't retrieve them so instead he watched them hang in the air.

"No." She offered a tepid smile for him and his mother.

"Right . . . okay." He bobbed his head in understanding and endured the torrent of perspiration that emanated from his crotch and stung the flesh of his thighs. "Of course. Well, it was wonderful to see you. You look . . . *wonderful*. Have a safe trip." He kissed her on either cheek and remained standing until she walked back to her table. Noire felt his stare make mush of her belly. She dropped into her booth and stabbed the cold crepe in front of her.

Noire's rented cell phone vibrated on Pierre's nightstand. She pulled away from his body that had tensed in anticipation of the news to be delivered in a late-night call. Even though the New Year was five hours old, Pierre's instincts as a journalist for Haiti's most outspoken newspaper made him wary of such calls. He held Noire's naked thigh in support.

"Hello?" She clutched the phone and waited, the delay in transmission heightening her own anticipation.

"It's Dennis! We had the baby! Happy New Year!"

Noire exhaled. "Oh my God! Congratulations!" She listened to the static and fumbling on the other end.

"Thank you, Noire!" Arikè announced herself, her voice dancing across the choppy transmission in a fierce ragtime rhythm. "We're so excited! I can't believe it!"

Noire glimpsed the faintest haze of the first day of the year in the windows of Pierre's house. She smiled away the knot of confusion at Pierre's brow and asked the requisite questions: sex, time, weight.

Realizing that the news on the other end of the line was good, Pierre began to suck on Noire's nipples.

"He's a boy! Born at 12:02 A.M. And big, Noire. Eight pounds fourteen ounces. No wonder why I was huge! We were eating breakfast yesterday when my water broke. It was crazy! I pushed for like five hours! I guess he wanted to be Baby New Year! Well, this is long-distance and I know it's early, so I won't hold you."

Noire struggled to hear all that Arikè said. "You sound good! What's his name? Does he have one yet?"

"Well, Dennis won the bet, so he named him Purpose. The

name will grow on me, I guess!" She chuckled. "Noire, thanks for your prayers through all this. I love you!"

"Okay, good-bye." The phone went silent on Noire's last syllable. She felt bad. Arikè had thanked her for prayers she seldom remembered to say. She looked down at Pierre, whose nibbling had migrated down to the meeting of her thighs.

"Would you like me to give you a baby, Noire?" His words breathed hot air through her thicket of hair.

"Guess." Noire handed him a condom and let herself feel all the things that blocked the noise in her head that sounded like crying.

Abidjan

May 2001

Côte d'Ivoire's rainy season had begun in earnest. Innocent's latest trip home commenced over three months ago, when the heat was a welcome escape from the misery of February in New York City, the snowstorms no longer novel or festive. He watched sheets of rain slice the May sky into ribbons of cool air, making the city shine like new money atop broad boulevards and moist red earth. He felt antsy. His own business development had brought him there but Maman had seized the opportunity to resume her campaign to get him married in time for his ill father to witness it. And his many trips throughout the city on errands for Papa or in pursuit of his own business provided ample opportunity to indulge his penchant for seeing the buttocks of thick women straining against hastily tied wrapper skirts as they negotiated the marketplace. But he managed not to partake of the delights that dwelt behind those threadbare outfits, preferring discreet hand jobs of his own invention or his grade-school classmate's widow who had offered her oral skills for no more than an hour's conversation.

She talked about things that didn't interest him, and he began to revile their arrangement, and himself for consenting to it. He had weathered periods of celibacy before, and even enjoyed the opportunity for reflection. But this time he did not want to interrogate his restlessness, so he eventually succumbed to his mother's many suggestions of dates with the women whom she had deemed acceptable. And when Chi-Chi called and mentioned that May 4 was her twenty-ninth birthday, he wondered aloud if he could take her to dinner. She graciously accepted.

Her body had the roundness of a woman who had long passed the awkwardness of new womanhood and her mind percolated with more world events than local gossip. He greeted her with a kiss on either corner of her lips.

"You seem happy to see me."

"It's your birthday." He offered her a flash of his thoughts. "And it's my *pleasure* to see you."

She raised her eyebrows in response. "Perhaps it's not so bad to be an unmarried woman on the cusp of thirty after all."

"I think it's a good thing, Chi-Chi."

They drained a bottle of champagne before the main course was served, and by dessert, Innocent imagined the inside of her thighs hugging his and the softness of her belly promising a soft place to land.

Sex with Chi-Chi offered every physical thrill he had longed for. He closed his mind to his thoughts and focused on his urges. When it was over, Innocent slunk out of Chi-Chi's sister's house—which she had been minding in her absence—and walked six miles in the darkness back to his parents' home.

The main house was already closed up for the night, and Innocent was relieved to have some space for himself. He went straight to the boys' quarter and took a bucket bath, washing Chi-Chi off his body and out of his mind with black soap and cold water.

Part One

STRANGER
THAN FICTION

❧

CHAPTER ONE

11 SEPTEMBER 2001

5:45 A.M.

Innocent thrust his face up toward the showerhead, the hot water pelting his skin like a million rubber bullets shot at close range. The news reporter's voice slithered into the bathroom: *"Polls will soon open in New York City. Registered Democrats will be choosing their candidate for mayor during today's primary."* He opened his eyes into the hail of water, then stepped back. The bathroom was hazy gray, the only light a promise of a sun that was yet to rise. He made short work of his morning erection, relieving himself in a small, satisfied gasp as the reporter made predictions on who would win the primary.

Voting. Innocent had never concerned himself much with U.S. politics, only mildly chagrined that he paid taxes to a government that saw him as an outsider. But after the fiasco of last year's presidential election, he had managed a more robust interest in this country's system of government that impacted him in more ways than he cared to admit. He swiped a bar of soap across his body halfheartedly, knowing he would soon replace its scent with his own sweat when he arrived at his twice-weekly personal training session with Miguel. No longer a six-figure investment banker, Innocent knew his downsized lifestyle did not warrant Miguel's hefty price tag, but he decided to keep him even after leaving Wright Richards because Miguel knew how to get the results Innocent wanted.

Innocent stepped out of the shower, residual water making rivers of the ridges in his chest and muscles of his legs and landing in newly created puddles that he tracked from the bathroom to the refrigerator. He grabbed a banana and poured a glass of tomato juice. He ate standing up, dressed, and pulled on his in-line skates before leaving his loft in time for his 7:00 A.M. session with Miguel on the one hundredth floor of the World Trade Center.

"Where is Pierre?" Madame Jean-Juste crinkled the many folds of her eyes in Noire's direction from her perch on the porch.

Noire kept her gaze trained on Raynald, her landlady's driver, who was loading her last piece of luggage into his car. She had offered to have him drive Noire to the airport. "At home, I suppose." It was her final morning in Haiti and Noire didn't want to reveal the rest of the story.

Madame Jean-Juste sucked her teeth and put her hands on her hips, pulling her housecoat taut over her pendulous breasts and splaying at the bottom to reveal a wrinkled knee. "He loves you. You know that?"

She spoke as if Noire must not have known, as if her revelation would soften Noire's heart to him. Of course she knew how Pierre felt. He always said how he felt. That was the problem. Noire didn't want to know half of what he shared. She knew about his father's torture and death at the hands of the Tonton

Macoutes during the elections in 1987 and about his wife's mysterious drowning in 1999. He had more baggage than she wanted to carry. She had rented out her body to him for the price of an orgasm. Haiti had not been what she expected and had left her tired. "I'm going back home, Madame Jean-Juste. And, for better or worse, home for me is the United States."

"The U.S. is overrated."

Noire hunched her shoulders. Maybe that was true, but what did it matter.

"The two of you could live in Miami!"

Noire laughed now, momentarily entertained by her landlady's desire for a happy ending to a story she barely knew. At eighty-six years old, Madame Jean-Juste had outlived two husbands and complained to Noire about the erectile dysfunction of her seventy-four-year-old boyfriend. "If anything changes with Pierre and me, you'll be the first to know." Noire jogged up the stairs and hugged her good-bye. Madame Jean-Juste had been an unexpected source of delight for Noire during a year that had made her more cynical about the world's disregard for the black and the poor, of which Haiti had plenty.

Noire plopped into the backseat of Raynald's car and rolled up the window, adjusting her eyes to the tinted glass that cast a gray-green hue on a predawn Pétionville, Haiti's sole wealthy suburb that clung to mountains that rose up from the frenetic energy of Port-au-Prince. She relished the drive from Madame Jean-Juste's house to Guy Malary International Airport in Port-au-Prince for her return flight to New York. The flight didn't leave until eight forty-five, but she wanted to make the fifteen-minute drive to the airport before the crush of traffic threatened her ability to make her flight. Noire had enough international travel under her belt to know how unexpected and drawn out the whole process could be.

And despite her great affection for Haiti—and her elderly landlady in particular—she was anxious to get home. In her twelve-month stay, she had never adjusted to the country's peculiar brand of class discrimination and the fact that she always found herself on the side of the rich, the influential, and the mixed race. To be sure, her skin color matched that of many of the children who dodged open sewers in their bare feet to sell peanuts and beg for change. But her features, her not-quite-kinky hair, and, most important, her American dollars and accent gave her access to the rarified world of Haiti's elite. And even as she sought to understand the strange tension between Haiti's elite minority and its economically and politically disenfranchised majority who all spoke Kreyòl (whether they admitted it or not), she knew that it was her privilege that bought her entry into both communities, one out of a perceived sense of parity, and the other out of learned deference. Noire was anxious to leave this world whose social hierarchy placed her in the role that she despised yet understood in the United States. Once she saw her mother and father, Bonita, Jayna, Arikè, Dennis, and their son, Purpose, she hoped to reclaim who she was and where she fit into things. And besides, she needed to meet Purpose; she didn't understand how she had managed to become his godmother despite her absence during his first nine months of life and her own spurious godparent qualifications.

8:31 A.M.

Innocent stepped out of the sauna in the gym's locker room and walked toward his locker. He cupped his nearly bald head in his hands and let its weight pull the sinews of his neck to their limit. His muscles were flaccid, having put in an extra twenty minutes of cardio after his session with Miguel.

"You're naked!" Alexander laughed boisterously and continued fixing his tie.

Innocent jerked his head upward and looked at his former coworker and sometime protégé. "I didn't see you out there."

"Two thousand one and black men are still invisible, even to each other!" Alexander let out another guffaw before continuing. "Actually, I didn't work out. My night and morning was spent right in my fucking office. Figured that since I have an appointment, I'd do well to wash off yesterday's funk and change into a fresh shirt."

"Good move." Innocent wrapped his towel around him and opened his locker. "How's it going?"

"I'm alive, so I guess I can say it's going well." Alexander ran a pick comb through his corporate Afro.

"Mmm." Innocent stepped into new boxers and the clothes he arrived in.

"Hey, I'm meeting with Dennis Appleton." He looked at Innocent's blank expression. "You remember him. He's the husband of Noire's hottie friend Arikè. The chick who stripped off her bathing suit top that time!" Alexander licked his lips in remembrance.

"Oh yeah, I know, I know . . ." The unexpected memory of his trip to the South Carolina Sea Islands with Noire and a motley assortment of their individual friends rushed at him, nearly making him lose balance.

"So, we're doing some business. Seems he's trying to raise some capital for a deal he wants to get up off the ground."

"And what has that got to do with you?"

"I'm a power broker! He needs capital and I know where to find it." Alexander chortled. "Man, you know me. I have to keep the hustle up. This job could be gone today or tomorrow. A man needs to diversify his lines of business."

"But on company time, Alexander?"

"The workday is from nine to five. Our meeting is at eight forty-five."

"My bad."

"Oh shit!" Alexander looked at his watch. "It's eight thirty-eight. I need to get back to the office. I told him to come in on the ninety-second floor so that I don't have to sign him in at reception on eighty-five. So I have to be there to let him in."

"Okay. Well, let me walk out with you. It'll be a full day for me as well, but mostly just mundane stuff. No power broker moves for me this time."

"In time, Innocent. It'll happen in time."

"I'll remember that."

Innocent rode down to ninety-two with Alexander and Alexander stepped out.

"There he is." He pointed at Dennis. "Why don't you hold the elevator? Then I can just grab my briefcase and we can keep it moving."

"You know these elevators alarm if you hold them for too long." Innocent shook his head at Alexander's irrationality.

"Alrighty, brah. Then you go on and take over the world. But we right on your ass!"

"Easy, Alexander." He gave him a quick pound and waved at Dennis standing behind the glass door. The elevator doors closed and Innocent started to scroll through the day's errands in his head. He needed to pay Howard University an additional twenty-five hundred dollars for his sister Mireille's recently secured dorm room single, e-mail one of his father's business partners about importing a new line of textiles, and respond to Mamadou's request that he join the board of directors for his thriving Parisian art gallery. Landing at last at the ground floor, Innocent fished a nutrition bar out of his jacket pocket and walked out of the building.

The weather was brilliant, the sunlight blinding him as he sat on the nearest bench to put on his in-line skates. That done, he looked up toward Tower One and tried in vain to locate the Calhoun Masters Wright Richards office windows, which spanned from the eighty-fifth to ninety-third floors. Though he had worked there for his first four years out of Columbia Business School, he hardly missed it. Now, nearly two years after he was unceremoniously downsized when Calhoun & Masters acquired his firm of Wright Richards, he could say that his departure had been a blessing. His severance had ended nine months ago and he was beginning to feel the effects of not having a six-figure salary, but he was his own man. He had managed to cash out his company stock while it was still high and had plenty of money to float his boat for quite a while. And since he no longer had to make appearances on a daily basis, he was spending more conservatively. This was a good thing. A man only needs so many tailored suits.

Innocent's thoughts were jarred by what sounded like a small explosion. He squinted up at enormous plumes of white and gray smoke that sullied the vivid blue of the morning sky, and was accosted by a shower of debris. Innocent flinched and shielded his eyes. He jumped up from where he sat on the bench and skated away, leaving his sneakers where they sat on the ground. He looked up again, this time from a distance of about five hundred feet, and saw violent balls of orange flame shoot out from the smoke nearly ninety stories above him. The tower a lit match, the top of the structure was obscured by a growing inferno. Innocent's body shook with the ferocity of his fear. He rammed his hands into the pockets of his pants, his fingers finally grasping the cell phone that he thought could do something. He dialed Alexander's office but got a busy signal. Then he called the main number for Calhoun Masters Wright Richards but the same thing happened.

He tried Alexander again, this time on his cell phone. The phone rang incessantly. Desperate to confirm that Alexander and Dennis had made it out of the building ahead of the explosion, he tried again and again, ignoring the mechanical voice that announced, "All circuits are busy now. Will you please try your call again later?"

Innocent was at a loss for what to do. His face coated in a film of debris and his temple trickling blood from an errant shard of glass, he skated back to the building but was stopped by the mounting presence of police, firefighters, and emergency vehicles. Returning to his perch a block away, Innocent stared at the burning building. He had been on the one hundredth floor only five minutes before. With Alexander and Dennis. And now . . . Innocent retched all of the contents of his stomach.

Noire balled her airline pillow into a knot and tucked it into the crook of her neck. She leaned her head against the window and feigned sleep. It would not be a good flight. She could feel it. Her stomach was rejecting her early-morning breakfast of porridge and black coffee and she couldn't find a comfortable position for her legs on either side of her overstuffed carry-on under the seat in front of her.

Her eyes scrunched into hard balls of tension, Noire listened to Lizz Wright's rendition of The Wiz classic "Soon As I Get Home" spill out of her earphones like prophecy: *Don't want to be afraid / I just don't want to be here / In my mind this is clear / What am I doing here? / I wish I was home.* . . . She didn't want to be in Haiti. Not any longer. She was spent from the effort of being the African American girlfriend of one of Haiti's most eloquent critics of the United States. Their relationship had begun as the ultimate challenge to Noire, their spirited arguments settled in equally vigorous rounds of sex. Being with Pierre blew the boundaries of her understanding of her own country with every caustic op-ed he published on the U.S. role in unwarranted economic sanctions against Haiti that held ransom hundreds of millions of dollars in international aid from the Inter-American Development Bank. So she downplayed her Americanness to the cohort of Pierre's friends and colleagues who challenged her to defend policies that she was ashamed she knew little about and did not support.

Pierre raised the stakes, challenging her to repatriate to another country—perhaps Haiti—and let her life be a testament to her disavowal of a country that oppressed black and brown people all over the world. But it wasn't so simple. The United States was what she knew, where she was from, where her family and friends were. She couldn't just leave. And Haiti seemed to be doing a good job of oppressing its own people. She argued as much. But when the United States pulled out of the World Conference Against Racism a week ago under the pretenses that it was protesting anti-Semitism rather than dodging its own racial problems, she was defeated. It was time to leave, even though it meant returning to a country that didn't give a damn that she was a part of it.

She glanced at the child seated next to her. He bounced his behind in his seat, unleashing the foul aroma of his soiled diaper with each landing. She had already determined that the plane was full, so she put her barf bag in easy reach and issued a feeble prayer: God please don't let me puke.

Fitful sleep claimed her body and dulled her senses. She was naked and alone, her ankles shackled to the floor of an empty airplane, the crust of old tears and mucus polluting her face. A cold prickliness burned through every layer of her skin like acid but she could find no source to her pain. No wounds, no blisters. Just pain, flowing like lava, under her skin. . . .

"Ladies and gentlemen, this is your pilot." Noire awoke to

the stilted French of a man's voice. "Please be advised that this plane is safe. However, due to a situation in the U.S. in which airports have been closed, our plane is being returned to Haiti. Again, please remain calm, as our aircraft is safe. We do not have additional information at the moment, but upon our arrival, we will learn more. Please return to your seats and fasten your seat belts. We are making our initial descent and should be landing within the hour. Thank you."

A chorus of prayers, spoken in fervent Kreyòl and in the English of Southern Baptist missionaries, broke out around Noire, masking the sound of her heaving into her barf bag. Spent from the effort of vomiting, Noire turned her head toward the seat next to her, now occupied by a woman younger than her who was tying fabric across the little boy's body up against hers, fashioning it into a kind of harness. That done, she bounced the baby lightly, trying to calm his whimpering as much as her own. She looked at Noire and, seeing her mostly recovered, grabbed her hand in hers. "We are okay, sister. Your people are safe. Do not worry."

Noire wanted to believe her, so she clung to her neighbor's hand with the strength of her soul. Something was terribly wrong. She knew it.

The emergency landing of her American Airlines flight gave her little time to collect her carry-on luggage. She had stuffed her wallet, passport, and telephone book into her pants pocket before deplaning just in case she got separated from everything else. But she no longer had the cell phone she had rented and was delirious with worry to call her parents. Unlike most of the people on the plane whose families and church missions were there to receive them at the airport, she had no one. Madame Jean-Juste was not her family and couldn't come to her aid without the help of her driver, whom she knew to be running errands.

And Pierre. She had specifically instructed him not to see her off at the airport, noting that it would only be a pose at relationship where a real one did not exist. But now he was the one she most wanted to see. As a journalist, he would certainly have the most current information about what was going on.

The walk from the airstrip to the airport was somber, all of the passengers following the flight attendants' orders out of fear. Arriving in the terminal at last, they were greeted by Haiti's national French language radio station blasting a news report about a terrorist attack on the United States that included the collapse of one of the World Trade Center towers in New York City, an attack on the Pentagon, and at least three downed airplanes in the process.

Noire's body crumpled under the weight of the words, her tears silent from shock. She could barely hear the flight crew's announcements on procedure but was given a sheet with instructions about how to find out if and when a flight back to the United States would take place, and the promise of a meal and assistance from the airline for temporary accommodation if passengers were unable to make their own arrangements. Noire's steps were those of an ancient woman slowed by the burdens of too long a life. She was following an airline employee when she heard her name from a distance. It was Pierre. He accelerated toward her, took the papers out of her hand, and led her to a seat.

"When I heard that flights to the U.S. were being halted, I came here to find you. Come with me to the news office. You can try to call home then."

❧

"More food or sex?" Pierre paused in clearing away the empty bottles of Prestige beer and discarded bowls of rice *djon-djon* and *lambi* stew that littered his living room long enough to look at Noire scooped down in his favorite chair, a pillow propping up her head.

"I would think you've had enough of both."

"I didn't ask you about *me,* Noire, I asked you about you."

Noire didn't respond. In the span of sixteen hours, she had become Pierre's live-in girlfriend and an unwitting celebrity. Noire's presence had made it the appropriate place for Pierre's circle of journalists, professors, and economists to argue the implications of this act of aggression against the United States and the country's myopic foreign policy that policed the world while exacting its own form of imperialism laced with paternalism and a heavy dose of ignorance. It was nearly two in the morning, and, finally exhausted from milling around Pierre's one-bedroom bungalow talking about the U.S.'s woes alternately as tragic or as a sign of a crumbling empire, they had left at last. But before the first person had even arrived, Pierre had managed to console Noire with his lips, his tongue, and then his penis. She had allowed the sex because then she didn't have to talk to him. Or even think. And she didn't want to answer him now. Pierre never asked just one question.

"So, has anyone convinced you to stay?" He dipped his finger into the empty pot of *lambi* stew brought over by his best friend and fiercest journalistic competitor, Dumal Emmett. It had been made by his wife for the night's dinner but was repurposed for a better reason, Dumal explained when he arrived with the pot in hand.

Noire watched Pierre lick his finger. The perversity of his tongue made her quiver and then hate him . . . momentarily. She saw the simmering lust in his eyes and closed hers. But that only replaced his image with that of CNN's incessant broadcast of the Twin Towers tumbling to the ground or the soot-covered New Yorkers walking barefoot, their stunned faces etched in horror and loss. She lacked the emotional reserve to place one more failed phone call to her parents or Jayna or *anyone* in New York City just to know that they were alive and safe.

Pierre plopped down on Noire where she sat, his hand landing on the crest of her jean-covered crotch. He gave a rub. "I put your clothes away."

Noire opened her eyes but kept her head turned away from Pierre. "Why?"

"You can stay, Noire. I told you that."

"I'm going home." She spoke into the pillow.

"You don't even know what home is anymore, Noire, or when you can return."

She sat up and pushed daggers under his skin with her eyes. "So I should just wipe my hands of it and just stay? Fuck the family and friends; I'll just stay here and play house with you!"

He stood up and pulled her to her feet. "That's not what I'm saying."

They walked into his bedroom and she crumpled to the bed. Where was she supposed to go? She wanted to be home, but home could have been another planet. So instead she sat on Pierre's bed.

He unbuttoned her jeans for the second time that day. "Noire, I love you. I want you with me. Is that a crime?"

"I don't love you, Pierre."

"Would it be so bad if you did? You just haven't allowed yourself to."

He was right. Noire had never given Pierre a chance. It never seemed necessary. She'd be leaving anyway, so what was the point? She had come to enjoy his generous and patient tongue that never tired of pleasing her, his strident newspaper editorials even when they did cause her grief in her position as a reluctant American apologist, and his surprisingly large personal library in his stunningly small house. And he had stuffed her full of sad stories of loved ones who had died, disappeared, or emigrated to France, Guadeloupe, or the United States. Sometimes she blocked him out, giving the occasional grunt or head nod when it seemed called for. But she resisted being sucked in. Because then maybe she'd become invested. And then she'd be leaving. That was more drama than she needed.

"Noire?"

"What?"

"Have you ever had a man love you?"

Noire hesitated long enough to make sure that his question was serious. Then she slapped him.

Pierre's head turned on his neck without effort; he let it return to its original position equally effortlessly. "I guess that's a no."

"It's an 'of course' and you're an asshole for asking."

"Any man who really loved you wouldn't let you go."

"Not that you have the right to *let* me go anywhere, but have you forgotten that I was on a plane back to New York this morning, Pierre? Or are *you* the reason for the terrorist attack?"

"That's nasty, Noire."

Her words stung her own ears, but she didn't flinch.

He cleared his throat. "Noire, planes only create physical distance, but I've never had any intention of letting you go." He glided his fingers along the seam of her panties and let them land in the center of her V, his thumb rubbing the hood of her clitoris nonchalantly.

"You don't know anything about me."

"I know that you are in my bed at my house for at least the two hundredth time since I met you eleven months ago. I know that every tear you've shed here has been a bitter one and its cause was not me. I know that you are a thirty-year-old black woman who needs love in her life more than you'd care to admit. And I know that I love you." He broke into a smile. "That may not be everything, but I have a tremendous capacity to learn." Pierre tapped the flimsy cloth of her panties.

Noire grabbed his wrist and pulled his hand up to his face. "I'm not here to *fuck* you, Pierre. And I don't need you to fuck me."

He stared at her with hard eyes. "You make my love sound so wicked, Noire. But you're really speaking for yourself, not for me." He rolled over, clicked off the light, and pulled the sheet over his head.

Noire stared into the darkness. The air was thick with the lingering smells of tobacco, beer, and Haitian food. Lizz Wright's plaintive voice echoed in her head: *I wish I was home.*

CHAPTER TWO

FIRST

Dennis's funeral was only the first. Noire sat beside Arikè, who held nine-month-old Purpose's chubby body across her chest like a shield. The church—one of the storefront varieties that catered to many a tortured heart and hungry soul in Flatbush, Brooklyn—was full of sad faces steeled against the fact that Dennis's funeral was only the first.

Noire's hands were kept busy by a travel pack of facial tissues cradled in the lap of her brown pleated skirt. She hadn't wanted to wear black, as if the color was too final a good-bye. Brown seemed softer, like waving through a train window at a relative left at the station.

The funeral—a "celebration of life" the preacher called it—had a curious incompleteness. A closed casket with a poster-board photograph of a smiling Dennis standing by it and a worn Bible propped at its foot only suggested that his body lay inside. But though she was sure she didn't want to see it, she nevertheless imagined that it was not him. That he was alive. Somewhere.

Studying the picture, Noire wanted to tell Arikè how beautiful Dennis's smile was, that she never realized what a nice smile he had, but it didn't seem appropriate. So she sat silent, the plastic wrapper for the facial tissues making an occasional crackling noise in her hands.

And then Arikè got up with Purpose still clutched to her chest and shared the story of her and Dennis's last full day together. Monday, September 10, 2001, had been their first anniversary. Dennis had taken the day off from work to spend it with her and Purpose. The day was full of chores and naps and playtime, but that evening, he hired a babysitter for Purpose and a personal chef to prepare a gourmet dinner for him and Arikè. After dinner, Arikè wanted to stay in and snuggle but Dennis insisted that they take a walk in the neighborhood. Once outside, she found a vintage New York City taxicab and driver who drove them down to Fulton Landing. There they ate ice cream from the Brooklyn Ice Cream Shoppe—butter pecan for her and peaches and cream for him—while gazing at the commuter ferries on the East River and the glowing New York skyline.

Pointing to the World Trade Center, Dennis explained that he had an eight-forty-five meeting with Alexander before work in order to talk about additional financing for the music distribution company that he had been trying to launch over the last six months.

On the morning of September 11, Dennis left Arikè lying in bed, still barely awake. Kissing her on the forehead, he placed a Hershey's Kiss atop a piece of paper by her head as she continued to doze. Fully waking to Purpose's wailing perhaps an hour and a half later, she took him downstairs to nurse him while she had a protein shake and watched a rerun of *Girlfriends*. She also had Dennis's note, which she began to read only moments before the breaking news of the World Trade Center attacks interrupted the show. Arikè opened up the paper:

Mornin' Beautiful,

This Hershey's Kiss is my stand-in 'til tonight. Just place it wherever you want it and I'm kissin' you right there.

Love, Dennis

Arikè sat the paper down on the podium and squeezed her eyes shut in an effort to hold in her tears. Then she continued. "So, even though this is the hardest thing I've ever had to deal with, I have to believe that Dennis died as happy as he made me. And I feel thankful for that." She folded up the paper with her free hand and grabbed the podium for support.

Innocent blinked back the tears that stung his eyes as he sat in the back of the church. He had seen Dennis's face only moments before the attack. Smiling and waving. And if he had waited for Alexander and Dennis instead of claiming to be in a rush—where was he going, anyway?—Dennis would still be alive. He looked away from Arikè, huddled in front of the mike, speaking to the closed casket in front of her. He was afraid to take in any more of her pain. It made it difficult to breathe. So he pulled himself into a ball. But it was made of glass.

Noire saw Innocent weaving through the crowd toward Arikè. She didn't know he would be there; his unexpected presence uncoiled her reserve as well as her bladder. She was sure she would urinate on herself. By the time he inclined his head toward her cheek, she had fidgeted enough to move her lips into the path of his approaching mouth, and he gave her a percussive kiss.

Now Innocent became unhinged. "Ooh! Um, sorry. I mean . . . it's good to see you. Not for this reason, though. Of course."

"Um-hm." Noire shook her head so that he could stop. She

needed to use the bathroom. She reached out to touch Arikè's arm. "Innocent's here."

Arikè turned away from her other conversation. "It's because he was meeting with Alexander, you know." Her voice had an edge Innocent didn't expect.

He nodded quickly. Yes, he knew. Innocent had accompanied Alexander to the meeting with Dennis that would end both their lives. They were to meet at his office on the ninety-second floor before heading to coffee somewhere off-site. He knew more than he wanted to know. If he had held the elevator and waited for Alexander to collect Dennis and his briefcase, perhaps they both would have gotten out in time. Perhaps he and Dennis would have been out of the building by the time the first plane struck instead of stuck above the crash site. The memory of Dennis's smiling face only minutes before the attack plagued him with guilt.

"I wish he never had that goddamn meeting." Arikè's eyes flooded with a new wave of tears. Innocent wondered if she could see his last memory of Dennis reflected in his own eyes but reasoned that she could not. Then Arikè walked away.

Winded, Innocent stumbled into the church pew and looked up at Noire, returning from the restroom.

Noire saw guilt-streaked grief in Innocent's face and gave him an anxious stare.

"Alexander died, too," he offered as an explanation.

"Yes, I'm so sorry." Noire acknowledged their friendship.

"I'm sorry, too."

∞

Noire counted the number of e-mail messages from Pierre and blocked his address. Too much had happened, and she didn't want to know what Pierre thought about it. With Dennis's funeral only a few hours ago, Noire's emotions were wrung dry; the past week had aged her. Only a week before, Dennis and Arikè were celebrating their first wedding anniversary and Noire was spending her last full day in Haiti with Pierre: eating Madame Françisque mangoes, talking politics, and enjoying the delights of the flesh that Pierre lavished upon her in his tiny house. His wit was as sharp as his intellect, and his tongue was fearless, so she returned his affections in kind. But in the four days that she stayed with him post-9/11 until air travel to the United States gradually resumed, he displayed a seamier side to himself that took perverse delight in Noire's anxiety. She had been unable to reach either of her parents for the better part of two days, and she couldn't reach Bonita or any of her friends at all. So he filled her mind with worst-case scenarios that left her with nothing and no one to return home to and his love as the only thing that she knew to still be alive. Alarmed and depressed, Noire walked out on him, spending her last night in Haiti at the airport awaiting the first available flight out and she didn't look back.

Innocent had what he called "people fatigue," his euphemism for "dead people fatigue." He kicked off his shoes and set Dennis's funeral program on his desk. His eyes went from his smiling face frozen on the cover to the blinking light on his answering machine. Today made four days since he had answered his telephone. After reaching out to Mireille and his family in Côte d'Ivoire on the evening of the eleventh to let them know that he was okay, he had been bombarded by improvised telephone chains composed of students and alumni from his alma maters of the Sorbonne or Columbia Business School, former coworkers at Calhoun Masters Wright Richards, and an odd assortment of colleagues and acquaintances who still had his outdated business card with his old cell phone number that forwarded to his home phone. It had seemed like a good way not to lose touch with associates whom he might want to cultivate for future business opportunities, but now it had become a hot-line to bad news.

After the greeting of "Innocent Pokou, happy to know you're alive," and putting a check next to his name in the "living" column on their lists, they would tell him who was missing or recount unsubstantiated stories they had heard of final calls to loved ones before phone lines went dead or desperation made people leap to a certain end. Two days of it was already too much. He already had two faces etched in his mind. He couldn't bear to grow the list of casualties to include more. So he simply turned the ringer off and let his answering machine take any messages. He knew that he should show concern for everyone, but he could not. The grief center in his mind was overloaded and his heart hurt so much that he simply couldn't touch it. He put his feet atop his desk and quieted his thoughts.

His private cell phone vibrated on his hip. Startled, he fumbled and dropped it before answering on the fourth ring. "Pokou here."

"I'm happy you are. I've been trying to reach you for days. I got this number from your mother."

Innocent strained to hear the soft voice that spoke French on the other line. He couldn't place it. "Please, you haven't told me who this is."

"It's Chi-Chi Abiokun, Innocent." She said her name slowly, as if she expected him to write it down.

"Oh, Chi-Chi. I'm surprised to hear—"

"I'm pregnant with your baby, Innocent. I wanted to let you know."

Innocent was sure he had been punched in the groin. He looked at today's date—September 17—and calculated that he hadn't seen her since two or three days before his return from Côte d'Ivoire four months ago.

"If this were true, you would have called me before now."

"I'm nineteen weeks pregnant. I'm due February sixth."

"February 6th?!" Innocent jumped out of his chair and tried to shake the nightmare he was sure this was.

"Innocent—"

"When were you going to tell me?"

"I never planned to make this your problem. But then my boyfriend broke up with me—"

"Your boyfriend? You had a boyfriend? Chi-Chi, you were fucking your *boyfriend* and now you're calling *me* to tell me this baby is *mine*?"

"Because he was away, Innocent. I never loved him. He returned to Côte d'Ivoire on June ninth. He was in school in Paris. He would have married me, too, but only because I'm the only one left to marry. We didn't love each other; we both knew it." She paused, her breathing labored from the effort of purging her secret and the pain of the truth.

"I told him it was his, but . . . When I told him in mid-July, he didn't believe me. He thought I knew too soon. And my doctor broke my confidence. He told him that I was already ten weeks pregnant after I told him it was just four weeks."

Innocent's mind was reeling. He was going to be a father in five months. And with Chi-Chi for the mother. He was shamed by the realization that Chi-Chi had used him as much as he had used her. And look where it had gotten both of them.

He didn't hate Chi-Chi. But he had never bothered to know anything about her. He had taken the sex she freely gave him in the final weeks of his visit home without so much as a backward glance. She entertained him well enough; her sense of humor made the time pass when they weren't having sex. Her thighs were succulent, their meatiness enfolding him in moist warmth and holding on to him even after his postorgasm sensitivity made him want to let go.

But his child's mother! He counted up the condoms he had

used and knew they came up short as compared with the number of times he had parted her legs and enjoyed what awaited him there. He had mumbled, "Are you taken care of?" only once and had satisfied himself with her grunt in response. But somehow he never thought it would happen to him.

The tears that flowed so freely at Dennis's funeral could not come. He knew he wasn't dead so he could not weep. But he knew that his life—the life he had called his own—would never be his alone anymore.

∞

Noire made a beeline toward the produce aisle at Utopia Foods. This was her third early-morning shopping excursion in as many days and once again her EcoBag was overflowing. This morning it was organic fruit: blackberries, apples, peaches, plums, oranges. There was something about shopping for food that made her feel safe and in charge of the world, or at least her corner of it. She stopped at the peaches and locked eyes with Marcus Gordon, Innocent's business school buddy whose name-brand family and conviction that she was not of Innocent's caliber made him their relationship's worst adversary from the get-go. His frown inspired her own. She feigned a cough, hoping to dodge the courtesy of saying hello, but he just stood there until she finished.

"Are you okay?" His face was a mixture of concern and distaste.

She was not. "No." Noire was hoping he would take the hint to disappear.

"I saw you in aisle six but wasn't sure it was you." Marcus cleared his throat and waited for a response.

"Well, it is." She manufactured a smile and dropped three peaches into her bag.

"So what brings you here at six-thirty on a Thursday morning?"

"I should ask you what brings a 'Harlemite' like you all the way to Brooklyn to do the same?" She made quotes with her fingers. "I thought that you had shepherded in a wave of gentrification that had brought organic produce to your 'hood as well." Noire let her face drop. Why was Marcus playing at civility now when he had waged a successful campaign against her when she was with Innocent, citing her lack of family pedigree as her biggest fault? She had little tolerance for his trust-fund-baby antics then and even less now. Irritated by the memory, she added, "In case you didn't know it, Marcus, we are *not* friends." She turned her back to him and picked up two more peaches.

"I'm not pretending that we are." He touched Noire's arm, commanding her attention. "I guess I shouldn't be asking so many questions. It's just—it's nice to see you. See that you're all right." His expression was devoid of the arrogance that usually resided there.

Noire nodded her head, her face a picture of surprise. "Thank you, Marcus. That's . . . kind of you." She furrowed her brow. "So, how are *you*?"

"Not great. My father-in-law—Lydia's dad—died last week. On the thirteenth."

"The *thirteenth*?" Noire's preoccupation with the September 11 tragedy had made her forget that people died on other days, for other reasons. She made an apologetic expression. "I'm . . . I'm sorry." She shook her head. "Wow. I hope it wasn't due to an accident."

"I think it was." Marcus's face twisted in anger and shame. "He had a heart attack. While screwing their next-door neighbor."

"Oh my God." His admission smacked astonishment onto her face. Noire jerked her head away, not wanting to compound his embarrassment with her own surprise.

"I shouldn't be sharing that. It's just—things are really pretty fucked up right now."

"Damn. So sorry. Really."

"Thanks." He shook his head in acknowledgment. "I figured you'd understand."

Noire replaced her surprise with suspicion. *What is he trying to say?* They had no more in common than friendship with Innocent and the three degrees of separation that linked every other college-educated black person in New York City to her past, present, or future. But what was that? She wanted to ask him, but remembered his wife's kindness toward her when she met her several years ago and felt her heart ache for her and her mother. "Actually, I can only imagine, Marcus."

He read the question in her eyes and sidestepped it. "Lydia's mom lives around the corner right on Clinton Avenue. Lydia and the kids and I, we've been spending some time over here; helping her go through paperwork and everything."

"Of course."

"I just needed to get out of the house, you know."

"Yeah, I know." Noire moved her shopping bag laden with fruit she didn't need to her left shoulder.

"Hey, I'm sorry to lay such a jacked-up story on you so early in the morning."

"New York City is one big jacked-up story these days."

He didn't respond but let his eyes wander over her hasty getup that was both tighter and brighter than it needed to be. "Well, *you* good, Noire. Very good."

Noire traced the path of his gaze to her yellow GOT MILK? T-shirt. It clung to her braless breasts in answer to its own question, so she clutched the EcoBag to her chest, crushing a peach in the process. The juice oozed down her shirt and settled into a sticky mess at the top rim of her sweatpants.

"I hope I didn't do that." Marcus's look was saucy.

"Don't ruin my high opinion of you." She pinched her mouth

into a smile and decided that the conversation had been too long. "Okay, Marcus, take care." She turned her head and expected her body to follow. But he caught her waist with his hand.

"Hey, I just— You know, I've been trying to get in touch with Innocent since like"—he counted the days on his fingers—"last Thursday, but he hasn't returned my calls or anything. Is he, you know, *okay*?"

Noire read his meaning. Marcus didn't even know if Innocent was alive. It wasn't a given anymore. If it ever was. "I saw him at the beginning of the week. At a friend's funeral."

"Wow." His voice was a whisper. He let his hand drop from Noire's waist belatedly.

"But if I talk to him, I'll tell him you were trying to reach him."

"Let me just give you my card. For Innocent." He gave a hint of that same saucy smile. "And I'm happy that you're well. Count your blessings."

"I hope that you're counting your own, starting with your wife. Give Lydia my condolences." Noire punctuated her words with a squint and let Marcus walk away from her. Then she grabbed a handful of peaches. She needed more.

Innocent skated south along West Broadway, a fraction of the normal morning rush of buses, taxis, and cars creeping along beside him. Recovery workers, the National Guard, and city and state police officers outnumbered pedestrians ten to one and dozens of stores stood shuttered along a route normally teeming with foot traffic and commerce. He turned off along Canal Street, and away from the crater of foul air and crushed hope at the foot of Manhattan Island. The muscles of his legs were a concert of movement propelling him first along the streets and then onto the Brooklyn Bridge's pedestrian walkway. He was almost alone, and the silence—except for the drone of traffic below—created a haven for his thoughts, thoughts he had been avoiding.

Since Chi-Chi's revelation three days before, Innocent had been awash with shame and compounded regret. He felt responsible for an emerging life that connected him to a woman he didn't love even as he wrestled with his unwitting role in the deaths of two of his contemporaries. And his mind somersaulted into the memory of his fourteen-year-old brother, Serge, who had mounted the back of their neighbor's motorcycle with Innocent's seventeen-year-old consent and met his death in what would have been a minor accident had Innocent been the one in his place. All of the biggest decisions of his life—which had seemed trivial at the time—turned out to be wrong and to have catastrophic consequences. And as he found himself on the wrong side of the life-and-death equation once again, he questioned other decisions he made, including whom he had let into his life and whom he had let go.

Innocent was surprised to find himself at Noire's doorstep and even more surprised to see her lugging two string bags laden with fruit.

"I don't believe this" were the first words out of her mouth.

"Hi." Innocent couldn't justify why he was there so he didn't say more.

Noire searched his face for a motive for his seven A.M. visit and remained silent.

"Can I carry those for you?" Innocent reached toward her bags.

"Is that why you came here? To carry my *bags*?" Noire was incredulous.

"I guess I wanted to see you. To talk."

"Oh." Noire registered the same sadness she had seen in his face at Dennis's funeral. Why did he look like that? She couldn't even account for his presence at the funeral other than the fact that Dennis had been meeting with Alexander, Innocent's former colleague. But that didn't seem to be enough. "Suppose I have something else to do."

"Then I'll go home, Noire."

She read the longing in his eyes that mirrored her own. There was something needy in his expression and it made her want to fill it. In that moment, it gave her a purpose, and that felt better than the restlessness that darted in and out of her heart without rhyme or reason.

She led the way up to her apartment. "Things are a mess."

The door slammed shut, sucking out all of the air in the apartment along with it. Innocent stood still in the vestibule and willed the torrent of perspiration and the hardness between his legs to retreat. "Um, I should take these off." He handed the bags back to Noire and stooped to unfasten his in-line skates.

Noire felt her skin melting into puddles of inexplicable emotion. She hadn't been so close to Innocent—alone and in private—in more than a year and a half when they had hurled words at each other that were meant to wound. But now she couldn't remember why the anger had been so ugly and so necessary to express. Noire turned and walked into the kitchen. She began unpacking too much fruit into a refrigerator brimming with more produce and dairy products than she could eat. "Would you like a peach?"

"Yes." Innocent's words burrowed into her Afro, his hands relishing the curve of the ass he still worshipped. He ran both his pointer fingers along the meeting of her cheeks, making an identifiable lane in her sweatpants. Landing at the base of her spine, he circled her waist with his outstretched hands, letting them sink into the exposed skin and kneading the lip of flesh that lived between her navel and her untamed copse of hair. "Oh, Noire."

The utterance began a chant of her name that beat back his sadness and his shame and his fear.

She turned to face him, to feel his hard presence against her and allow her hands free rein along the grooves of his back and a behind that rose to fill the palms of her hungry hands. His body felt like a prayer answered and she didn't care what it all meant or if it meant nothing more than that she was needed. Right now that felt like enough.

She pushed her hands into his shorts and led him to the bedroom, her fingers wild and insistent. Innocent groped for a condom where he knew she kept them and Noire put it on with her mouth. She was awash with something beyond lust and not unlike love. It made her clamber on top of Innocent's body and envelop him with her own vulnerability.

Innocent wanted to swallow Noire whole. Her juices flowed into his fallow spirit, coating it with something mystical. And for as long as he stayed there, him inside of her inside of him, she plugged the holes in his pockmarked soul.

∞

CHAPTER THREE

NORMAL PEOPLE

Noire tapped her clove cigarette with her pointer finger and watched Bonita Fuentes's dangle out of her mouth while her head turned in time to read the first few pages of her dissertation. They were in a neighborhood park near Bonita's Bronx apartment, since Bonita still was not riding the New York City subways after the 9/11 attacks. But the early October chill was making it harder and harder to sit outside for long periods of time and the opportunities to smoke were wreaking havoc on Noire's lungs. Her habit—which had been dead for eleven times longer than it had been alive—was revived when she began her outdoor meetings with Bonita.

"I like it." Bonita spoke out of the left side of her mouth while blowing smoke out of the right. The old cigarette was already crushed underfoot. "It's strong. Really strong. You don't even need me."

Bonita's eyes told Noire that she'd always have her, even if she didn't want her, but Noire humored her nevertheless. "But,

Bonita, you're my inspiration. My muse. You are the reason why I can even express myself!"

"Don't you ever forget it." Bonita laughed and lit another cigarette. Noire grabbed one from the pack sitting between them, stuck it in her mouth, touched it to Bonita's, and inhaled. "Seems that I've also inspired another habit in you."

Noire smiled. "The original inspiration was a trip to Paris during high school and my short-lived career as a photographer my first year in college. But it just got too expensive. Smoking like this, however"—she tapped Bonita's pack of cigarettes—"is very cost-effective!" They both laughed and puffed, imagining themselves to be old girlfriends in a Hollywood film.

"Well, *mi cariñosa*, you'll have to buy your own for a couple of weeks next month. I'm going to DR."

Noire was shocked. Bonita wasn't even taking the subway; how would she manage to fly to the Dominican Republic in an airplane. She said so.

Bonita removed the cigarette from her mouth. "I figure that lightning doesn't strike the same place twice so I'm safer now than before 9/11." She shrugged her shoulders. "Besides, my only granddaughter called me herself. She's ten. According to her, my son is organizing a family reunion and she begged me to come. So I said yes."

Noire had never heard Bonita talk about her family or the Dominican Republic except to recount the hardship of her pregnancy at seventeen, her grandmother forcing her to leave her son and move to New York City shortly after his birth, or her parents' fatal car crash when they had traveled home for her *abuela*'s funeral. The stories were always tragic and she often ended them by caressing Noire's cheek and thanking her for being her nondysfunctional family in addition to being her friend.

"I didn't realize you were even in touch with them."

"I'm not. But my number has been the same for twenty years.

So I guess it's not hard to find me." She pulled her lips into a tight line across her face, signaling an end to that part of the conversation. She uncrossed and recrossed her legs. "So, how's your sex life?" Bonita never acknowledged anyone's love life. She believed everyone's life included both love and hate. Sex—having it or not having it—was what changed.

"How dare you ask?" Noire was annoyed but acted amused. She didn't want to tell her.

"What? Should I go first? Well, my vibrator's batteries went dead last night. Right before I came. But I bought some more at the drugstore before coming here." She tapped her pocketbook. "You? I saw on the news that everyone's having sympathy sex these days. That, and deciding to get married. It's a part of post-traumatic stress disorder, it seems."

Noire shook her head. She knew about it. She was having it with Innocent. It started with him wanting to talk, presumably about losing Alexander and about Dennis's funeral. But they never got to that. When she told Innocent about running into Marcus and about the loss in Lydia's family, Innocent tensed his jaw and pressed his finger to Noire's lips. Their fear and neediness and the pain that clung to Innocent's skin like dew seemed too hard to discuss, so mostly they didn't. Mostly, they watched reruns of *The Cosby Show* before climbing into bed and having sex.

"I guess we all could use a little comforting." Noire deflected Bonita's question.

She redirected it. "Who's been 'comforting' you?"

"I saw Innocent the other night."

She pulled on her cigarette dramatically. "I was hoping you'd say Nácio."

"You know I've never slept with Nácio!"

"It's time for that to change!"

"We're not meant to be, Bonita."

"That's the other thing. Everyone's become so goddamn fatalistic. 'It wasn't meant to be.' 'I guess it was their time to go.' That's *bullshit,* Noire. No one is ever meant to be blown up in an airplane or have a skyscraper burst into flames and crash down on top of them! Who makes that shit up! We're supposed to live until we die! Of *natural* causes . . ."

"Then I guess we should stop smoking." Noire tried to lighten the mood but Bonita's glassy eyes made her get choked up. She didn't want to talk about it. She didn't want to imagine death, even though it was all around her. She didn't want to think that Dennis and Alexander and people she had gone to high school and college with were a part of the crater of death at the foot of Manhattan. That the cloying smell of human decay that turned her stomach whenever she was within a mile of the World Trade Center site was composed of people she knew.

Innocent had told her that Alexander's mother was still holding out hope. "Until they find something of his," she told him, "I won't believe that he's dead. I can't. What's there to live for if my only child is gone?" So Innocent became Alexander's family's first point of contact for the recovery mission. And while he waited for information about Alexander, he found out that the four people he had been closest to when he worked at Wright Richards before it was taken over by Calhoun & Masters had all perished in the towers. And he knew that he hadn't held the elevator for Alexander and Dennis.

Bonita reached over and hugged Noire. "I'm sorry, *morena.* I can see this is hard for you. You lost people, too. I guess we all lost someone or something that day. And with your president threatening war, the dying has just begun."

∞

Innocent got off the Amtrak train and headed toward the taxi stand at Washington, D.C.'s Union Station. Despite the dismal mood in the nation's capital post-9/11, or perhaps because of it, Howard University had decided to host a homecoming weekend even more uplifting than usual. The freshmen especially were feeling a little less like the adults who had tramped off to meet their destiny at college only a month and a half before and more like overgrown children who craved their parents' affection and deeper pockets to finance the weekend's enjoyment. Innocent was there for his sister Mireille; once again, he was happy to play the role of big brother/surrogate father and to spoil her as best he could.

He gave the taxi driver the address to Akwaaba D.C.—the bed-and-breakfast that Mireille had insisted he stay at so she could brag that she had been there, too—and settled into the backseat of the car. He marveled at the number of American flags he saw—in windows, on buildings, and as stickers on many of the cars that whizzed by him. It was America's response to grief, it seemed. As though symbols of patriotism could quell the pain or answer the difficult questions blanketing the country and world like a field of land mines. He couldn't be sure if any of the rhetoric he heard was sound or helpful, but he knew better than to raise even one question or voice one critique in his accented English and with his African passport.

Akwaaba D.C. was as stately as its Brooklyn cousin and had the benefit of having a smiling Mireille waving at him from the picture window towering above him.

"I just couldn't wait," Mireille's jubilant voice chirped in a French lilt he had longed to hear. Every time she spoke she offered him a bit of home and he was happy to receive it. He couldn't wait, either.

She gave him a tour of the parlor and salon, taking care to explain the literary theme of the place—interspersed with her recently acquired knowledge of African American literature—before settling him into the Langston Hughes room and heading out to the Howard campus.

"There's a woman I want you to meet," Mireille said as they exited the taxi. "She's a postdoctoral fellow here and one of the faculty liaisons for the African Students Association. She's from Rwanda. I told her a lot about you."

Innocent felt his stomach clench up. He had no business meeting anyone. He still needed to work up the nerve to tell Mireille about the child he was expecting by Chi-Chi in February. And he had somehow managed to fall back into a sexual relationship with Noire. He didn't need another woman to worry about. "I hope you didn't tell her that I'm available."

"Well, I didn't tell her you're married, because you're not. And neither is she. But she has a child, a son. He's seven. A very beautiful boy. Very big eyes." Mireille spoke quickly, as if giving Innocent more information would ensure that he had to meet her.

"It's not that simple, Mireille."

"You always like to make things complicated. Just meet her, Innocent. I'm sure you will like her. She's beautiful, too. Very tall. With eyes like her son's. Or perhaps it's the other way around." Mireille giggled and grabbed Innocent's hand, ushering him toward the main hall.

"How's Noire?" She kept her head faced forward but slid her eyes into the corner so she could see him.

"I knew this was about more than introducing me to someone."

"I just asked a question, big brother. You've made it more. And from the look on your face, I'd say it's quite a bit more. Innocent. I may be your baby sister, but I wasn't born yesterday. College opens your eyes to a lot of things."

Innocent changed the subject. "Have you spoken with Maman?" He wondered if maybe she did know about Chi-Chi. But his mother only learned about it two weeks ago and Mireille was already in Washington, D.C. Besides, if she knew, she wouldn't have been able to keep it to herself. He barely understood why he was so secretive about it, but then he knew he was ashamed that he had gotten Chi-Chi pregnant and had no intention of marrying her.

"Whenever I speak to Maman, she tells me how sad she is that all of her children have left her and Papa to die alone. But of course, *I* plan to come back." She eyed Innocent before introducing him to some of her classmates.

Shema was beautiful. Innocent was watching the candlelight flicker in eyes that were rimmed in wisdom and laced with pain. At thirty-nine years old to his thirty-five, Shema felt like an adviser as much as a potential lover. And whatever Mireille had told her about Innocent, she seemed willing to be both. Her voice was rich and low and she slipped into one of a handful of African or European languages when French didn't adequately capture what she felt. Innocent reveled in the unrehearsed sophistication of her conversation and the complete attention she lavished on him as he offered his own reflections.

Their acquaintance had begun only five hours before when Mireille seated Innocent next to her at the panel on the African experience at Howard; by its conclusion, they already had an easy rapport that clearly delighted his baby sister. Mireille soon left them to enjoy the more youthful activities planned for students; without a plan for the balance of the evening, Innocent readily agreed to accompany Shema to an Ethiopian restaurant in Adams Morgan that Shema swore by.

They lingered over dinner for three hours before finding a speakeasy with close quarters and dim lighting that set the stage for an intimate tête-à-tête.

"Even though I am a postdoctoral fellow, I'm clear when I'm accepted by the other students and when I remind them of their mother."

Innocent chuckled. "My ex-girlfriend was pursuing her doctorate. Still is."

"Mireille counted that among the reasons why you would like me."

"What were the other reasons?"

"She said you liked tall, beautiful women with skin the color of toasted almonds."

"My sister knows me well."

"She also said that you lost friends recently and that you could use some company. I told her that I often feel the same way."

Innocent looked at her face again. He knew that her eyes told a story. But it didn't scare him; in fact, he wanted to know. "You're from Rwanda." He started her off.

"I am Hutu and Tutsi; my father was Tutsi, so that made me Tutsi, but my mother was Hutu. And since my husband was Tutsi"—she looked for surprise or disdain in his eyes and, finding none, continued—"he was killed. Hacked to death by our neighbor. His killer raped me and kept me as his pet. He is Nakem's father." She paused.

Innocent reached for her hand, signaling her to continue when she was ready.

"I was so distraught about my husband's murder and the repeated rapes that resulted in my pregnancy that I tried to give myself an abortion. I didn't want to bring another Hutu into this world that would kill more Tutsis just because they're Tutsi. But when my rapist—he called me his wife—found me bleeding from my vagina, he called me a Tutsi slut, put a hot poker inside of me, and then threw me out. I crawled to the house of a Hutu woman who took pity on me. She saved my life. And Nakem's, too. Nakem is my only child."

Innocent stared at this beautiful woman who had just shared her tortured story over port and bittersweet chocolate cake. It was hard to believe that she could come out of that and still look normal. He said as much.

"A lot of people walking around look normal, if there is such a thing. But we are not. We all have stories, experiences of pain and loss. Regrets. I'm no different."

Innocent felt the beginning of a tear forming in the corner of his right eye. "Does Mireille know all of that?"

"She does not. She knows that my husband is dead and that Nakem's father is dead. But she probably thinks they are the same person. I didn't want to burden her. She's been so sweet to me. She's a lovely young woman. Maybe I wanted to protect her. But more likely I wanted to protect myself. From what she might think."

"But you told me."

"Because you have a story, too."

Innocent offered a fragile smile that melted into a frown. "I am going to be a father."

"That's a blessing."

He looked up at her. He had never thought about it that way. A responsibility. A source of shame. But not a blessing. "I'm not in a relationship with the mother. She is at home. Mireille doesn't know, yet."

"You should tell her. She is to be an auntie."

"Yes."

"Don't ever let this child be ashamed of himself. We are not responsible for the circumstances of our birth. And if we make it to this world it is because we were meant to live. Nakem was meant to live. And I am happy to have him."

Innocent paid the bill and they held hands as they left the speakeasy and sauntered back to the inn at which he was staying. He opened the door and Shema walked in. She followed him into his room. The chocolate walls and dim lights made her a burnished goddess. Innocent studied the lines of her body, her ample breasts and belly and buttocks that restated her connection to their continent of origin.

"I cannot make love with you, Shema."

"No, you cannot, Innocent. You do not love me and I don't love you. But sometimes we don't have to love each other's bodies to affirm each other's lives. In the dark, a man does not see my body, the body that reminds me of my history every day. Look at me, Innocent. Look at my scars and respect my history." At that, she disrobed in the soft light of the room. With his eyes, Innocent traveled the scar that began at the hollow of her neck and drew X's on her belly. It left a thick, mottled scar across the mound that had once been covered with pubic hair before the follicles were destroyed. And at the meeting of her thighs he saw the beginnings of a ring of scar tissue that forever stamped her vagina as the focus of her degradation.

When he was finished, he looked back into her eyes that were filled with tears. "That you can look at me without disgust or judgment is better than love. It is respect for me as a woman."

∞

Innocent zipped up his luggage and glanced at Mireille. "Did you know you look exactly like you did when you were a baby . . . only taller?"

He smiled at her smile and saw the look of expectancy that he had come to know so well. Mireille had sensed all weekend that he had something to tell her, and the nearness of his departure made her anxious to know. But now that he had nothing to distract him—no more people to meet or functions to attend or luggage to pack—all he could do was talk to her.

"Do you remember Chi-Chi?" Innocent began.

Mireille rolled her eyes. "One of your masses of admirers!" She referenced the daily dinner guests that their mother had invited to attract his attention when he spent the holidays there for the last two years.

"Don't act like that, Mireille. She's a nice woman and Charlotte's classmate from secondary school." He cleared his throat. That wasn't the direction he had wanted for things to go. "Well, I found her to be a very nice person. In fact, we went out—on some dates—in May. When I was home."

Mireille raised her eyebrows in surprise. "How come I didn't know that?"

"Perhaps you were occupied with your boyfriend, Abdul? He *is* still your boyfriend?"

She took on none of Innocent's implied reference to the male attention she was now receiving and redirected the conversation back to Chi-Chi. "I was sure she had a boyfriend. Or maybe I should call him the one who was to keep her from being an old maid. He never treated her well, you know. Charlotte told me that he had contacted her while he was studying in France. He wanted to catch up on old times, he said."

Innocent didn't know about Chi-Chi's ex-boyfriend's connection to his sister Charlotte. He knew very little about Charlotte's relationships. But he nodded his head nevertheless. "I'm aware that she was in a relationship but they are no longer together." He cleared his throat.

"So, what of Chi-Chi, big brother?" She studied his face.

"Well, we got to know each other a bit better . . . while I was there. And, well, she's—we're expecting—"

"You got Chi-Chi pregnant?!" Mireille's voice rang out.

"Yes, she's pregnant. But you needn't yell."

"My brother is about to be a *father* and I needn't yell. Is that what you told Maman and Papa? That they needn't yell?! Or are they still in the dark, too?" Mireille was incredulous.

Innocent wasn't prepared to share his parents' response, so he didn't. "They know."

"Am I the last to find out?"

"I'm not sure if Maman has told Charlotte."

"You know they're not talking."

Innocent looked concerned. "I didn't know that. Why?"

"Wow. You'd think that this family had a hundred people in it for as long as it takes us to share news! Charlotte and Michel are separated; he has taken custody of Bibi. Something terrible happened, it seems. Charlotte won't tell me and neither will Maman. But Charlotte said she is staying in France no matter what; she doesn't feel welcome at home."

Innocent's head was spinning. This was the first time he had heard that Charlotte and Michel were having problems. But he knew that his ignorance was partly his fault. He never reached out to Charlotte himself and seldom asked his mother about her. He had resigned himself to having a distant relationship with her and made no effort to strengthen it.

"So how does Maman feel? And Papa? I'm so hurt that you didn't tell me first. When is the baby due?"

Innocent couldn't tell if Mireille was happy or merely curious. "I'd like to know how you feel first."

"That's the question I should be asking you, big brother. You haven't shown an ounce of pride."

"It's not as simple as all that, Mireille."

"Well, simple or hard, the baby is coming! How has her pregnancy been? When is the baby due?"

"February sixth. And Chi-Chi says she's okay. Tired mostly. She's still working."

"She's due in"—Mireille calculated in her head—"a little less than four months' time. Tell her to stop working, Innocent. You can send her enough money so she doesn't have to!"

"She works for the UN and gets very good benefits. She *wants* to keep working. And I *am* sending money." Innocent grew defensive. "I am trying to do right by her."

"Then will you marry her?"

"We're not in a relationship, Mireille."

"If you were at home, perhaps you would be. She's going to be the mother of your child, Innocent."

"I know that. But you can't make yourself love someone who's five thousand miles away."

"So then maybe you shouldn't be five thousand miles away!"

They stared at each other, both caught up in their own thoughts, pulled apart by their own emotions. Innocent watched dozens of questions march across Mireille's mind; she was determining which she would ask. He was sure he didn't want to answer any of them, but took their conversation as penance for all of his sins of omission.

"You're not starting anything with *Shema*?" Mireille's tone stated her disavowal of any hand in setting them up only two nights before.

"She's a very nice woman—thank you for introducing us, Mireille—but no."

"So you told her?"

He shook his head.

"And Noire?"

He creased his brow. "What of her?"

"When I asked about her the other day, you seemed . . ." She searched for the right word. "Ruffled somehow. Do you still see each other?"

"If you're asking me if I've seen her recently, I have."

"Is she hurt?"

"Why are you asking me that?"

"She loved you and you loved her. Maybe she thought that you would start a family with *her*."

Innocent stood up and walked into the bathroom, signaling the end of the conversation. "Let me just take care of my own affairs, Mireille. I have enough issues to sort through."

"You're not the only one affected, Innocent. This baby is a part of *my* family, too."

※

CHAPTER FOUR

ARRANGEMENTS

Washington, D.C., blurred into Maryland as the train lurched toward New York City. Innocent closed his eyes to the dizzying scenery outside and saw Shema, her scars cleaving her body in two and ending at her vagina, her words a disclosure and a declaration: "That you can look at me without disgust or judgment is better than love. It is respect for me as a woman."

But if that were so, then why was his romantic life a tangle of frustration and failure? In his thirty-five years, he had managed to kill every serious possibility for marriage or have it killed for him. The women in his first two years of college didn't count; he had spent that time at the Sorbonne delighting in the challenge of bedding as many women as he had the energy for. French, Italian, and German women seemed most willing, so he started there. But once, in one of the record shops crowded along Boulevard Saint-Michel, a diminutive Cameroonian woman came over to him where he stood in front of the African music section.

"I didn't think you liked *our* music. None of us did."

He turned to look into her face. He was sure he didn't know her or the others she referred to. He said as much.

"If you don't know me, it's because you haven't wanted to. I suppose that European women take up all of your time." She narrowed her eyes at him, sending a small, sharp arrow into his chest. He flinched.

There was nothing to say. He didn't have to explain himself to her or anyone. So he excused himself and left the store without purchasing the new Salif Keita cassette he had come to buy. But for the balance of the day, he redrew her features upon a canvas of his memory: lips that fanned out like the proud plumage of a peacock, eyes that promised secrets shared, skin that would impart warmth with every touch. In an instant, his twenty-year-old sex-starved body changed course, imagining berry black nipples and high, round asses sloping into thick brown thighs in every wet dream.

When next he saw the new object of his desire, she was holding hands with one of his Malian classmates. His pants tightened in spite of himself as he eked out the most ordinary good morning that he could.

"Ah, ah! My brotha. Good morning, heh!" she said in playful greeting to him. Then, letting go of the Malian guy's hand, she came over to him. "You left your cassette in the store the other day. I have it for you in my room. Come by this evening to pick it up." She wrote her address on a torn piece of notebook paper and handed it to Innocent.

"Okay" was all he could mumble in reply. And that evening she taught him that he had the ability to make love to a woman's entire body, an hour for each region, before bathing in the recesses of her glorious dark haven.

Soleinie became everything to Innocent and he was sure he would marry her. But when she graduated—she was a year his senior—she said that she was already engaged to one of the big men back home in Cameroon. She would be leaving within the week and would never see him again.

Her words were curiously matter-of-fact, and it was he who shed tears of disillusionment and pain. But then he realized, she had known her plan all along. Innocent was her last conquest before becoming a wife to someone else. He tried to curse her for her cruelty but she bit back.

"It is men who are cruel, Innocent. How do you make a twenty-three-year-old college-educated woman marry a fifty-four-year-old man with children older than her? But my own father agreed to it. After my first-year scholarship ended, I came home for holiday and my father told me there was no more money to send me back. I was miserable. But then, a week before classes were to resume, he told me I could go.

"I did not ask him how he got the money; I was so happy, I didn't care. But the next year, when I came home on holiday, my mother had a special dinner and invited the man who had a business importing cars to Cameroon and Nigeria. He was a rich man. He sat across from me at dinner and asked me what I was studying. He encouraged me to take accounting classes and English. That night, my mother told me he was paying my school fees and my father had agreed that I could marry him after I graduated.

"Can you imagine my devastation, Innocent? You cannot. You don't know what it's like to be promised to someone whom you haven't chosen for yourself. As a man, you have all the choices in the world. But I had two choices: refuse and end up leaving school and returning to Cameroon with the reputation of being a difficult, half-educated girl, or stay in school and enjoy my life . . . until I had to come back.

"After my shock wore off, the choice was clear. He is not such a bad-looking man and he has a successful business and lots of money. I could do a lot worse than him. But in the meantime, I met and fell in love with you. And I thank you for being all that you have been to me: a lover and a friend. If I never again taste lips as sweet as yours, Innocent, I will know that I did have them once."

Innocent spent his final year recovering from the emotional devastation of his breakup. He was too hurt to let anyone in and, since he had learned to share love through sex, he was sure he would never again share his body without also giving his heart.

After a year of abstinence, Innocent was a newly minted Sorbonne graduate with a well-paying job. He was also twenty-three and horny. His celibacy resolve was broken weekly when he visited a forty-two-year-old Togolese au pair in her little room at the home of a French businesswoman. Their arrangement served them both for two years.

When he matriculated at the Columbia Business School, New York City's variety of fascinating and beautiful women nearly overwhelmed him. But when he met Lissette, his classmate whose status as a member of the Haitian elite made her both exotic and familiar, he allowed himself to fall in love.

Through his relationship with Lissette, he found his feet in New York. Her SoHo loft—which he subsequently bought from her—and her urbane sensibilities opened the entire city up to Innocent before he even knew what to look for. She was sophisticated, beautiful, connected, and on the "A" list of every player in the city's international social scene. With her encouragement, he found out that he was on several of those lists, too.

When Lissette left for Paris shortly after graduation, some of his social scene left, too. And he learned that their relationship hadn't made the trip. He was ready for a change. He wanted to remake himself, learn who he was as a cosmopolitan African professional in New York City. He had bought Lissette's loft from her, so he had a stylish address, but he had to build the rest for himself.

Noire was a part of the rebuilding. In her he saw someone who wasn't slotting him into a scene that they both already shared. She was outside of the flow: she was African American, she lived in Brooklyn, and she didn't make any claims of affluence. He also came to know her passion, her wit, her sincerity, and the depth of her beauty and love. She loved him as if her life depended on it and, despite his own reserve, he came to do the same. There was no choice. Noire demanded all of him. And she challenged everything he knew he wanted. Noire was like too much of a good thing. Too much of anything could be bad.

So their relationship became bad. Fraught with too many highs and lows, too much drama, too many things said that they could not take back. Every space they occupied together was crowded.

But yet he had come back. And things were different. They had traded words for action. Noire didn't ask questions he couldn't answer, accepted every raw emotion that exited his body without flinching, and held on as tightly as he did for reasons that lurked in the shadowy underside of her thoughts. Innocent didn't ask questions, either. Noire wasn't his girlfriend; she was his fix. And right now, that's what he needed.

∞

Noire stepped around the boxes that crowded the doorway of Jayna's cramped Washington Heights studio. The air was rank, filled with the smell of spilt beer and stale marijuana.

"Damn, girl." Noire kissed Jayna on the cheek and handed her a bag with a seven-dollar Dominican feast that she had picked up on her way in. "Who did you have living in *here*?"

"A white boy." She threw Noire a look, as if to say that no

more explanation was needed. And it wasn't. "Took him three weeks to move his shit out. Can you imagine? I had to sleep on tired-ass Wendell's living room floor for three weeks while he acted like I didn't exist. Prancin' his ass around naked!"

Noire had slept on that same living room floor for three weeks last summer and had witnessed Jayna's then-boyfriend's penchant for displaying himself to mixed company but said nothing. She needed to be supportive. "What caused the breakup?"

"What *didn't* cause it, you mean!" Jayna dished out the rice and beans onto styrofoam plates and pulled the roasted pork close to her. "I know you don't eat this."

Noire nodded and retrieved her own fried fish from its container.

"Wendell and his tired ass had me jumping through hoops. I mean, what does a homegirl have to do? I'm already a dentist, for godsakes! But he wanted me to get a weave. Offered to pay for it and everything. He had already gotten a referral."

Noire choked on a black bean. "A *weave*? Why?"

"He said I needed to walk the walk."

"Of what?"

"Of being his woman. Apparently my hair is too short for official appearances." Grabbing some hair between her thumb and pointer finger, she pulled it taut to its full two inches and snapped.

"That's bananas!"

"Who are you telling!" Jayna munched on her pork. "But the worst of it was the cunnilingus prohibition."

"What? He wouldn't go down on you?"

"No, girl."

"*Never?*"

Jayna shook her head. "He did once. The day before we broke up. But then he went through all this drama about how his previous girlfriends were understanding and never required it of him."

Noire was stunned.

"And I was like, 'Negro, how dare you tell me about other chicks' pussies when you're naked in *my* bed!' Then he corrected me, saying that the one-thousand-eight-hundred-dollar bed I've been enjoying these past seventeen and a half months belonged to *him,* as did the condo with a view of New Jersey."

"That's fucked up, Jayna." She saw tears well up in her friend's eyes. "Hey, I'm sorry. I mean, he's too raggedy to even cry over, but . . . I know it hurts."

"I wish it didn't but it does." Jayna let her tears flow in a rare show of vulnerability. "I was trying to love that asshole. In fact, I did love him." She blew her nose into the stack of napkins that came with their takeout. "You know I'm the only homegirl who goes and *breaks up* with her boyfriend after 9/11! You know Trina's man proposed to her?"

Noire didn't know Trina or her man. "Trust me, Jayna, you're not the only one. And don't worry about everyone else. You just need to take care of you. What your needs are. Wendell is not the one!"

She nodded in agreement. "But what does a black woman have to do to get some love?"

Noire wiped a tear from a corner of her eye. "*I love you,* Jayna." She smiled her compassion.

Jayna was wiping her own eyes with the used napkins and trying to set her face into its usual urban bravadista stance. "If I was a lesbian, maybe I'd try to work with that. But I'm strictly a dick-lover." She hunched her shoulders. "My shit's just too good for most homeboys. That's the problem!" She snapped her head in a fierce affirmation of her own words.

"Yup."

"So, is Innocent still tightening you up on the regular or is the sympathy sex over? It *is* November."

Noire was sorry she had let that slip a couple weeks ago. "I see him every now and again."

"Don't be cagey with me! Why don't you join the trend and get married? You know you'd say 'yes' if he asked you." Jayna bored holes into Noire's face.

"Sex isn't a relationship."

"But you two have *had* a relationship. You've had the love as well as the sex. I bet you still have both. So why be hardheaded about it?" She threw up her hands for effect.

"You make it sound simple."

"In your whole relationship, I never heard you say that Innocent complained about your hair or that bohemian way you like to dress. He didn't seem to give a shit. And even with all your proclamations about wanting a poor but righteous brotha when we were in college, I don't remember you protesting the major ducats Innocent was dropping on you in *that* relationship. You had a man who loved who you were, not who *he* wanted you to be. So, what's the problem?"

Noire couldn't answer her because, right then, she couldn't remember what the problem was. Every objection she had to Innocent got flushed out of her pores every time he made her come. Her thoughts were a chaotic mess. "It's just not that simple. I don't know if I'm in a good position to love him . . . or anyone."

"And what was the deal with that dude in Haiti? You said he was brilliant and that he wanted to give you a baby!"

A laugh rumbled in Noire's throat. "There are plenty of men right here in New York City who would be happy to give a woman a baby!"

"True." Jayna joined her laughter, then got serious again. "But that's not what I mean. You said he was nice and that he said he loved you. Don't you know how to love a man who loves you?"

Noire felt her muscles tighten. "Of course, dammit! Don't make me sound like some jaded black woman, because I'm not."

"Those are your words, not mine."

Noire glared at her before continuing. "He's just got a lot of baggage."

"Who's traveling light these days? Surely not you."

"Jayna, look. I came here to see how *you* were doing. Not to get grilled about my love life!"

"All I'm saying is, kill the nonsense, Noire. Your girl Arikè's husband is dead. Samantha from high school is dead. And she had just gotten married two weeks before. There's no time for waiting, Noire. If you've got something good, you need to act on it."

Noire thought about Arikè. She had called her a couple of days ago and dropped in just to check on her last week, but she seldom knew what to say. How many ways can you say "I'm sorry" to a woman who became a widow at twenty-nine years old? Noire didn't know if her awkward conversation comforted her or just highlighted Dennis's absence. And she didn't feel she had any right to burden Arikè with her own problems that must have seemed like self-created drama by comparison.

She returned her thoughts to the conversation. "It's not that simple, Jayna."

"Listen, Black, we're thirty now. Simple is just *not* coming back. Get over it."

❧

Innocent calculated the time in Paris. It was nearly one A.M. He had been trying to reach Mamadou for over a month, but the best he could do was play a game of one-sided phone tag or trade three-line e-mail messages. Mamadou was busy with the gallery, he knew, but he needed the compassionate ear and sage counsel of his oldest and dearest friend. He dialed and pressed the handset against his left ear.

"*Allô?*" His voice was still asleep.

"*C'est moi, mon reuf!*" Innocent smiled into the phone, hoping to jog him into wakefulness.

"*Pardon? Qui est à l'appareil?*" Mamadou's grogginess emerged as annoyance.

"It's Innocent, man. I thought you'd know your best friend's voice anywhere."

"It's late." Recognition hadn't yet softened his newly wakened edges.

"Hey, I know. I just—have you gotten my messages?"

"Look, I'm sorry, man. Things have been crazy with the gallery. I've got a slew of new investors—Spaniards and North Africans mostly—who are willing to underwrite anything I can dream up, but they're giving me a tough go of it. At literally a moment's notice I've got to be ready for breakfast meetings at dawn and dinner till midnight. This is my first day off so I tucked in early. These days, I'd rather sleep than have sex!"

"That's saying a lot, *mon reuf*!" Innocent tittered, his unease about his own news growing.

"So look, I'm sorry I haven't replied to your latest e-mail and call, and I really shouldn't talk long now, but—"

"Mamadou, I'm going to be a father!" Innocent shouted into the phone.

"A father?" He snickered. "A *father*!" He let the news sink in. "*MALPT!*" He guffawed.

"I need more than luck."

"Yeah, I guess you do." He chuckled. "So, is Noire the happy mommy-to-be?"

Innocent frowned into the phone. What did Mamadou know

about Noire that he didn't? He had only met her once. "Why are you saying *that*?"

"For the simple fact that she's the last woman I know you to have dated, and you love each other—at least you did then—*and* she wanted to have your baby from the time I met her on that crazy trip two years ago—"

"She said that?!"

"But I suppose I'm wrong." Mamadou cleared his throat.

Innocent searched for his words. "The woman . . . the *mother* . . . is a longtime friend of the family. My sister Charlotte's age-mate, actually." He jumped out of his desk chair and lunged toward the kitchen in search of a Dr Pepper that he knew wasn't there. He cursed himself for giving it up; he'd have to pick up a couple of cans. Just for emergencies.

"How long have you known—"

"Chi-Chi. I remember her from way back. They, she and Charlotte, went to secondary school together."

"But you were at university then. Here. In Paris."

Innocent remained silent. He was incriminating himself.

"Look, man, I'm not trying to grill you or judge you or anything. I was just wondering how you know her. If you know her, even. You wouldn't be the first." He sighed. "Does she live in New York now?"

Innocent relaxed his jaw. He hadn't known what to expect, but he imagined that Mamadou's view of him had shifted, lessened somehow. Innocent had prided himself on always being in control, and getting Chi-Chi pregnant was a stark departure from that. "She lives back home. We got together, you know, when I was there earlier this year."

"Mmm . . ."

Innocent could hear him get up from his bed, walk the ten steps over to his refrigerator, and pour himself a small glass of water. Mamadou drank water like most people drank vodka. Especially at night.

"So, are you going to try to make a go of it with her?"

He felt a dam burst. "I barely know her, Mamadou. That's the fucked-up part. I mean, with anyone else . . . But I just don't know what to do about it." He stopped short of mentioning his recent involvements with Noire, though he ached to know how Mamadou knew she wanted to be the mother of Innocent's children.

"*Do?* Seems like it's already been *done,* Papa. Now you have to support whatever *she* has to do. I imagine she's planning to keep it."

"She's five months pregnant now."

"*Putain!*" He breathed noisily into the phone. "Okay, okay . . . How long have you known?"

"A little over a month."

"Right, right . . . Look, Innocent, don't see this as a bad 'thing. Because whether you're happy or sad, it is what it is. You're going to be a father. That's a blessing. Really. Some of us should have a tribe by now; I'm convinced I'm shooting blanks!" He snickered. "But honestly, Innocent, you're thirty-five years old. I know that you had hoped to join families and kill a fatted calf and all that before fatherhood came along, but I know you'll do the right thing."

"That's just it. What *is* the right thing?"

"You'll have to pray on that, *mon reuf*. But the answer is out there. Somewhere."

Innocent felt less comforted than he had hoped. His thoughts somersaulted in a hundred different directions. "So, Noire wanted my baby?"

"That's the second time you asked me that, Innocent. Seems that you have a better answer than me. Does she know about the pregnancy?"

His words stung his ears. "No."

"Are you no longer in touch with her?" Mamadou's tone suggested that he didn't believe that to be true.

"We're in touch."

"In touch."

"That's what I said."

"So, where exactly are you touching her?"

"Man, fuck! Why are you asking me all that?" Innocent was indignant.

"Because you called me at one A.M. to 'talk.' And I want to know the answer."

He sighed. "We've been getting together. Hanging out some."

"At the *movies*? Come on, Innocent. I've known you since you were nineteen. You're not a hands-off kinda guy."

"We're *fucking*, okay? No relationship. No 'I love you.' We're fucking."

Mamadou sipped his water. "This is sounding unfortunate."

"Why is sleeping with Noire more unfortunate than having a baby with a woman from home whom I barely know?" He was incredulous.

"It's not. It's the two things together that concern me, Innocent. You can't think clearly about one thing because you're mired in the other. You need to extract yourself from something. And since you can't undo Chi-Chi's pregnancy, you need to undo your 'arrangement' with Noire."

Innocent scrunched his eyes into the back of his head until they hurt. If only that could be his penance. "I know, man."

"Noire's a beautiful woman. She doesn't deserve to be jerked around."

"I didn't force her into this."

"Maybe not, but she's not operating with full information and you are. That's the definition of jerking someone around."

Innocent nodded. He knew.

"Innocent, I don't need to tell you that you're in a tight spot right now. I'm a man, too, and I know that shit happens. But I'm also your friend. I don't want to see you go out like this. Tell Noire the truth and cut your losses. The truth can't hurt as much as this lie."

"You're right."

"Innocent, I've got to be up at six, or I would talk longer. But believe me, the sex is not worth putting yourself through all the hell. For you or Noire. She's a beautiful woman, man. Let her move on with her life."

He nodded his head. "I will."

"Hey, I'm going to be in Washington, D.C., in mid-November. I've got a solo exhibition at the Howard University art gallery."

Innocent's spirits brightened. "You know Mireille is there?"

"Oh, right. Of course. So if you can come down—"

"I'm there, Mamadou. You know it."

"And Innocent, I'm on your side. It's gonna work out for you."

"Thanks, man."

CHAPTER FIVE

BROKEN

Noire traced the steps she had memorized during the year and a half of her relationship with Innocent. She tripped over her feet, her eyes blurry and unfocused. She didn't know what she needed but she wanted to numb the crushing in her chest. She galloped the nine blocks that separated her from Innocent's apartment, knowing that he would be there and that he would soothe her. The doorman, reacquainted with Noire's presence since her and Innocent's recent trysts, nodded her up. She knocked on Innocent's front door and he opened it immediately.

"Bonita's dead," she said to his stunned face.

"Oh my God."

She allowed herself to be ushered in and guided to sit on his unmade bed. Her wails fractured the air. Innocent held her hand, and when she flailed about, he grasped her thigh.

When exhaustion robbed her of her sound, he stared into her glassy eyes. "I'm so sorry, Noire. What happened?"

"She was on that flight headed to the Dominican Republic that crashed this morning. She was going to see her son—meet his wife and daughter. She hadn't seen him since her grandmother sent her to New York to live with her mother like thirty years ago."

Innocent produced a handkerchief from his pocket and handed it to Noire. "My God." He shook his head.

They sat still on the bed, Noire's tears drawing silent lines down her face. Innocent studied her. Watching Noire cry always upset him. She looked like a watercolor whose delicate lines had been smeared by careless, wet hands. He reached for her and pulled her into him. He felt the urgency of an aching heart beating against his own chest. Noire's right hand crept up the side of Innocent's face in tentative movements. She pulled away from him just enough for her lips to brush his.

"Oh God, no. We— I-I can't," Innocent moaned.

"Please." Noire's eyes held the sincerity of her own desperation and grief. She pleaded with her eyes, her hand suspended at his ear.

"Noire, I—" His voice cracked so he stopped speaking and stared at Noire's eyebrows arched into twin question marks before she pressed her lips to his with an insistence that neither of them was strong enough to resist.

Innocent tasted Noire's pain on his tongue. Her body imparted every hurt feeling she had ever felt. He wanted to make her better, to ease her pain by making it his own. He pulled away from her, wiped her face with his hands. "This is not what you need, Noire. *I'm* not what you need right now."

"So then give me what I want." She challenged him with her stare and pulled off her jeans and panties. Taking his silence as compliance, she pushed his sweatpants to his knees. "Give me what I want." Her voice edged in despair, she gulped back the avalanche of grief that crashed inside of her. Noire was running.

Running from the pain that spilled out of her skin as sweat. She pushed it away from her with violent kicks, replacing it with Innocent just as violently. She dug her heels into his buttocks and her nails into his back, pulling herself up off the bed and latching onto him. She thrust her pelvis toward him, forcing him deep inside of her recesses.

Wrestling him down to the bed, she pinned him under her by sheer force of will and he poured everything he had into her in angry thrusts that drained the heat from his mouth, curled his toes, and wrenched a howl from the pit of his groin. Every inch of his body was exquisitely sensitive and burned from Noire's rough touch.

Noire's eyes stung from the salty mix of sweat and tears that bathed her face. Every sob pulled her body closer around Innocent still inside her and under her and holding her. He was the only thing that let her know she was really living the present moment. So she memorized the feeling: the resistance, the hardness, the support. Everybody was dying. Was she dying, too? The pain robbed her of her perspective. She held on to Innocent's body—in her, on her, under her—and told herself this was real. And that the pain meant she was still alive.

Innocent felt the curve of Noire's behind tickle the nest of hair between his legs. He opened his eyes. A new sun cast an ethereal glow across her shoulders and down her back, finally resting on the heart tattooed in the crevice of her back that bloomed into her proud behind. He longed to kiss her right there, his favorite place on her body at his favorite time of day. Right now, everything was simple. He didn't have to ask himself why he was in bed with his ex-girlfriend rather than in Côte d'Ivoire with the expectant mother of his child. Or why Alexander and Dennis and Bonita were dead but he was alive. He wanted to savor the moment by letting his tongue slip into the crease of Noire's back and between her cheeks. But he knew that once he did, she would awaken and begin the complexity of the day.

He heaved and tasted Noire on his tongue. This would be the last time. Nervousness crept along his spine. He stirred. He was at the wrong place at the wrong time. Noire needed to know about his child on the way, about what had been happening with him. He clutched his flaccid penis as though he didn't understand its actions and sprang out of his bed. Cold air greeted his skin.

Noire, scared awake, stared at Innocent's naked body shivering in the murky light of the morning. "What's wrong?"

Innocent watched the unrehearsed bounce of her breasts in an attempt to reclaim some of the enthusiasm he usually displayed for Noire. But he couldn't, and instead stood shriveled and alarmed.

"Innocent?" Noire clambered out of the bed and tried to hug her body into his, tried to soothe him and seduce him to soften her fear as much as his. Nothing was right, she knew. They weren't a couple. They weren't even dating. They had become the other's sex partner. Or at least he had become hers.

The phone tore a hole through the stillness of the morning. Noire frowned at Innocent fastened to the spot where he stood, more fearful than she had ever seen him. "Innocent, get it," she pleaded on the third ring. She knew just how much she didn't belong there.

Innocent broke free of the hold on his body and dropped onto his cracked leather banker's chair. It let out a groan before he answered the phone. A voice he didn't know spoke words that changed his identity. He was a father. Of a baby girl. She was born twelve weeks too early. She was in intensive care. Fighting for her life. Chi-Chi hemorrhaged but they think she should be okay.

A tidal wave welled up inside of him. He was a father. To a

girl. A sick, premature, tiny baby only eleven hours old and without a name. He was not there for her.

Innocent spoke in a rough whisper, his rudimentary Abure inadequately expressing his worry. Yes, he would fly out immediately. Of course, he would pray for his daughter. Yes, the child should have his last name.

He looked up at Noire and felt ashamed. Ashamed that he hadn't told her about his child. That he had had sex with her so many times, exposed her weaknesses in his bed, so many times, but he hadn't shared his own secrets.

The call finished, he held on to the phone to buy himself some time. But Noire knew he was finished. He had stopped talking and she could see he was no longer listening. His mind was somewhere else. In that instant, she became scared to stand there naked, as if putting on clothes would protect her from what she was about to hear. She knew she shouldn't be as vulnerable as she had allowed herself to become. It didn't feel safe.

She turned her back to him and stooped to retrieve her panties still sitting inside her jeans like she had jumped out of both and could easily jump back in. She knew Innocent was looking at her but his eyes upon her body felt uncomfortable. She lowered herself to the edge of the bed and hunched her body in upon itself as she wrestled her bra from her balled-up T-shirt. She prayed that Innocent would wait until she was dressed before telling her the news she knew would hurt her.

"I'm a father." He cleared his throat. "To a baby girl. My daughter— She was just born . . . in Côte d'Ivoire." Innocent listened to himself declare his new status to the woman he once thought would bear his children.

Noire felt her stomach wring out every bit of bile and push it to the top of her neck. The bitter taste sat at the back of her throat and made her nauseated. *A father? A FATHER!* She had been sharing her body with him, seeking comfort from him, even though she should not have, and he had failed to mention that somebody was carrying his BABY! But instead she said, "I don't understand," before lifting her body up just enough to slip her panties over her exposed crotch.

"I needed to tell you . . . before now . . . but— She was conceived when I went home." He made it sound like it was a lab experiment. "Her mother and I are . . . friends."

She narrowed her eyes at him. "More than *friends,* Innocent. You have a *child.*"

"Yes, well . . . yes. But we're not together. I wouldn't have . . . let everything happen—with us—if we were!" Innocent grew defensive.

"Does she have a fuck buddy, too? Is that how the two of you do it?" Her voice was too weary to hold any malice.

"Noire—"

"Oh, and my bad. Congratulations." Noire wasn't sure what she had a right to feel, but she felt anger, jealousy, and betrayal churn in the pit of her groin, nevertheless.

"Please . . . Noire, the baby's so sick. She was due on February sixth." His voice was thick with tears.

Noire's roar was cut to a whisper. "I'm sorry."

Innocent was awash with pride and fear and shame. He looked at Noire and knew he didn't have any more space inside of himself to take in all that she felt. He was sorry about it, but he was too full. "Noire, look, I'm really sorry, but I can't— I just need some time to get myself together. I have to go to see her."

He pushed his forehead into his hands clasped on his desk. He was the father of a two-pound baby born five thousand miles away. He listened to his breathing to block out Noire's muffled sniffling across the room. He couldn't comfort her, nor could she him. They were both too broken for that. So he didn't allow himself to hear her or see her. When he finally turned around, she was gone.

Part Two

ACTION AND REACTION

CHAPTER SIX

DAUGHTER
OF MY SOUL

Noire started with the bananas. She lined them up by height—shortest to tallest—and carefully returned them to a cake pan repurposed to contain her overflowing assortment of fruits and vegetables. A cluster of eyes dotted three old potatoes in the bottom of her produce drawer; she'd have to throw those away, too. The pile had grown: one withered bell pepper, four prunelike kiwis, a fuzzy orange, six brown avocados that burst at the slightest touch, and three slices of watermelon swimming in their own smelly overripe juices. Pinching her nose with one hand, she pitched the bad fruit into her kitchen trash can with the other. She removed her foot from the trash can's pedal and pulled her face into a frown of disgust. It had all been a waste, a terrible waste.

She padded over to the refrigerator and began a new shopping list:

ERICA SIMONE TURNIPSEED

ORANGES

AVOCADOS

PEACHES

She would be more judicious this time. No sense in buying more produce than she could eat. The November sun darted out from behind a cloud and the indifferent light of normalcy poured into the room. It was just another day. Yet another airplane had been ripped out of the sky so pointlessly but the sun shined like it always did. It seemed cruel.

Noire retrieved her last peach from the refrigerator and left the room. She went to her dark bedroom, the air smelling of half-eaten peaches, and climbed into bed. She took a few bites before the cloying in her empty stomach stopped her and the effort of thinking overcame her. So she balled her body into a knot and fell asleep.

For eighty-six thousand four hundred seconds, Noire did not answer her phone nor did she cancel the Wednesday afternoon class she taught. Instead, she wallowed in restless sleep that dulled the sharp edges of her angst and transported her to a liminal state that slowed her body and mind.

Noire dreamt of fried catfish. Trays and platters of fresh fried catfish being passed around a hut. Bonita was breaking off bits of fish with her fingers and guiding them into Noire's mouth while Innocent held open her legs, spread-eagle in the air, and told her to push. She pushed until beads of sweat rimmed her forehead. She gave birth to Dennis, and Purpose and Arikè both squealed with delight. Noire kept on eating catfish. Kept on eating it. But then she had to go to the bathroom. She turned around and Bonita was gone. Arikè was teaching Innocent to breast-feed the baby she had birthed. But the baby didn't belong to Noire. It was Innocent's. Everyone seemed happy, except for her.

She woke up and screamed. Her apartment smelled like catfish.

"I didn't mean to scare you, baby."

Her mother's voice reached her only moments before she appeared in the doorway. *Her* doorway to *her* bedroom.

"Put that bat down, baby. I'm making catfish." Flora wore Noire's apron over her business suit. "You could wash this, you know." She tapped the apron stiff with Noire's recent cooking mishap.

Noire stared at her mother. When had she arrived?

"Wash your face and brush your teeth, Noire." She surveyed her daughter. "Actually, why don't you get undressed and take a shower." She turned on the bedroom light and stared at Noire as she pulled off a T-shirt and panties that had worn out their welcome.

Naked, she looked at her mother sheepishly.

"I'm throwing these away. You don't need them anymore. Go on, Noire. The shower is calling your first and last name."

Noire obeyed her mother.

Flora finished frying up the catfish and threw together a salad. She looked up at her clean and wet daughter wrapped in a towel. "There was a sale at the fish market near work so I bought this at lunchtime."

Noire nodded and walked back toward her bedroom.

"You might want to put some oil on your skin, baby; you're looking ashy."

Noire slathered cocoa butter onto her skin before putting on the fresh panties, T-shirt, and yoga pants that her mother had laid out for her. "Why did you come?"

"NYU called me to see if you were okay since you left screaming Tuesday morning, and I couldn't give them a good answer. Your phone seemed to be out of order, so I decided to confirm your status for myself. In person."

Noire looked at her mother and could see that Flora knew about Bonita. She hadn't remembered screaming when she got the news of Bonita's death. She could barely remember leaving Innocent's apartment before dawn yesterday. But she remembered the pain in his eyes that mirrored her own.

She was sure her mother knew nothing about Innocent and was content to keep it that way for now. There was no way she could utter the words that told his story, so she wouldn't even try. Instead, she attempted to give Flora her childhood smile that said "I'm okay, really," but it wouldn't form on her lips.

"Your Big Mama always said that she could never be too happy or too sad." Flora confirmed the statement with a nod.

"Because Big Mama could censor her emotions doesn't mean it's that easy for the rest of us."

"It's not censorship, it's wisdom. And it's not easy for any of us, Noire. Lots of things are more painful than anything we thought we would ever live through. But we've *got* to live through them."

"Not everyone can."

"You're right. But right now I'm talking about you."

Filling two plates with food, Flora carried them into the living room. "Still don't have a table?" Her eyes scanned the hodge-podge of furniture: four overrun bookshelves, a well-loved love seat, her father's old computer desk, and a desk chair Noire had rescued from her neighbor's garbage heap the summer before she started grad school.

Noire ignored the question and brought out two TV trays. She set them up in front of the love seat, the only comfortable seating she had, and turned on the TV as a reflex.

"I'd like to talk, Noire."

She clicked the TV off and popped a piece of catfish into her mouth. Her appetite surprised her. She was sure that it should have been gone.

Flora held out her right hand toward Noire and suspended it there until Noire grabbed it. She cleared her throat. "Dear God, we thank you for another opportunity to be in your presence, to partake of your bounty, and to carry out your will one more time. We ask for your strength in times of great trial and your grace that surpasses all understanding. Amen."

Noire mumbled an "amen" and took an overlarge bite of her catfish. She chewed the food violently and gulped it down prematurely. Her stomach thumped, shocked by its new diet expanded from her peach and the nuts and dried fruit she had nibbled at Innocent's loft the day before. She let out a percussive burp, excused herself, and tried to eat more slowly.

"I know about Bonita Fuentes. And I'm so sorry. Especially for her family."

It hurt her just to hear her name. Bonita. *Noire* had been Bonita's family. She had said so herself. Noire had become an odd mix of child/protégée/confidante/girlfriend to Bonita in the three years that they had known each other. She believed in Noire's academic voice and took as an unqualified given that she should use it whenever and wherever she saw fit. Bonita was her strongest advocate and harshest critic. And she loved her with a fierceness that scared and flattered Noire. She didn't fully understand why Bonita had adopted her as she did, but she knew it felt good.

Bonita's "family" didn't know any of that about her. She was the old maid eccentric academic who had been sent to New York City as penance for her pregnancy and then never came back. They thought she hated them. And sometimes Bonita claimed that she did. But what she hated was the pain they had caused her and that she imagined she had caused them. So she protected herself. And Noire received all her displaced love and allegiance and hope. Noire was the family that Bonita *chose*.

Noire watched her mother's eyes survey her face. She knew

her thoughts had betrayed her, so she shared a portion. "I was like family to Bonita, Mom. And she was to me."

Flora nodded her head. "Well, I can't pretend to understand your relationship with her. I'm sorry I never met her." She blotted her eyes and looked at Noire. "But I'm here for you, baby. And *I* love you."

She hugged Noire into her ample bosom, and for a minute, Noire felt safe. But as quickly as she felt it, she resigned herself to the fact that her mother wouldn't understand. Noire was no longer the girl whose mother orchestrated her life. She had relationships Flora didn't know about, wounds she couldn't heal, and desires she couldn't change. They both knew it. Noire studied her mother's melancholy frown with a curious detachment that preempted her own sadness. Noire handed her the folded paper towel that she hadn't used and wiped her mouth with the back of her hand.

"Let me share some good news, baby."

"What is it?" Noire didn't think that there was any more good news left.

Flora's mood shifted quicker than her appearance had. Jagged bits of laughter erupted from her mouth as she wiped the remaining tears from her eyes.

"Mom, are you okay?"

"Ooh! I guess I still don't know myself!" Flora dabbed new tears from her eyes and fought to regain some semblance of composure. "I'm getting married!" This time her laughter came in a wild torrent that slapped Noire in the face.

"*Married?!* To whom?" Noire was afraid her mother had decided to do something rash.

"To your *father*!"

Noire gasped, her face stamped with shock. How could she be marrying her father? "But, I don't . . . quite—" She didn't know what to say. Of course, she knew her parents were friends and that they occasionally did things together. And in the last few years, they had been willing—even encouraging—of spending Thanksgiving and Christmas together. But Noire had naively thought that was all for her benefit. Though, of course, she *was* thirty years old.

"It kind of surprised me, too, baby. But I'm happy. Paul popped the question"—she fanned herself with Noire's copy of *The Sista's Rules*—"well, almost four weeks ago now. I just— we've both kind of been in shock. I still don't know how to act," she said, almost to herself. "We weren't sure how best to tell you. It's just, with all that's been happening, the terrorist attacks and everything, we figured, why not? After all, we love each other. And of course none of us knows how long we have. Why wait for tomorrow?"

Why wait for tomorrow? Because you waited *for thirty-one years!* Noire looked at her mother and waited for a punch line that never came.

"Noire? I expected you to be surprised, but . . . Well, say something! Aren't you excited?"

"Of the thirteen million things I imagined you might say, this was not on the list."

"Mmm." She shook her head. "Paul told me not to expect a big reaction. Not immediately." She paused, looked almost sedate. "I guess there's just been a lot going on. I had gotten my hopes up. Well, I'll give you a little time to . . . sit with it, you know. But I'd like you to be my maid of honor. I'd be happy if you would."

Flora's face told her she was looking for a response. "Okay." Noire felt trapped.

"Oh, it'll be wonderful. I'm so happy!" Flora hugged Noire and this time Noire hung on for support. She didn't get it. Just like that, out of the clear blue, her parents had become engaged. Thirty-one years after they met. Thirty years after having *her.*

Somehow, they never saw fit to jump the broom. Until now. What was that? She witnessed her mother's excitement but couldn't match it.

"Noire, you should eat your food. The fish will get cold."

She got up and dug a lone cigarette out of her jacket pocket. One of Bonita's cigarettes. Fighting the urge to scream, she retrieved a book of matches from the kitchen and lit it, plopping onto a pillow in the center of her living room.

"I didn't know you smoked." Flora sounded reproachful.

"I do a lot of things." Noire slid her eyes over at her mother and savored the wicked pleasure that had been hers and Bonita's.

She was the woman-child who fought her little-girl's need for reassurance that she was still first in her mother's life and the adult who desperately wanted not to care. But because she could be neither completely, she was a dueling duo who felt hurt by her own confusion.

❈

Innocent stared at the tiniest living body he had ever seen. Hooked up to breathing devices and poked with IV needles, she lived in the shelter of a plastic igloo—an isolette—that enclosed her. "Can she hear through it?" he asked the nurse who hovered at his right.

"The sounds are muted, but yes."

He reached into his bag and pulled out the tiny music box that his grandmother had bought him when he was a baby and wound it up. Sitting atop the isolette, it issued the tinkling notes of a French lullaby he had known all his life. The baby, his baby, flexed her feet in a full-body yawn as her lips readjusted around the breathing tube that sustained her life.

He counted her toes and studied her features before his tears made her a blur.

"You can touch her. But please wash your hands first."

He washed his face and hands, then opened one of the doors to the isolette and reached for one of her perfect feet. Her skin was so fragile and new, unexposed to the world's roughness. Her entire leg was smaller than the span of his hand. He touched the underside of her right hand with his finger and she held on.

"I am your father," he whispered, "and I love you. I will always love you." Innocent marveled at her tiny ears and the eyelashes on her closed eyes. Her pinky-brown skin and downy baby hair completed this new being. At three days old, her two-pound body fought to carry out the tasks that were too difficult for a baby who was still twelve weeks away from her due date.

"You were supposed to be a Valentine's baby. But you just couldn't wait, could you?" Innocent's voice was low, his words soothing himself more than the little person who lay before him. He looked at the depression her chest made with each breath. She seemed to be working too hard. He turned to look for the nurse who had been hovering near him only a moment before. At the sound of a piercing alarm, she rushed past him. She was joined by another nurse who, together, worked feverishly on his daughter, leaving him to watch. Their actions were punctuated by one-word commands and they worked with a determination he had never before witnessed. The younger of the two started to mumble something in a barely audible Dioula. He knew she was praying. He was praying, too. For his daughter, whose isolette read BABY GIRL POKOU. She was a Pokou. The next generation of his family. She had to live.

It took fifteen minutes to stabilize her. She lay there, her mouth pried open even wider, full of larger tubes, her body attached to more IVs. She wasn't getting enough oxygen, he was told. Her lungs were very premature, even for her age. Her mother's ruptured placenta and preeclampsia—a pregnancy-induced illness that caused dangerous hypertension and organ failure—had restricted Chi-Chi's blood vessels, thereby depriving the baby of some of the nourishment that she needed. The nurse added, in a gentler voice, that his daughter's condition was very fragile and that things could change at a moment's notice.

Innocent nodded without understanding. All he knew was that she had to live. He reached down to the music box, broken on the floor, and promised he would fix it for her. Overcome with emotion, he was directed to leave for a while; it wasn't good for the baby. He left her reluctantly.

Chi-Chi's skin looked like a crumpled paper bag and her body was an ill-fitting mass inside. Her lips were cracked and her closed eyes caked with old tears. Her mother looked at Innocent with a start. "Oh!" came out in a burst. "Let me wash her face." She grabbed a washcloth off the nightstand and rubbed it quickly over Chi-Chi's face before Innocent could stop her.

Standing over the bed, Innocent was gripped by a wave of pity quickly followed by a sense of awe. Chi-Chi was the mother of his child. She had given birth to his daughter—their daughter.

"Sit on the bed." Chi-Chi's voice was stronger than her body. "I nearly died, Innocent. And so did Bisi." She used a family pet name for their unnamed daughter.

He shook his head.

"I'm sorry I couldn't hold her, couldn't keep her inside me."

"You brought her this far, Chi-Chi. We thank God for that."

"She's beautiful, heh?" A flash of pride flickered in her eyes.

"Like her mother." Their daughter's crisis of the moment before choked him up. He closed his eyes.

"You don't have to say what you don't mean."

"Chi-Chi, she is beautiful and she looks like you. I mean both." He didn't know how he felt about Chi-Chi. She was a beautiful woman shrouded in the skin of sickness. And though he didn't love her, he loved what she had done and admired the determination that was the reason both she and their baby were alive.

"What will you do, Innocent?"

"I will stay here until she—until you both come home."

"What is home for us, Innocent?"

Innocent felt the sting of the question. "I can always call my father's house my home and you can call your father's house home as well."

Chi-Chi rolled her head to the other side of her pillow and Innocent studied her ear. Just like their daughter's ear. He knew that she had become a part of him because she had borne their child. No matter what happened in the future, she was a part of him and he her. Their celebration of Chi-Chi's birthday had given birth to another life.

"I'll come to see you tomorrow."

"Please don't, Innocent."

He nodded at the back of her head and raised his eyes to meet those of her mother, who stood pinned into the corner of the room. He bounced his head again, sharply, and walked out of the room. He had to get home so he could fix the music box. His daughter needed it.

〰

Noire pulled her hair into a severe bun, an erratic Afro-puff exploding out the other side of the hairclip. Red lipstick accentuated the pout of her lips, and her dress—a vintage black-and-white polka-dot chiffon that had been a thirtieth birthday gift from Bonita—gave her the appearance of Bonita's beloved flamenco dancers whom she had often imagined herself to be.

Dressed for a dance more than Bonita's memorial service, Noire nevertheless saw her outfit as a declaration of love for a woman who had cultivated a passion for her field that she didn't know she had. Bonita had been more than her mentor, and she was more than her protégée, she had been a sista-friend who allowed Noire her quirks and shortcomings. Bonita had lived with her own longings and regrets, so she didn't discourage Noire from having her own, just from succumbing to them.

Noire walked through the doors of the Church of Our Lady of Refuge in Bonita's beloved Bronx neighborhood and stopped short. A closed wooden casket lay stretched out in the center aisle. Noire's eyes began to water when she glanced at the picture of a much younger Bonita in the same dress that Noire now wore. It was a professional black and white and the interplay of light and shadow, along with Bonita's proud stance and castanets in both hands, made her every bit the Andalusian Gypsy. In all of their long-winded conversations, Bonita had never said that she had danced on any more than a social level, but the picture told a different story. Noire's eyes grew moist with tears of sadness and humility. Bonita had given her a piece of her history, of her passion, when she gave her the dress, but Noire had neglected to ask about the story that went with it. She realized that she had been afraid to ask Bonita much about herself because she didn't want to cause her to recall painful memories. But not everything was painful. She studied Bonita's piercing eyes and saw playfulness and sensuality. And happiness. Noire would never know the story of that happiness.

A small, slight man tapped Noire's shoulder. "Would you like me to direct you to a seat?" His words were in Spanish, and he spoke them with gentle authority. Taking Noire's silence as an answer, he began to march her down the aisle and along the side of the casket, depositing her into a wooden pew in the first row.

"I can't— Can I move . . . back just a bit?" Noire fidgeted.

"Aren't you the daughter of the deceased?"

Confusion lined her face and weighted her tongue. He must have read her frown as agreement because he patted her hand and left her sitting where he had placed her.

Noire made a careful sign of the cross, the reverent gesture taught and reinforced through weekly Mass attendance during her childhood summers in New Orleans with devoutly Catholic Grand-mère. She hadn't stepped foot inside a Catholic church since her last Louisiana summer when she was twelve, but the memory of Mass on Sundays—conducted in a thick Louisiana French and populated almost exclusively by quadroons and octoroons—lived as a vivid, bittersweet memory. She remembered her feeling of accomplishment when she could rattle off a memorized prayer with the same French cadence as Grand-mère, and she liked the lemon verbena toilet water that her grandmother would dab on her neck only on Sundays. But she dreaded the weekly hair-straightening exercise that Grand-mère thought necessary and the unanswered prayers to God that he give Grand-mère a steady hand so she wouldn't burn the backs of Noire's ears. At thirteen, the recent memories of those hot-comb burns, and the constant teasing from her "redbone" cousins for her dark skin and nappy hair outweighed the summer's pleasantries and she declared her independence. That summer she went to summer camp.

A man the size of a newly sharpened pencil eased into the pew beside Noire. He nodded at her briefly before sinking onto the kneeler and plunging himself in prayer.

Noire had forgotten that she should be praying. She had never considered whether or not Bonita believed in God, attributing the ornately carved wooden cross in Bonita's bedroom more to her Latino heritage than to any pose of Christianity. She turned her head toward the casket. Was Bonita really inside? She thought of the news reports that said only pieces of bodies had been recovered, and became weak with nausea.

The man pulled up from the kneeler and returned to his seat. "I'm Eduardo, Bonita's son." He kissed both of Noire's surprised cheeks in greeting.

"And I'm Noire. Nice to meet you," she whispered, her Spanish self-conscious despite her fluent mastery of it.

"Yes, I know. My mother had e-mailed me about you. She called you '*hija de mi alma*' and she told me that you were a beautiful woman whose love made her happy in a way that she hadn't been in a long time." He wiped his eyes with a handkerchief. "Thank you for being that to her."

Noire tried to smile. She turned the phrase over in her mind—daughter of my soul. The line came from the Andalusian flamenco song "Trigo Limpio" that Bonita played incessantly in her office. That song, coming from a beat-up tape recorder, was the only piece of her personal life that Bonita would ever bring to her NYU office. She didn't know that Bonita had called her a daughter, least of all to her own son. "I didn't realize . . ." Noire pulled out her own handkerchief and blew her nose.

"And did you know that our birthdays are the same day? But I think you're older." Eduardo smiled cautiously, unsure of whether he should have said the last part.

Noire smiled. "By three years. Yes, she told me." She grabbed his hand. "She really wanted to meet you. And your wife and daughter."

Eduardo blew his nose. "I don't remember her, of course. She left when I was only a few weeks old. But— Well, she had you. And now I have you, too. Please, I would love it if you could tell me more about her."

"I will." Noire stared at the picture of Bonita, the dress she now wore falling against her graceful curves. She had known things about Bonita. Things no one else knew. She looked at Eduardo's profile; he looked like Bonita from the side. Maybe she still had her, too.

CHAPTER SEVEN

NERVOUS

Noire sat stock-still, her unwilling body absorbing the vibrations of her mother's stifled giggles. Flora imparted unsolicited smiles to the groaning masses that pressed into their overfull subway car as it lurched through Manhattan at evening rush hour. Why had she made the appointment now? Noire wondered. She eyed the commuters' faces: their sullen expressions of post-traumatic stress had replaced the normal chatter of parents inquiring about their children's homework, the playful repartee of coworkers blowing off steam after work, and the good cheer that Thanksgiving season usually ushered in. Instead, a tense silence ruled; they were just holding on till home. She turned toward her mother and saw her fondling her three-week-old engagement ring, its sapphire, diamond, and yellow gold bigness more gaudy than anything Noire had ever seen her wear. Why were her parents going through all these changes, anyway? They'd already known each other for thirty-one years!

"I'm thinking of wearing a white dress" sprang out of Flora's mouth like a leprechaun toward a pot of gold.

Noire winced.

"I mean, I *am* a first-time bride!" She giggled again, this time uncontrollably.

"Mother, you're fifty-two years old; you don't have to go through all the hoopla. Why don't you just go to City Hall?" Noire's voice was strained.

"Since when is a woman's wedding 'hoopla'?" Flora's eyebrows came together in a momentary frown before an unexpected view of her engagement ring distracted her from its purpose.

Noire cowered in her seat, afraid of what else she might say. So she chose to keep quiet.

The subway deposited them below West Forty-second Street and Eighth Avenue, at the far corner of the Garment District. The late November chill filtered into the station and made her cold despite her coat as they climbed aboveground and onto the street. They weaved west toward Ninth Avenue, to Cassandra Bromfield's unassuming design studio on the third floor of a small commercial building. Cassandra greeted Flora with a hug and clasped Noire's hand hello. Noire could not match their enthusiasm but she managed a tiny smile.

Flora and Cassandra spoke in the shorthand they had already established over the phone, Cassandra's sketches of a spring wedding dress materializing in quick strokes. Noire tried to picture her mother, clad in white, kissing her father for the first time as his wife. She tried to imagine them as a couple, a package deal, and not just her mom and her dad. They would be husband and wife, legally recognized lovers, and each would be considered the other's next of kin. In the time it took for them to say their vows, Noire would cease to be their primary connection to each other.

She looked at her mother's simple joy, saw the happiness in her eyes, and felt none of it.

Cassandra turned her sketch pad toward Noire and said, "What do you think?"

Noire nodded in simple acknowledgment of the question.

"Noire's my maid of honor." Flora beamed.

"That's me."

Cassandra gave a quizzical glance to Noire before returning her eyes to the sketch pad. "Your mother will make a beautiful bride."

"No doubt." Noire's voice was flat.

Flora and Cassandra chatted, laughed, and produced sketch after sketch of the wedding dress, each a bolder revision on the last. Noire sat in a daze, a headache claiming most of the space in her brain and migrating into her heart. An hour passed before Flora looked at Noire again.

Recognition of Noire's silent pout crossed Flora's face. "You look ill." There was more anger than concern in her eyes, but Flora's voice oozed concern.

"Then I guess I am." Her feelings were inexplicable and strange, her mind's eye plagued with the image of her mother and father kissing, their declaration of their marital union, and her feeling outmoded.

"Maybe you should go to the restroom, baby, and get yourself together."

Cassandra pointed to the studio door and a lone key dangling from a loop of satin ribbon adorned with cowrie shells that hung from its handle. Noire snickered. Even going to the bathroom was a joyous event for brides-to-be, it seemed. She left the room, only realizing belatedly that she didn't know where the bathroom was. She wandered the entire floor before stumbling upon it. Once inside, Noire understood her mother's expression. Her face was creased into a long-held frown. She looked angry. And perhaps she was. Noire was afraid to ask herself why right then. She was afraid that the answer would take a long time to emerge and even longer to resolve. So she smashed her emotions into the most remote corner of her mind she could find, relieved her bladder of its meager contents, and splashed cold water on her face before returning to Cassandra's studio.

"Well, okay, Flora!" Cassandra's voice sounded nervous and like she hadn't been responding to anything Flora said.

Her mother was on her feet, hugging Cassandra good-bye. "We'll be in touch . . . soon." She gave her a familial kiss on the left cheek and turned toward Noire. "Let's go." She moved toward Noire while Cassandra stayed where she was, blocking Noire from offering more than a verbal farewell.

But Noire was too surprised to speak; her frown, smoothed into submission only a moment before, had returned, this time in confusion. The heat from her mother's body pushed her out of the door and back into the hallway. Flora brushed past Noire and headed toward the steps. Noire followed abruptly behind her.

Noire wore her unease like a cape, her shoulders hunched together and hands clutching the center of her chest. She looked down as they walked, her feet a few paces behind her mother, unable to face Flora's anger. They were in the heart of Times Square, and the bustle of commuters competed with intrepid tourists whose trips to Ground Zero during the day gave way to pretheater prix fixe dinners and a cut-rate Broadway play in the evening.

They walked to the subway station in audible silence, Noire struggling to keep up with her mother's nearly six-foot-tall stride. Panting from their sprint through the crisp fall air, they arrived at last on the subway platform.

"Noire"—her gravelly voice stopped them both in their tracks—

"a daughter is supposed to support her mother, and a maid of honor is supposed to support the bride. Which one are *you*?"

"What's that supposed to mean?"

"It means, what the hell is your problem?! Why can't you be happy for me?"

"Maybe I'm not happy for *me*! Or did it never occur to you that I could feel anything other than joy?"

Flora stared in stunned silence, her lips pinched into a dark brown line of tension.

Noire glared in return, righteous indignation filling her. Her mother was being thoughtless and selfish, she told herself.

Flora pointed at the train coming on the Queens-bound side. "Okay, Noire. Good-bye."

"Good-bye?" Noire was incredulous.

"I'm leaving. It's my train." Flora stepped forward, the noxious breeze produced by its rapid appearance blowing her off balance.

Noire nodded only belatedly. She watched the doors open, accept the bodies of dozens of commuters including her mother, and shut. She stared at Flora's face through the window as the train pulled off and noticed that it no longer displayed anger or its former glee but had morphed into an expression as sullen and fatigued as the rest.

Noire felt responsible for her mother's changed mood. She was awash with a mix of annoyance and guilt that proved to be easier emotions for her to deal with than the more confusing feelings that inspired her own funk. She allowed herself to feel miserable as the minutes of her wait for her own train became double digits.

At long last her train entered the station. She was greeted by a raft of people who appeared to have been out to sea for far too long. The train inched along the tracks, stopping every eighth of a mile to adjust its speed back to a crawl. The commuters' anxiety was palpable. Noire held her breath as the train crept through the tunnel that linked Manhattan Island to Brooklyn. Finally at her stop, she breathed a sigh of relief as she climbed back to street level, mounting the steps two at a time.

"Hey, Noire. Thought I'd meet you here rather than at your apartment. I didn't want to scare you."

Noire recognized the face as it came closer to her to land a kiss on her forehead. "Dad?!"

"I know you just met up with your mother, so I figured you'd be coming through pretty soon. That is, unless you decided to make another stop!" He forced a chuckle. "But here you are. I got here a few minutes early so I stopped by that little fish shop around the corner. I got some catfish and breadcrumbs. Figured I'd fry it up."

Noire was sure she had entered the twilight zone in which her parents arrived unexpectedly bearing gifts of catfish. "*Why* are you here?" She squinted her eyes through the evening blackness and focused on the back of her father's left ear as he led the way to her apartment a block and a half away. It was red from the cold.

"Like I told you, I knew you and Flora had your appointment and that you should be coming through." He kept his head forward and his hands rammed deep into his pockets. The bag of fish swung freely from his left wrist.

They walked up the steep staircase that led to her brownstone's front door. Paul stepped aside and let Noire unlock it. Then they climbed three more narrow flights up to her apartment.

"What's up with you? And Mom, too? Has 9/11 made you both overly romantic and overbearing parents, or what?"

"Or what."

"*What?*" Noire turned around to look at her father. He was

hanging his coat on a hook by the door. Paul was barely a quarter inch taller than his daughter's five foot eight, and his rosy cheeks, widening midsection, Mighty Sparrow T-shirt, and unruly shock of curly gray hair coming out from under a red, gold, and green Rasta cap gave him the look of a real soca Santa. Noire smiled despite herself, then remembered she was annoyed by his unexpected appearance and restored a frown.

"Flora told me about your tantrum."

"I didn't have a tantrum!" Noire put her hands on her hips.

"When your nearly thirty-one-year-old daughter crushes the joy of your upcoming marriage, your mother believes that that constitutes a tantrum. And I tend to agree. She was upset, so I told her I'd deal with it."

"This is *bullshit*!"

"I'm not one of your friends, Noire."

"I'm sorry." She cleared her throat. "But how dare you come here to 'deal with' me! What does that even mean? You're right, I am almost thirty-one. I don't need my parents 'dealing with' me because I don't react the way they expect me to. The age of majority came almost thirteen years ago, Dad."

"Don't be snide with me, Noire. Poor choice of words, perhaps. I'll accept that. But that doesn't change the fact that you are having a problem and have hurt your mother."

Noire looked at the hazel brown of her father's eyes and could see that he felt justified in standing there as he was, saying what he was saying to her. It fueled her with fresh venom. "Okay. You're telling me that I've hurt *Mom's* feelings, but neither of you have bothered to check in on *my* feelings. You're talking about 'your mother and I' as though that's been the normal course of things. Well, Dad, it's *not*! In all the years since you accidentally had me—and recall you told me that you and Mom's May 1970 drug binge led to Mom getting pregnant on your first date—you two have *not* been together. Even when I was wetting the bed from nine to eleven years old because of the way children would tease me and I begged you two to get married. In all the years that you were raising me, all the years that I was young, you told me that your love for me had *nothing* to do with each other. That the two of you just weren't meant to be but that it said nothing about me, about us and our family.

"And so now September eleventh happens—tragedy that it is—and you pop the question. Just like that. I am thirty years old and you tell me that *September eleventh* made you decide to get married!"

Her skin was hot with anger, years of anger she didn't know she had. Tears sizzled on her cheeks as she relished the pain on her father's face. She hadn't expected to bring up his bit of verbal diarrhea when he shared the circumstances of her conception, but she wanted him to feel at least a taste of what she was feeling. She felt vindicated by the tears that pooled in the corners of his eyes.

"Noire, I— I don't know what to say." He wiped his face with the back of his hand. "This isn't about you, Noire. About loving or not loving you enough for us to have gotten married when you were young. Flora and I loved you with our whole hearts. With everything we had. And we still do. But our love—the love that Flora and I have for each other—has taken a different course, Noire. A much slower one. And of course there was my marriage to Celine and Jabari's birth . . .

"Maybe 9/11 became a convenient excuse for us to take this love, which has been growing over all of our years of loving and parenting you, to this next step. But more than likely, it made us think about our own mortality. And yours, too.

"Noire, on the morning of 9/11, your mother and I kept a vigil for you. We knew you were up in the air on an American Airlines plane and there was nothing we could do about it. All we could do was pray that we'd see you again.

"Life can be over in the blink of an eye, Noire. The blink of an eye. And when I was forced to think about death—my own or that of you or your mom or Jabari—it forced me to think about the things *I* need to do before I leave this world."

Noire collapsed onto a floor cushion and rocked herself back and forth. "I didn't know."

"I know you didn't know, honey. But it was just too painful to tell you all of that. We just wanted to share the happy news without the accompanying sad thoughts, I guess. After your academic adviser died—"

"Bonita."

"Yes, Bonita. Your mom—we—just wanted to share a little happy news with you. News we thought you'd be happy about."

Noire nodded her head.

"I'm sorry we didn't do this the right way, Noire. And you have a right to feel all the things you're feeling. Maybe in trying to rescue you from the grief of so much loss, we didn't allow you the space for your own emotions. And that's wrong." He sat down at last on the floor beside his daughter and held her hand as she sobbed.

Noire's free hand clawed at her body and the air, her skin spilling grief-filled drops of sweat. Her father grabbed that hand, pulling her into him, and rocked her like the little girl she no longer was. Then, pulling away just enough to see her face, he asked, "How about some fried catfish?"

❧

Stepping out from the air-conditioned interior of Polyclinique Internationale Sainte-Anne-Marie for a breath of fresh air, Innocent was instead greeted by plumes of cigarette smoke rising from clutches of nurses on their lunch breaks and a small band of Japanese tourists whose attire suggested a day of fun and frolic rather than a trip to a hospital emergency room. The fumes, combined with the November harmattan winds that sucked the air dry and draped the sky in red dust, made Innocent feel like he was walking through soup. His lungs gasped in search of a fresh breeze, his bloodshot eyes for moisture.

He walked away from the hospital's imposing edifice that shot out of the ground like a small white mountain range right in the middle of Abidjan's cushy Cocody neighborhood. Innocent had had Chi-Chi and their as-yet-unnamed daughter transferred there four days before, when she was then only three days old. He blamed himself—his absence—for why they hadn't been taken there immediately upon Chi-Chi's health crisis. The other hospital had managed to save Chi-Chi's life and deliver the baby, but PISAM, as the hospital was called, was his daughter's best chance of long-term survival. He had gotten Chi-Chi a single room and his daughter a private nurse who sat vigil over her when sleep or his own father's failing health kept him away for more than ten minutes. She had to live. He knew that his life would mean nothing if she didn't. He had to get this part right.

So he used all of his resources and his family's influence to get her the best care and best medications on the continent. And he prayed with a fervor he never knew he had. His prayers came out in mumbles and moans and erratic tears to the God he had learned to fear as a boy in boarding school but never to love. But now his desperation made him believe in God's saving grace and in miracles performed for the poorest, the weakest, and the least deserving. In the space of thirteen days, Innocent had become more of a father than he had ever known in his own childhood. He was his daughter's champion, medical advocate, and prayer partner. When he stroked the whisper-soft underside of her tiny feet, he imparted his hope and was strengthened by her own will to live. They were a team . . . and they always would be.

But Chi-Chi was afraid to name her. She looked at the frail-ness of her body during her once-daily visits to the neonatal intensive care unit and said "Not yet." She feared that naming this child whose blood still flowed cautiously through her veins would mark her for death. So she referred to her as "my little Bisi," her eyes hard with fear, and refused to touch her. She blamed herself for Bisi's premature appearance in the world and was afraid that she would make her daughter worse instead of better.

Innocent knew that there was no changing Chi-Chi's mind. As her hormones churned and breasts filled with milk she could not give to a child who was still too fragile to hold, she would not be swayed. "You stay with her. Be her mother and her father, Innocent. I'm of no use to her."

So Innocent traced hearts onto the soles of her feet and whispered words of love and encouragement to this new creation lying out before him. He wound up the music box every morning and hummed along to let her know he was there, and he instructed her nurse to play it for her if she fussed.

The rest of Abidjan became no more than a backdrop for the most dramatic chapter of his life. He went home to his parents and performed the role of dutiful son in the crevices of the day. But his heart remained in the hospital, tethered to his daughter.

CHAPTER EIGHT

✤

THE REALNESS

Noire pressed REPEAT on the remote for the fifteenth time in two hours, skipping immediately to "Fool of Me" on the *Love & Basketball* soundtrack. She was overdue to buy Me'shell NdegéOcello's entire album, so for now playing "Fool of Me" incessantly would have to do. The song depressed her. And since she was officially depressed, it was perfect.

She gnawed on what remained of her peach and watched the sunset outside her apartment window. It was the day after Thanksgiving and yesterday's blessings—from volunteering with her dad at the Resurrection Church Soup Kitchen to her mom's deep-fried turkey at their own Thanksgiving dinner-cum-engagement party—had already joined her overrun pile of Things Wrong With The World. And Me'shell was her coconspirator. She concentrated on the despair in her voice:

Does she want you with the pain that I do

Life was fucked up. With the cancellation of Bonita's class since her death—of which Noire had been a teaching assistant— she finally had more time on her hands. But her avalanche of grief and hurt had made her of little use to everyone, including herself. Her colleagues in the Comparative Literature Department tiptoed around her for fear that she would lash out with a sarcastic quip. Her mother asked very little of her as her maid of honor and her father called only to say he loved her and to see how she was feeling. Jayna was pounding the pavement to find a replacement for Wendell and had opened up her field of potential suitors to include French men under the rationale that they loved black American women even more than black men did. And Arikè. She had nothing to offer Arikè but concerns that had to seem trivial compared with her own, so she kept her distance. Noire's world was contracting. She tried to convince herself that it was a good thing, that she needed some downtime. But she knew it was a lie.

She pressed REPEAT on the remote control and closed her eyes.

The telephone jangled into her consciousness only on the fourth ring. She grabbed it into her hand. "Hello?" Her voice was a mutter.

"Goddammit, Noire" was Jayna's greeting.

"Jayna?" Noire sighed.

"Noire, turn that sad shit off and put on . . . some India.Arie or Kevin Webb or *something*! What's *wrong* with you, anyway?" She crunched down on what sounded like a carrot.

She pressed PAUSE. "Are you calling to cheer me up? Because you're not." Noire got indignant.

"My calls always cheer you up."

Noire was silent.

"*Anyway,* I was calling to invite you to something tonight."

She perked up momentarily. "What?"

"I joined this sistas circle last month."

"Oh, Lord . . ." Noire raised her eyebrows at the phone.

"It's kind of an empowerment group, actually. Today's topic is 'A Holiday for One.' This sista named Milagros thought we should invite other sista-friends. I thought you might enjoy it."

"Enjoy talking to a roomful of single black women I don't know about being lonely over the holidays."

"Not lonely, Noire, *alone*. And some Latinas are a part of it, too."

"Oh, in that case."

"You just need to lose all this sarcasm and depression shit."

"Okay, I'm cured."

"I'm disappointed in you, Noire."

Her words stung her. "Well, you're not helping me, Jayna."

"Maybe you need to direct *that* statement to yourself."

"Thanks, Jayna."

"Look, I'm sorry about all the jacked-up shit that's messing with your mind, Noire. Your mentor's—"

"Bonita—"

"—death and Innocent, and whatever's bothering you about your parents getting married, and whatever else. But you need to just, like, get out more, and try to get past it. God knows, nothing good is coming to you in that stuffy, book-infested apartment of yours. *That's* the realness."

"I'll reflect on that tonight in my stuffy apartment, Doctor."

"So you're not going to come to the meeting."

"No, I'm not."

She sighed. "I figured as much. Well anyway, *Boomerang* is on Black Stars in like . . . eighteen minutes."

Noire gave a small guffaw.

"I'm taping it."

"I thought you had bought a bootleg copy?"

"I forgot it over at Wendell's when I moved, along with my Ebony's Secret edible panties! And Negro's too cheap to even mail that stuff back to me!" She gave a knowing *humph* in Noire's ear.

Recalling Jayna's admission that Wendell wouldn't go down on her, Noire blushed for her friend. "Damn."

"Yeah. Anyway, call me tomorrow, okay?"

"All right, Jayna. And give all the sistas a raised fist for me!"

"That's old, Noire." And she clicked her phone off.

Noire pressed the PAUSE button and Me'shell continued where she left off: *You made a fool of me, tell me why?*

Noire was giggling in spite of herself at Grace Jones's perfectly bawdy Helen Strangé character in her not-quite-ready-for-prime-time Strangé perfume ad when the phone rang. With laughter still in her throat, she answered on the third ring.

"I knew you'd be happy to hear from me." Cudjoe's island-tinged West African accent splashed into Noire's ear like an enchanting wave from a distant shore. She squirmed.

"This is a surprise." Noire succeeded in taming her voice despite the fact that Cudjoe still aroused her basest emotions a full ten years after their relationship when she was a study-abroad student in Ghana during her junior year in college. And when she and Innocent saw him in Jamaica nearly two years ago during their first-anniversary trip, she had again responded to the sight of Cudjoe despite her best intentions. She had spent the balance of that trip erasing Innocent's memory of that fated dinner with Cudjoe and his Jamaican relatives on day one of their vacation. But here she sat, aroused and alone in her living room, hearing the voice of the first man to make love to her body *and* mind.

"A pleasant surprise, I'd say." His voice had the silken quality of a man who knew exactly which lie a woman wanted to hear.

"Not unpleasant." She crossed her legs.

"Well, then perhaps this next piece of news will tip it into the positive. I'm here."

"Here *where*?"

"That's not grammatically correct, Noire."

"Fuck you." She regretted her words.

"We can arrange that." His laughter was a dare. "I'm in New York City. In Queens, actually. Is Brooklyn close by?"

A flash of fear replaced her flippancy. "Why are you here?"

"Airfares to the U.S. are cheap these days. Thought you knew that."

Noire sucked her teeth.

"Why do you sound like that, baby? *I'm* not Osama."

"That's not a joke."

"I know it isn't."

Noire hesitated, unsure of Cudjoe's motives for contacting her and apprehensive about the sudden appearance of moisture that drenched her drought-stricken body from the inside out. "So then stop being cagey!" she said finally.

"Damn, Noire. I thought you'd have a little more love than that." He cleared his throat. "I've been here for the last three weeks. Celebrated my first Thanksgiving and everything! But this morning my cousin Kwame said that my time was officially up. Seems that the red carpet had been rolled up a week ago, but his blond live-in girlfriend drew the line yesterday. She said my stomach full of her turkey and stuffing should hold me long enough to fly back to Jamaica or Ghana or wherever I bloody hell chose to land. But I don't feel ready to leave. I mean, I definitely had to see *you*."

Noire was silent, her mind a desert and her loins an oasis.

"So, where's your man? I thought he might not let you pick up the phone after ten on a Friday night."

"Is that why you called? So I wouldn't pick it up."

He licked his lips. "Touché."

"How is your Head-Negro-in-Charge anyway?"

"You know what? Fuck you, Cudjoe."

"Now that's the second time you said that. And of course, your wish is my command. But how would your man feel about me taking up the challenge?"

"He's— We're no longer together, *okay*." Noire immediately regretted sharing that information.

"I knew he was stupider than he looked."

"It was *mutual*, Cudjoe."

"Well then, you were smart and he was stupid."

"I don't need your commentary."

"You're right, baby. And I sure as hell didn't call to give it to you." He made his voice suave. "I called because I'd be much obliged if you could clear a small space on your living room floor for an old friend. It would be great to just catch up . . . see how Santa Claus does it in New York City, you know." He waited only a moment before continuing. "And besides, one good turn deserves another, don't you think? My family in Ghana *and* in Jamaica still talks about you. I'd like to think that African Americans haven't lost the hospitable spirit of their ancestors to the south and east."

Noire pursed her lips together, then, realizing that he couldn't hear that, said, "No need to guilt-trip me, Cudjoe."

"No guilt meant. But you still haven't given me an answer."

She hesitated long enough to glance at Strangé on the television screen. "Okay."

"Great. Give me your address; I'll take a taxi."

∞

In the wake of Côte d'Ivoire's 1999 coup d'etat, the December 7, 1993, death of Félix Houphouët-Boigny—the country's first postcolonial president—had come to be commemorated as both a day of mourning and a day of hope. From the darkened windows of his father's SUV, Innocent eyed the flickering candles and eight-year-old obituaries propped against homes and vendors' stalls as shrines to the nation's father of independence. There were bigger, more "official" tributes as well, but it was the sincere emotion of these small gestures that affected him. His country was hemorrhaging under the strain of an illegal government that had overpromised and underdelivered and an economy that had lost international support and, therefore, credibility. In the month since he had returned home, the burden had become visceral. For thirty-five years, his life had taken him farther and farther away from his country of origin, but his daughter's birth had made its every wrinkle his problem.

The car neared the hospital, and his thoughts shifted to the morning's task. Chi-Chi's mother had been curt when she instructed him that he was to bring all of Chi-Chi's belongings back home on this, the day she was being discharged. Though he couldn't imagine what she could have accumulated in her twenty-five-day hospital stay that would warrant its own means of transport, his guilt made him agree to it and offer to hire a private nurse for Chi-Chi during her continued recovery.

Innocent was greeted by silence when he walked into Chi-Chi's room, the happy chatter of her, her mother, and her sister quickly hushed and replaced by suspicious stares. His own words of greeting rang hollow, even in his own ears. He cleared his throat. "I've come to collect your things . . . to take them home."

Chi-Chi nodded her agreement and pointed to a stack of folded boubous and wrapper skirts.

"You look well." He said it because her ashen skin held less of the sickly gray of the weeks before. He wanted to be complimentary.

"Thank you." Her whisper of a smile was shut down with her mother's disapproving stare.

"Thank you for your call this morning, Madame Abiokun." He landed his gaze squarely upon the surprised face of Chi-

Chi's mother. "I didn't want to be an intrusion, so I was happy to know that I was welcome."

"Of course!" Her surprise came out in a high-pitched burst of sound.

Satisfied that he had replaced the tension that his presence had introduced with a more manageable unease, he placed a fatherly kiss on Chi-Chi's forehead and grabbed up her clothes with both hands. "I'll pick up some meat from the Lebanese *supermarché* on my way to the house. Do you need anything else?"

"I don't. Um, thank you, Innocent."

"It's all I can do." Innocent offered a sincere smile that he hoped would mask his pain and walked out of the door. He knew that for as long as Chi-Chi felt wronged he could never be right, but it took none of the sting out of his predicament.

∞

The hospital coffee scalded the back of Innocent's throat. He grimaced and held it in his mouth until it cooled. Its sharpness bit into the sides of his mouth. It was too strong. He stared at his sister, marveled at all the experiences he saw in her face that he did not know. Charlotte's eyes were decades older than the rest of her thirty-two-year-old body. Her fingers gripped a tall mug of hot chocolate. He smirked at the incongruity of her wizened demeanor and child's drink. It had been only a year and a few months since he had seen Charlotte last, but it had been their grandmother's passing on New Year's Day in 2000 that had them both back in the country of their birth at the same time. Now nearly two years later, everything had changed: Innocent was a father and Charlotte was separated from her husband *and* her daughter.

"Are you bitter, Charlotte?" The cafeteria table rocked beneath his hands.

"This conversation isn't about me, Innocent." Charlotte ran

her fingers through recently cut hair that gave her the boyish looks of their brother—and her twin—Serge at the time of his death when he was fourteen.

"It's about whatever we want it to be. And we're all caught up on my life." He motioned at the four corners of the cafeteria that had supplanted his own kitchen in the five weeks he had been in Côte d'Ivoire.

"I don't want it to be about me."

Innocent wanted to know more about his niece, now two years old and living with her father. He wanted to know about Charlotte's reliance on sleeping pills that had grown into an addiction as the months of Bibi's colicky nights wore on Charlotte's nerves. Becoming a father had given him newfound interest in his family of origin. And he knew Charlotte least of all.

"I'm your brother." His voice pleaded.

"Brothers know what's going on in their sisters' lives, Innocent. When was the last time you called me just to say hi? You abandoned our relationship eighteen years ago." Her voice was matter-of-fact, her words neither callous nor hyperbolic.

Innocent tacitly agreed. "I will always love you and you will always be my sister. I've been far from perfect, I know. But perfection is not a requirement."

She bobbed her head unconsciously as she lost her battle to fight back tears. "Maman isn't speaking to me. To her, every African woman is born knowing how to be a good mother. She thinks Paris has made me weak. And maybe it has."

Innocent thought about Chi-Chi, her resistance to pumping breast milk to freeze for their daughter, her tentative strokes on her little Bisi's five-week-old body during her visits to the neonatal intensive care. She had finally been given a name, Awura, but Chi-Chi still refused to use it. Innocent shook his head. "That's not it, Charlotte. You're not weak."

She hunched her shoulders. "I just—I couldn't take not sleeping. I couldn't. I wanted to stop the pills when Bibi started teething. And mostly I did. But then I would have insomnia. Michel didn't understand why I couldn't keep up my end of the bargain when he was managing all of our major finances. And so, I started taking them again. And when I became pregnant again, I couldn't stop the pills. I just felt so nervous. Bibi was only nine months old. I kept taking them. I lost the pregnancy in the fourth month. Michel blamed me. I was neglecting Bibi, neglecting him, and now I killed our child with the damn pills. That's when he decided to leave me and take Bibi with him. He told me that Bibi is French and I couldn't take her out of the country even if I decided to leave myself. But I wouldn't leave her. She's all I have."

Innocent reached out for his sister's hand. They were small, but gnarled. Her cuticles were shredded from biting and picking. Before Awura, he would have rebutted her statement; Bibi wasn't *all* she had; there was family and friends, as well as her career as a speech pathologist that she could easily revive. But looking at the vacancy in her eyes, and the pain that manifested itself in her body as an actual hunger, he understood what she meant. He knew that pain of wanting and hoping intermingled with an indomitable fear and profound sense of unworthiness. For, even as he prayed for Awura and shepherded her through her first five weeks of life, he knew that God didn't owe him anything and he deserved no favors. It was lonely. Bibi was all Charlotte had and she was barely in her grasp.

"I'm so sorry, Charlotte."

She grabbed his hand in return. "I'm scared."

Innocent studied the feeling of his sister's hand, the hand that had been withdrawn so many years ago when their brother—her twin—had died. It gave him hope.

Noire returned to an apartment that smelled of jerk chicken and fresh rum punch. Her keys still in the door, she was greeted by Cudjoe clad in her apron and Santa Claus boxers, a tall glass of punch extended toward her face.

She giggled in spite of herself. Cudjoe always kept her guessing, and the novelty of his presence was a welcome addition to Noire's shrinking world. "To what do I owe the pleasure?"

"It is because you give me pleasure." He gave her an exploratory kiss before taking her backpack and handing her the glass.

Noire took a gulp, tasting Cudjoe on her lips as she did so. "You're spoiling me."

"A flower as fresh as you cannot be spoiled. All you can do is bloom."

She propped her left hand on her hip. "No need to bullshit me."

"Why do you call a compliment bullshit? Sometimes the truth can sound sappy, but that doesn't make it any less true."

Noire rolled her eyes.

"Please, accept my deep and abiding admiration." He bowed reverently. "It's Christmas Eve."

Her laugh was boisterous.

"So, you think I'm kidding."

Noire nodded.

"I'd like to make you believe me." Cudjoe removed Noire's coat and let it drop down beside her backpack. Then he put his hand down the front of her sweatpants and tapped her clitoris with a cold, wet finger.

Noire jumped but he pulled her into him with his right hand. The rum punch dangled precariously from Noire's hand. He took it from her and took a swig before sharing it with her through a kiss. His fingers mimicked the exploration of his tongue, plunging and tickling without rhyme or reason, exciting her body as much from anticipation as actual sensation. Her body was on fire. The rum punch had ignited a flame in the bottom of her belly and his bold hand was fanning the flames of lust.

He pulled her into the kitchen and sat her on top of the counter. He pulled her sweatpants and panties down around her snow boots and pushed her shirt above her breasts. Then, with his mouth, he grabbed a piece of jerk chicken off of a plate and sat it at the base of her stomach, right above her line of pubic hair. He took a bite and chewed before kissing the heat onto her own lips and into her mouth. He took another bite and licked the soft strip of exposed skin between the chicken and her mound of unruly hair. He then removed the food and licked away all traces of the juice and spices before moving lower.

She felt his peppery lips excite the nerves in every millimeter of her skin. He inserted his thumb and pointer finger into her before his tongue, holding her open to allow her own juices to flow freely. Then he ate and drank everything she had to offer with a fervor that made her an ocean at high tide. The force of her orgasms wrenched her body up into his hungry mouth and guttural yelps from the pit of her gut. Her state of ecstasy kept jumping like electrons to ever more excited states. When she felt she could go no further, she banged at Cudjoe's head in a desperate attempt to make him stop and slumped back onto her counter once he finally did. Then he lifted her up and placed her atop the apron before pushing himself into her wet recesses and allowing himself to come.

∞

Innocent watched his father ride into the living room, his spindly legs hanging limp from the seat of his electric wheelchair like ornaments on the Christmas tree in the corner of the room. These days, his father seldom came out of the master bedroom suite. Or if he did, Innocent was never home to witness it. He hadn't seen his father since Christmas two days ago. The evening news was just coming on. Papa positioned himself directly in front of the television and watched the first ten minutes in complete silence. Then he clicked off the TV and wheeled himself around to face Innocent. "You've lost weight."

Innocent took in Papa's withered body. He had once been Innocent's ideal of what a man should look like, but now he appeared to be little more than one hundred pounds on his strongest day. "Yes, I have."

"We still have that workout bench you begged for when you were sixteen."

He nodded.

"Nasima's boys use it sometimes." He referenced the woman who had long been the Pokou family's house help and who occupied the modest house at the back of their property.

"Happy to know it's being used."

They both bobbed their heads.

"So, how is the baby?"

"Awura."

"Of course." Jean nodded his recognition of the name that honored his own family's prestigious bloodline.

"She's gained a bit of weight. Hopefully she'll be discharged from the hospital within the month."

"That's good news." He offered a reserved smile.

Innocent studied the veil that had covered his father's face since his own boyhood. He could never tell what Papa felt and seldom knew what he thought. Even sitting in a wheelchair his father was a marvel in self-control. Innocent hated the mask and the fact that he, too, had mastered it. "Do you have something to say to me, Papa?" His voice was like a paper cut on an unsuspecting finger: it drew blood belatedly.

Papa's narrow smile shrank. "Isn't it enough to spend time with my son?"

"We're not 'spending time.' We're occupying the same room." Innocent watched his father's face fall into another kind of pain, one that was personal and raw. It gave him smug satisfaction.

"Sounds like you've indicted us both."

Innocent buttoned his face in annoyance. "I suppose I learned it from the best."

"Don't disrespect me, Innocent." He turned his face away from him in a show of disapproval.

"Is respect the most important thing, Papa? Even now!" Innocent's words quivered in the air. Though the space was difficult, he relished the charged energy that he and his father shared. He could not remember the last time they had been more than cordial to each other.

At last, Papa returned his eyes to Innocent's. "Even now . . ." The words trailed but his gaze remained steady. "My son, you are not the first one to feel this kind of anguish. It has called my name many times in this life."

Innocent saw the memory of his fourteen-year-old brother Serge's fatal accident eighteen years ago appear in Papa's watery gray eyes and felt badly. He remembered his father spending every moment of Serge's three-day coma by his bedside until he succumbed to death. Yes, he knew what that kind of pain was like.

Innocent's heart softened along with his voice. "Tell me about Serge, Papa, please."

Jean looked at his son, his only living son, and blinked tears that he knew Innocent had never before witnessed. He forced a cough to mask his weeping and steadied himself before he spoke. "By the time we knew about the accident, he had already been at PISAM for about a half hour. When I saw him, I knew he would die. It's not that I had lost hope. I just had to recognize that, once again, my child would die and I could do nothing to help him. But I didn't want Serge, my frail little son, to walk into death alone, so I stayed with him. I told him it was okay for him to find rest and that we'd be all right. That I wasn't angry with him. That I loved him and always would. And before dawn of the third day, he left us."

A lump formed in Innocent's stomach and his eyebrows knit together in confusion. He remembered his own guilt and grief when Papa arrived home from the hospital and announced "my son has died" before going into a week of seclusion that was only broken by Serge's funeral. "My son." He had said it as though Innocent was not also his son, or at least, not the son who should have lived. Innocent bore Serge's accident as his own fault for allowing his little brother—who at three years his junior was only half his size—to ride on the back of their neighbor's motorcycle. And his father's statement confirmed for Innocent that he thought so, too. But even as Innocent digested this story, two words rang in his head. He repeated them. " 'Once again.' Papa?"

He nodded and leveled his gaze on Innocent. "Death claimed your oldest sister years ago." His voice had the curious strength of a man who has learned to bear burdens rather than make peace with them and his words steeled Innocent for a story he felt ill-prepared to hear. "My benefactor thought that graduating me from the French missionary boy's boarding school would better prepare me for university in France than the nonsectarian Ivoirian school that you and Serge attended." He snickered at the condescension that the phrase implied.

Innocent stared at his father; he had always thought that he and Papa shared the same alma mater.

"So I transferred in my final year of secondary school. I was devastated. I had come to enjoy my role as the jocular athlete at Abidjan Collegiate. Now I would be the lone African kid at a school that was predominantly populated by the sons of French governors and other colonial magistrates. My schoolmates referred to me as the benefactor's houseboy.

"The Burkinabè woman who cleaned my dorm had a daughter, Awa, whom she sometimes sent in her stead. Since I chose to study in my room as a refuge from my schoolmates in the library, I was often there when she came to clean. It gave me an opportunity to talk to another African who was my age-mate without the judgmental eyes of my fellow classmates for fraternizing with African staff.

"Out of a mixture of curiosity and boredom, our friendship slipped into sexual experimentation quickly. I found out she was pregnant in an emergency meeting called by the headmaster and attended by my benefactor as well. They said they did not plan to tell my parents and suggested that I refrain from mentioning it to anyone, though they had taken the liberty of telling all of the lecturers so that they would 'be on guard' for bad behavior from me. Awa had already been sent back to her father's village to live with her grandmother—a medicine woman—so she could give birth. They did not ask me how I felt or what I wished to do. Not that I knew. I was just told that I was on probation but that, if I followed what they told me, this should not jeopardize my chances to attend a French university. It was 1951 and, at nine years before official independence from France, the winds of change were beginning to blow. They assured me, in language that was more threatening than encouraging, that if I played my cards right, I could have a future as a governmental peon in the new Côte d'Ivoire. They booted me out the door with an admonition that from now on I had to study in the library with the rest of the boys and keep my penis to myself.

"I saw her mother only occasionally and could never ask her about Awa without facing recriminations. I learned that the baby was born—a girl—only after Awa had killed herself and our daughter with a lethal combination of her grandmother's herbs." He closed his eyes—gray with age and illness—to the re-activated pain of memory until the wave had passed. Then he opened them and stared at his son.

Innocent was incredulous. He looked at his father with new eyes and felt the burden of his father's tragic—and apparently secret—story. "I'm so sorry, Papa."

"Me too, Innocent. Life can be very hard, and it is especially cruel for some. But I know that I am luckier than Awa. She had no choice. I only *felt* that I didn't."

Innocent puzzled over his father's words. *No choice about what?* he wanted to ask, but his father's stoicism prevented him from asking. "Did you ever tell anyone?"

"Your mother, two days before we were to get married. I was afraid she would reject me but more afraid of what kind of per-son I would be if I *didn't* tell her. She had a right to know. But she didn't speak to me until a week after our wedding. And now I've told you."

Innocent's own silence about Chi-Chi's pregnancy to his par-ents, Mireille, and Noire had nursed an ulcer that still hadn't gone away. He couldn't imagine how his father had managed to conceal this heavy secret from his own parents and practically everyone else for years. His face reflected his question.

"Sometimes the time for speaking passes us by and it seems that mentioning it would cause more harm than good. The time for me to have spoken was when I first learned Awa was preg-nant. I should have told my parents, spoken to her mother, and most important, talked to her myself and told her that I would be responsible to her and our child. But I didn't. She must have felt that I had rejected her and the baby. And in a way I did. Because I put my needs before everyone. But after a while, I knew I would only rip open wounds and create fresh ones for my parents if I told them. My father died unexpectedly during my first year at university. I didn't want to compound my family's pain." He added, as a somber postscript, "But I couldn't let Serge die without me, too. I had to be there for him. And to say sorry to Awa and my daughter."

Papa produced a wrinkled handkerchief from the inside of his robe and wiped away a bubble of saliva at the corner of his mouth. He straightened his body in his wheelchair and trained his gaze on the television, now airing a soccer game. Innocent allowed his father the privacy of his thoughts and lowered his head heavy with his father's revelation. He, who had grown up as the oldest Pokou child, had an older sister. The television announcers masked the yawning silence. The time for speaking had passed for Papa, but not for Innocent. His daughter was still alive and he still had the opportunity to do the right thing. He just didn't know what the right thing was.

≈

CHAPTER NINE

B U S H . B A B Y .

Noire crossed and recrossed her legs. She looked around the room. There had to be at least fifty women present, and including her, Jayna, and Mama Nature—the session leader—there were three black women there. It was an odd assemblage of women: eighteen were divorced, half had children, and, with the exception of her and Jayna, they were either twenty-five-year-old women who had lived with three previous boyfriends, or women over forty-five who were reentering the dating world. One twenty-nine-year-old, who made a beeline over to the two of them during their midmorning break, described herself as a survivor of a two-year starter marriage—"when I lived in Iowa"—who wanted to reclaim her virginity.

Mama Nature stood in the middle of the circle of women and pulled off her wrapper skirt. They all stared at her suddenly exposed bush of salt-and-pepper pubic hair. She scanned the room, daring anyone to speak. No one did. "*This* is currency." She made a triangle of her fingers and placed them atop her crotch, outlining the obvious. "And until we, as women, under-stand how valuable this is, we will always sell ourselves short."

Noire watched all of the women shaking their heads in agree-ment. She looked at Jayna and rolled her eyes. But Jayna had picked up her pen and added Mama Nature's latest proclamation to a page full of scrawled sentence fragments. She gave Jayna's notes the once-over, then inclined her head toward her. "Why did we come to this?" Noire's words were a furtive whisper.

"Because our sex lives are fucked up. No pun." Her words were equally furtive.

"What do you think, Noire?"

Noire looked toward the voice to find Mama Nature's ex-posed crotch hovering over her. She cursed the name tag that had been given to her to wear when they arrived.

Noire tried to look past Mama Nature's vagina so she could respond to her face. "I just don't understand why you're naked."

"I'm showing you my *pussy*"—she gave the word emphasis—"because that's what you do when you meet a man. He doesn't ever have to wonder *if* he'll get inside of it. It's just a matter of *when*. And when's never that far away!" She lashed Noire with her gaze before looking around the room. "I'm talking about *all* of you. You knew what this was about before you got here. The workshop title—'A Pussy's Worth'—made it quite clear. And you're here because your pussy has been sitting in the discount aisle for too long!"

The room broke into nervous laughter.

"How many of you have fucked on a first date?" Mama Nature hesitated. "And don't tell me it wasn't a fuck. If you had sex on a first date, it was a fuck by definition. Now, let's see a show of hands."

Every hand went up.

"And how many of you have fucked a man the very day you met him?"

About twenty hands made a timid ascent, including Jayna's. Noire crossed her arms over her chest and poked her lips out.

"That proves my point, women. We have all given our pussies to a man—and maybe a woman—before we knew that they cared about or respected us. Before we knew if we cared about or respected them. That's like walking around like this"—she pranced for the women—"with our pussies exposed for all the world to see."

Noire didn't like Mama Nature's tone. Surely she wasn't suggesting that every woman there had slept with men simply because the man wanted it. Maybe the women wanted it, too. They were making choices, not just waiting to be chosen. She said as much.

"Noire, tell all of us about the man you're letting fuck you now." Mama Nature's words were a command, full of unconfirmed presumption and arrogance.

"I didn't tell you I was seeing anyone."

"But I know that you are, Noire. It's written all over your face. So, please share."

"He—we have a history. We were a couple a . . . few years ago."

"Then what are you *now*?" Mama Nature's smirk made her question an accusation.

Noire seethed, her face hot with embarrassment and indignation.

"*This* is my point, women." She threw her arm out in Noire's direction. "This is *exactly* my point. You didn't come here for me to tell you that every messy situation you're in is just fine if it's what you want. You know it's not fine. If you thought it was, you would not have come."

Noire thought of Jayna's explanation that if they both registered at the same time they'd each get the promotional price of $49.95 instead of the usual $75.00, and cut her eyes at her deceptive friend. She looked at Jayna's notebook and saw "PUSSY" written in all caps. Weren't feminists supposed to reject that word, anyway? Why was Mama Nature using it with abandon?

". . . so I challenge all of you to go on hiatus. As of today. Put your pussies on lockdown for everything but your own fingers for the next six months and see how things change in your relationships with men and especially with yourself."

Mama Nature picked her skirt off the floor and retied it around her waist. Noire wondered if that was somehow unsanitary and wished that she would put on some panties and wash her hands, not necessarily in that order.

Beginning at the far end of the circle, Mama Nature approached each woman individually and sat next to them on their gym mats. Her voice was low, but her hands were expressive, and she tapped the crotch of each woman freely and often. One by one, the women broke into tears, some more loudly than others. Mama Nature ended each miniconsultation with a tight hug followed by a hand over the woman's crotch and the words "I know your pussy's worth and I want for you to know its worth as well."

Noire put her snow boots on and stood up.

"What'd you think?" Jayna snapped her notebook shut and craned her neck up at Noire's frown.

"Are you serious?" She studied her friend's hopeful smile and found not a trace of insincerity.

Jayna crossed her arms over her chest. "I found it very helpful. And with your years-long struggle to get me into therapy, I thought you'd be tickled pink that I finally took your advice."

"Having an abrasive 'Mama Nature'"—she made quotes with her fingers—"show us her graying vagina and tell us that we're whores is not therapy! She is *not* a psychologist, Jayna. She's an angry exhibitionist who likes the word *pussy*."

Jayna jumped up. "Is that what you heard, Noire?! I heard her tell us to value our bodies and not give in to every man who wants some just because he's a little cute! That's empowering."

"If that's all you needed, I could have just taken *my* panties off every time you told me you couldn't leave a homeboy alone because he's doin' you too right! And if I had collected $49.95 each time, I'd have made more money than Mama Nature does in a *month* of workshops!"

Jayna sucked her teeth and prepared to reply when Mama Nature came and sat on her mat.

"Sit down, Jayna. And you too, Noire." She tapped the mat. "I can see you don't want to sit with me, but you should reject your own belligerence, Noire." She turned her attention to Jayna. "Did you find this workshop helpful?"

"Very." Her nodding was vigorous. "You helped me to decide to do something I should have done a while ago. I'm going to be celibate for the next six months. At least."

Noire stared at Jayna in disbelief. She had never heard anything like this.

"Jayna, that statement sounds like it's coming from a place of strength. It will be good for you. And for this." She rested her hand on Jayna's jeans-clad crotch. She let it remain and turned toward Noire. "And how about you?"

"I'm happy my friend found your workshop so . . . inspirational"—she made her tone intentionally mocking—"but I can't say the same."

"Did you not find anything you can apply to your own life?" She stared into Noire's blank expression. "Don't confuse the messenger with the message, Noire. You don't have to like anything about me. But you need to *love* this."

Noire's hand beat that of Mama Nature's to its intended destination of her crotch. She pushed her offending hand away.

"My touch is not meant to take advantage of you, Noire. But I can't say the same for the hands, mouths, and penises of the men who you let visit your pussy regularly."

"You don't know anything about that." Her words were a threat.

"But *you* do." Mama Nature stood up. She gave Jayna a hug and left the room.

"So, when were you planning to tell me about your born-again virginity?" Noire nibbled at her grilled veggie panini. She and Jayna had deposited themselves at Bite, yet another trendy TriBeCa eatery that charged too much money for not enough food. Or space. She motioned for the waiter to remove the ketchup, unlit candle, and salt and pepper shakers from their postage-stamp-sized table.

"Wait." Jayna took the salt from the waiter and sprinkled a little more into her skimpy BLT before responding. "Today."

"Mama Nature had that much of an effect on you, huh?"

"Don't be like that, Noire! Look, after Wendell, I realized I had really compromised myself. I mean, girl, I almost got that weave he was forcing on me!"

"You didn't tell me that!"

"I know. When I realized how ashamed I was, I knew that things had gotten out of control. And the thing is, the sex with him wasn't even that good. I mean, if he diddled my clit for long enough, of course I'd come, but most of the time I could just take it or leave it."

Noire thought about Cudjoe's tongue caressing her clit until she had to beg him to stop and felt a zing tickle her groin.

"I just— I want to get married, Noire! And not five years from now, either. Nana and Papi are already seventy-five. And my hateful mama has even asked me if she'll ever become a grandmother. Can you imagine? She gave me to her parents to raise, and now she's looking for a grandchild to bounce on her lap. Anyway, everyone's waiting for me to find a man and push out a kid."

"But, Jayna, you can't just do stuff because it works into someone else's timetable."

"But it's mine, too!"

Noire was exasperated. "Well, in that case, your moratorium on sex won't get you very far toward becoming somebody's baby mama!"

"See, Noire! You're not even trying to understand what I'm saying." She took another bite out of her BLT. "You know, this white woman who's been coming to my office to get all kinds of dental work done—I mean six crowns, three fillings, a root canal, and a little bleaching before her wedding in June—told me that her fiancé proposed to her after five months and that they're getting married on the first anniversary of their first date. And she *hasn't had sex with him*."

Noire's face was twisted into a knot of confusion.

Jayna continued. "Once he saw that she was serious about not giving it up, he had to decide if he was serious about her or not. And he realized that he was."

"That sounds passive-aggressive to me."

"I felt that way for a minute, too. Until I really thought about it and heard what she was saying. It's not about being passive, Noire. Or even trying to manipulate a situation. It's about seeing what a homeboy's coming with and making your own mind up without thinking you love him because he can make you come." Jayna took too big a bite of her sandwich and it was gone.

"So? That doesn't prove that she should be marrying homeboy! All it says is that dude is desperate to have sex with her." Noire bit into her panini, finding it cold and soggy. She set it back down on her plate.

"Are you really that cynical?"

"I think you're just seeing a moral to the story that isn't there."

"You don't know that!"

"And unless you're in their relationship with them, neither do you."

"I'm taking the chick's word for it, Noire. I mean, why would she lie to me? There's nothing in it for her."

"Well, Jayna, you sound pretty convinced. Maybe I can use my dress for my mom's wedding for yours, too."

"Don't sleep, Noire. It only takes one homeboy who's ready, willing, and able—"

"And *love,* Jayna."

"—and weren't you Arikè's maid of honor, too? Don't let that 'always a bridesmaid, never a bride' saying be you!"

Noire's mind wandered to her mother and father and then to Arikè. She hadn't talked to any of them in weeks. But she couldn't think about that. Not right now.

Satisfied that Noire's extended silence marked a victory for her, Jayna decided to change the subject. "So, sex with Cudjoe is still off the hook?"

"I wouldn't want to tempt you by talking about *s-e-x*!" Noire teased her.

"Oh, come on, Noire. What'd you do for New Year's Eve?"

Have doggy-style sex in the snow on her building's roof deck and then again when they came back inside. To warm up. It had been thrilling at the time, but, after listening to Jayna proclaim her New Year's resolution of celibacy, Noire didn't feel like her story had enough zip. "Girl, wouldn't you want to know!" She sounded more enthusiastic than she felt.

"Well, damn! Sounds like Cudjoe is showing some real long-term potential! Girl, you may hear wedding bells after all!"

Noire averted her eyes from Jayna's inquisitive stare and finished her soggy sandwich in silence.

❧

Every millimeter of Innocent's body exploded with joy as Awura's four-and-a-half-pound body nestled along the underside of his chin and warmed the center of his chest, from the skin straight down to his heart. He carried her through the hospital doors and into her first breath of fresh air. It was January 16 and, at nine weeks and two days old, she was still three weeks ahead of her February 6 due date. With the receiving blanket that Maman made to ensure Awura's survival, Innocent shielded her from the harsh harmattan winds and an unforgiving sun that parched the midday air. Chi-Chi busied herself with a tiny bag that held Awura's burping cloths and a few diapers. Unlike most babies her age, she was still traveling light.

Chi-Chi eased into the backseat of her parents' SUV.

"Can you please hold her?" Reluctantly, Innocent placed his precious cargo in her mother's lap.

"You're so good with her." She held her daughter with hands as unaccustomed to the task as they had been the first day she was allowed to breast-feed Awura over two weeks ago. "She's a papa's girl."

Innocent studied Chi-Chi's discomfort and smiled at Awura's oblivion to it; her body—curled into her mother's midsection—mimicked what he imagined to be her favorite position when she was in utero. "And a maman's girl, too. Look at her."

"I'm just—I don't know how to handle her. She's too tiny."

"She's getting bigger."

"But she's so . . . needy. She can't even see me."

Innocent smarted. He still could not accept that, due to her severe prematurity, Awura might never gain more than the sight of colors and fuzzy outlines of well-defined objects. He adjusted the car seat he had ordered from overseas and tested it for stability before reaching in to place Awura into it. Then he tucked a blanket around her body and another one around her head. Satisfied that she was secure, he climbed in beside her.

"The therapist will come tomorrow to explain how best to handle her and compensate for her limited sight. And of course you have the live-in nurse."

"She's blind, Innocent." Her tone was sharp.

"Her doctor said that retinopathy of prematurity *can* be treated and that some babies have significant improvements in their sight."

"Many don't."

The driver took off. He maneuvered the car carefully from the relative serenity of the hospital's Cocody, Abidjan, neighborhood, through the bustling city center of Le Plateau and along the periphery of poverty-stricken Treichville, where the midday calm was replaced with chaos restrained by the menacing presence of armed soldiers whose weapons dangled from shoulders and sprouted out of holsters. Crossing the inlet, they landed at last in Marcory, the ethnically diverse neighborhood that was the home to many West African émigrés, including Chi-Chi's Burkinabè father. Stepping outside of the car after they pulled into the family compound, Innocent was confronted with the tense calm of the neighborhood that was becoming a target of anti-immigrant violence. He saw the tension in Chi-Chi's face and shoulders as she first fumbled with a sleeping Awura and then prepared herself to exit the security of the tinted-window SUV.

Once inside the house, Chi-Chi traded her Western dress for a breezy *boubou* and wrapper skirt and returned to where

Innocent sat with Awura, asleep in his arms. She hovered above him, her arms akimbo. He looked up at her and frowned.

"I do not want our daughter to be circumcised. Ever. It's mutilation."

"Of course not. I wouldn't want that either."

"But of course that won't matter; she will never get married. Like her mother."

"Chi-Chi, *please*." Innocent's voice was a hiss. Why did every pronouncement come down to how he had wronged her?

"I'm just talking, Innocent. Aren't I entitled to express my own feelings?" Awura stirred at her mother's voice, then settled down. "I want her . . . to be proud of herself, no matter the circumstances of her birth."

At that, Innocent stood up and stepped close to her, Awura's body resting comfortably between them. "Are *you* proud, Chi-Chi? Because you'll be her biggest influence. Or do you want to see her suffer in life just to prove a point?" His eyes were hard, boring the question into her body. "Don't make this child the reason why things didn't work out for you, Chi-Chi. She's already got enough to deal with!"

"Coming from you, that's almost laughable. Maman still sucks her teeth when she sees me with Awura. If this child had been my boyfriend's baby, we would have gotten married and my mother could have accepted it. But she sees me as a slut, desperate to land a rich, Ivoirian man with a family name. And once you hop on a plane back to the U.S., it'll look like she was right!"

Innocent felt all the barbs that she had intended for him, even more than before. He thought about his father's story—shared only two weeks before—and felt the weight of his silence in response to Chi-Chi's anguish lay upon him like a blanket of guilt. But what if he married her? Would that really make things better? He was sure he didn't love her, and her disdain for him was visceral. Is that what Awura needed? Parents who married out of obligation and who grew to hate each other for it. He couldn't be sure if that would happen, but he also didn't feel prepared to jump from one hasty action into another. That didn't seem fair to anyone.

"Listen to me, Chi-Chi. We have a child, a beautiful little girl for whom we will always be her parents. She needs us to be her protectors, her providers, her advocates, and the ones who love her more than anyone. What happens between you and me remains to be seen. But I will not allow this little girl to feel any responsibility for that, or any shame about it. Her shoulders are too small, and her challenges far too great for us to place one more burden upon her. Do not make her a *pawn*, Chi-Chi. She won't feel shame unless you teach it to her, so *don't*!" Innocent's voice reverberated in his chest, jarring Awura from her nap. She started to cry in short, hard gasps. He bounced her and rubbed her and rocked her in vain, guilt twisting a knot in his stomach. "Shh, shh," he murmured to her. He was helpless to soothe her, but Chi-Chi's hands remained punched into her sides.

"That's easy for you to say, Innocent. In two days, you will be immersed in your New York City life, living the life of a Westernized African bachelor and sending dollars to cover up his Third World *mistake*." She rescued Awura from his arms and calmed her successfully before continuing. "See, Innocent. You can be a father, when you *want* to be, but I *have* to be a mother even if I don't feel up to it. I am a single mother to a blind girl who will be pitied her entire life. So, don't give *me* a lecture about how to be a mother to this baby. You haven't earned the right!"

Innocent wanted to pry Awura away from Chi-Chi and out of the path of Chi-Chi's words before they landed on her. But he couldn't. Nor could he answer her because he knew she was right—at least on some counts. In two days' time, he would return to New York and the world he knew would be none the wiser about his new fatherhood. He could continue as if nothing had happened. But he wouldn't do that.

In the two and a half months that he had been in Côte d'Ivoire, his single-minded prayer for Awura's survival and improvement had left him little time to think about what would come later. He skipped from a series of nows like rocks in a stream. But he would think about Awura and his future. And he would act in his daughter's best interest. He just had to figure out what that was.

Part Three

ALL FALL
DOWN

CHAPTER TEN

UNINVITED

Whereas Abidjan had been a myopic lens for Innocent in which Awura was at the center and Chi-Chi, his father's revelation, and his sister Charlotte's family problems were fuzzy images at the periphery, New York City was shattered glass in blinding sunlight, magnifying and distorting everyone and everything, including himself. Returning to the States was an ordeal in itself: Innocent had found himself a temporary ward of the government thanks to newly heightened airport security that had identified him as a potential terrorist because he shared a similar last name and "distinctive features" with a suspected terrorist. Sixteen hours after landing in New York, Innocent finally arrived at his loft, disheveled, disillusioned, and missing Awura.

Throwing his right leg out of the open door of the taxicab, Innocent recoiled at the damp January cold that crept up his pant leg and dove into the corners of his summer-weight B. Oyama jacket. He had left New York more than two months before with two hastily packed bags full of linen slacks and

T-shirts; and now, the bitter winds assailed his body and blew frigid thoughts into his mind.

"You must be cold." His doorman stepped toward the cab and pulled the door open to full stretch.

Innocent looked into Vladimir's smirk and nodded.

"Long trip?" His question was loaded with something beyond curiosity.

Innocent had no desire to engage Vladimir in more conversation than was necessary. "Anything happen since I've been gone?"

"Nothing bad."

"Good." Innocent's voice was matter-of-fact. "Good night, then."

Vladimir's smirk grew more menacing. "I should say the same to you." He tipped his hat.

Innocent looked askance at Vladimir before accelerating toward the elevator. The door shut his thoughts on the doorman, and his body went into autopilot. He arrived at his floor, walked the nineteen steps to his front door, rammed his key into the keyhole, and flung the door open. Dropping his bags, he frowned at the loft's dark draftiness. Noticing the open window close to the bed, he walked over and slammed it shut.

"I thought things needed a bit of airing."

Innocent shivered at the sly sweetness of Lissette's voice breaking through the dark of the apartment. She rose from her seat on his desk chair across the loft and began to shrink the distance between them, her petite frame shrouded in a black silk cape and her face lit from the yellow glow of streetlights.

"Why the hell are you here?" Innocent felt the power of Lissette's intentions seep into the underbelly of his thoughts. She looked like the female incarnation of Satan.

"You must be surprised. Yes, I can see that you are." She craned her neck upward and breathed warm air into his face.

"Vladimir let me in. He's still sweet on me, the dear." She referenced her previous ownership of Innocent's loft when they were still at business school . . . and still a couple.

The lilt of her melodic Haitian French curled around his body and the glint of her gray-green eyes dared him to seize the opportunity they offered.

"Lissette, you didn't answer my question." His words were deliberate, his voice even.

"Tsk, tsk, Innocent. I should be offended. I would think you'd be happy to have a beloved friend's welcome after such a long and difficult trip."

"We haven't spoken in nearly two years. Why would I seek your 'friendship' now?"

"That's the problem, Innocent. You haven't spoken to anyone: Marcus's phone calls have gone unanswered for months. Ali says you haven't replied to his e-mail, and you've all but written *me* off. But I know you, Innocent. You're a recluse like me. When you're hurting, you don't seek anyone's friendship. But that doesn't mean that you don't need it." Lissette pulled off Innocent's blazer jacket and hung it and her cape on a closet doorknob. Then she walked to the kitchen and produced a bottle of his favorite Thabani Pinotage and two wineglasses before sauntering back over to him and coaxing his tired body down onto the bed, where she sat as well.

"I know everything, Innocent. Your baby sister told me. I prayed for little Awura." She said his daughter's name with a familiarity that made Innocent bristle.

"I'm sure Mireille didn't call *you*."

Lissette twisted her mouth into a smile. "Please. Innocent, calm down. It was all quite . . . innocent." She gave a light chuckle. "I contacted Mireille last week when I was in Washington, D.C., for work and she told me that she had just returned from spending Christmas break in Côte d'Ivoire and that you were still there tending to your daughter, the precious little lamb. I didn't want to bother you, but I asked Mireille to call me once she knew you were coming back. I traveled to the city this morning and tried calling your cell phone then but apparently it was still switched off."

Innocent thought about how the immigration officials confiscated his cell phone and other personal effects for the duration of his detention before offering him their heartiest apologies and force-feeding him what he imagined was their standard line: *We have done this for your safety and the safety of all American citizens. Though you are not a citizen yourself, Mr. Pokou, surely you benefit from this country's vigilance. We trust that you understand that occasional inconveniences are a part of the privilege of living in this country and that you won't jeopardize our ability to protect and defend these borders by filing a needless complaint.*

"After not hearing from you for five hours, I became worried about your state of mind and decided to come over."

"I didn't know that I had a time limit in which to return your calls."

"Please don't be snide, Innocent."

"You're at *my* house, Lissette. Uninvited."

"Perhaps I shouldn't have come." She picked up a wineglass and took a sip. "You can tell me to leave."

Suspicion sloshed around his mind. Why *had* she come? And why was he allowing her to remain? He looked at the heart-shaped lipstick imprint on the glass and wished that he had never allowed himself to be her lover. She knew too much about him. And that scared him. "You are the last person I need to see right now, Lissette."

"I don't believe you."

Innocent narrowed his eyes.

"If you wanted me to go, you would have said so, Innocent.

But you didn't. And that's because you want me to stay." She kicked his shoes off with her foot. "I've known you too long, Innocent. You need me here. Because right now, I'm the only one who doesn't hate you." She smiled. "We're too similar for me to hate you. Chi-Chi's angry at you, your mother, father, and Mireille are disappointed. Even little Awura is wondering where her papa is." She moved closer to him. "But shit happens, Innocent. And I don't hate you for that. I love you." She squeezed his thigh.

He felt his blood turn to ice. "Get the fuck out of my house, Lissette. Now." He stood up and braced himself against the wall. He couldn't deal with this. Lissette was the voice inside of his head that he didn't want to hear.

"I know what it's like to have your every decision be the wrong one in the eyes of your family when all you wanted to do was make them happy."

Innocent closed his eyes. He didn't want her to see that she was right. Innocent felt like a well-educated, financially success-ful failure. He remembered his mother's face when she had asked him if he would marry Chi-Chi and he said no. He remembered boarding the plane back to New York and wondering if Awura would know him the next time he came to see her.

Lissette walked over to him and stepped into his space, cor-nering him.

He confronted the slate green coldness of her eyes. "Lissette, what the hell is going on?"

"Please, don't play dumb, Innocent."

Her face flushed. Lissette pushed it toward Innocent's, her breath hot on his cheeks. "This is your chance to finally get it right and you're messing it up. Again. I figured that since you were into making babies, you could give me one. We could be a family, Innocent. With Awura. I told you, I'm not angry at you, Innocent."

Innocent was stunned. "Lissette, we haven't been together since B-school . . . four years ago."

"And what has that gotten us, Innocent? You've got a baby mama back home and I've got nothing. But we could have been a family by now. We still can be."

"This is insane, Lissette."

"Is that what you said to Chi-Chi, Innocent? Is that what you said to your daughter when you saw her? That having her was insane. Is wanting a baby *insane*?" She spoke with an urgency that Innocent had never seen in her before.

As he listened to her, she almost made sense. He followed the lines that rimmed her eyes, battle scars, he surmised. "Lissette, I can't be anything to you; I don't *want* to be."

"Is that what you said to Chi-Chi?"

"You don't know anything about her."

"I know she's a thirty-year-old unmarried West African woman. I know that she lives in a society that values a woman's ability to marry well and produce children. I know that most of her age-mates are married. Like mine, Innocent. My parents can't figure out what's wrong with me. If I were back home in Haiti, I'd have been married for the last five years and had two children by now."

"But you didn't want that—"

"I didn't want it *then*, but that doesn't mean I didn't want it at all."

"Lissette! *Get. Out. Of. My. House.*" His voice was a roar.

She grabbed her cape from the doorjamb and pulled it on recklessly. "You can think what you want to, Innocent, but I'm just being honest with you. And if you were being honest with yourself, you'd see that we're not so different. You wanted to prove that you could do it. Or have you convinced yourself that forgetting to wear a condom was just an *oversight*?" She grabbed her bag from the floor. Then she slammed out the door.

Innocent stared into the space that she left. His mind was crowded with thoughts he was too scared to think. What if Chi-Chi had planned to get pregnant with Awura? Did he want it, too, or did he even care? The first question was well beyond the point of him wanting to know the truth; any answer would hurt him, and he loved his daughter. And the second. During his entire trip home, he hadn't given Chi-Chi more than a moment's thought unless he was coming between her legs. What did that say about him? His stomach retched, hurling bile onto Lissette's scarf, forgotten on the floor.

Innocent awoke on his bed in the middle of the night, his trousers still on, their hems crusted with vomit. He looked down at himself, the streetlight sending long shadows through the loft's window and across his body. He spent the first five minutes denying that anything had happened and the second five in disbelief that it had. His wall clock, a huge affair repurposed from an old French rail station, contended that it was nearly two in the morning. He pulled off his clothes and walked into the bathroom, hoping the spray of the shower would wash away the demons that had taken up residence in his mind. But the water was just water. He soaped and scrubbed and only succeeded in making his skin raw.

Slathering on cocoa butter in the cold of his loft, he thought of Mamadou. He had missed his exhibition at Howard in November because of his hasty return to Côte d'Ivoire. But maybe talking to him would give him the connection he needed. It was eight o'clock in Paris and, knowing Mamadou's grueling work schedule, he was probably already at the art gallery.

A strange voice full of youthful exuberance answered the gallery's phone on the first ring. They exchanged pleasantries, and he explained that Mamadou was in the United States on business.

"I'm a college friend and I'm in the U.S. Where is he, exactly?"

"Washington, D.C., monsieur, and then perhaps on to Montreal briefly before his return. But he is calling in for messages at least once a day. I'll tell him you called."

"Thank you." And he hung up the phone. Curiosity temporarily replaced his own self-centered angst. He wondered if Mamadou had tried to reach him, and realized that he hadn't checked his messages since returning because of Lissette's unexpected visit. He pressed PLAY on the answering machine; there were only two. The first, left by Mireille yesterday morning, sounded guarded.

"Brother, foremost, I hope that our little Awura is well and that you have traveled in good spirits, all things considered. My semester has begun well, so no worries at all. But I wanted to tell you that Lissette may be in touch with you. Also, I ran into Mamadou yesterday, having breakfast with Shema. I had brought her to his show in November, you know, but didn't realize that they had become friends. Have you been in touch with either of them? Brother, my message is—"

The machine cut her off. He waited for the next.

"I'm sorry, I'm too long-winded sometimes. But you should call him, I think. They seemed so surprised to see me. But not in a good way, you know. I mean, they were pleasant, of course. But neither asked about you. I thought that was strange. Okay, let me hang up before this machine cuts me again. I love you!"

Innocent digested his sister's messages. Shema. He hadn't spoken to her since their auspicious meeting in October, orchestrated by Mireille herself. But now he saw her body standing before him, cruelly scarred and yet so beautiful. Her fearlessness. Her story. The strength in her own vulnerability. She had shared something with him, and him with her, which felt private and special. It seemed that Mamadou had discovered that about her as well. He didn't feel jealous. He didn't have the right to. In fact, if he had had the presence of mind, perhaps he would have encouraged them to meet. But the words in Mireille's message— that they hadn't asked about him—made him uncomfortable. He wondered if Shema had told Mamadou about the substance of their encounter, and if the news wasn't setting well with his best friend. The prospect of a rift between them hijacked Innocent's reeling thoughts. He climbed into his bed and disappeared.

CHAPTER ELEVEN

NAKED

*7*18-867-5309. Noire looked at Arikè's phone number in her caller ID. She hadn't left a message. For the fifth time in as many days, Arikè had called and Noire hadn't responded. And she wouldn't again today. As the days since their last conversation stretched to weeks, Noire felt more scared to talk to her. What would she even say? *How were the holidays with Dennis dead? Did Purpose get lots from Santa? Oh, things are okay with me. My parents are getting married after thinking about it for thirty-two years and I'm fucking my live-in ex-boyfriend from about ten years ago. The sex is great. Very inventive. Oh, and I'm still in denial about Bonita's death but that's sure to come to a head sooner or later.* There's nothing that she could say to Arikè that would sound even remotely normal, so she didn't say anything. She looked at Cudjoe's slumbering body, spent with the exhaustion of their latest round of acrobatic sex, and got up. He pulled at her waist beads.

"I thought you were snoozing." Noire offered a preoccupied half smile.

"I was until the phone rang."

"Then go back to sleep." Noire walked out of the room and closed the door. She turned on the shower and heard the bedroom door creak back open. Jumping into ice-cold water, she cursed her anxious actions that were really an attempt to gain some distance between her and Cudjoe.

They were already nearly eight weeks into their de facto relationship. De facto because at no point did they ever discuss why Cudjoe's visit included weekly purchases of winter clothing that he housed in the spaces he cleared in Noire's cramped drawers and closets. To be sure, he did the laundry weekly like a real live-in boyfriend: washing his boxers alongside of her bras and panties and wheeling it all back in her shopping cart on Monday evenings. But he kept the destination of his daily excursions a secret, assuaging her growing curiosity with all the homemade Ghanaian and Jamaican cuisine and rounds of cunnilingus that she could stand.

And they didn't go out like couples did. Instead of Saturday afternoon brunch in the neighborhood and dinner with friends, they had midweek rendezvous in offbeat places too dark to be seen in and full of people who wouldn't know them anyway. It was the underside of New York City that Noire thought she had left behind along with her twenties—unsafe sex, her smoking habit that included a hit of the weed that Cudjoe had recently procured from somewhere, too little sleep for no good reason—but it all had returned and was more pitiful than the first time. Because now she was nearly thirty-one and old enough to know better.

"Baby, I need to take a leak." Cudjoe pushed the bathroom door open.

Noire remained silent. She listened to the toilet seat lid slap the tank.

"Aaaah." Cudjoe sighed his relief as he drained his bladder.

He didn't flush, knowing from experience that it would send an unwelcome blast of scalding water upon Noire in the shower. "You all right in there?" He pulled back the curtain to reveal Noire standing still in the corner of the tub. "Why so silent?"

"No reason."

"Do you need some help?" He dipped his hands into the water and sprayed it in Noire's face. Not waiting for an answer, he stepped into the shower with her.

Noire pressed her body into the corner of the bathtub. "I was trying to take a shower, Cudjoe."

"I'm not stopping you, baby." He ran the bar of soap across his hands before letting them slide down across her breasts and burrow into the V of her legs.

"Don't do that, Cudjoe. The soap stings."

He rinsed off his hands, then he kissed a path to the intended destination and let his tongue linger on her clitoris. He pushed her lips open with his fingers.

Noire spread her legs wide in spite of herself, her legs buckling from the spasms that ran from every part of her body and into her groin.

"Do you want me to stop?" Cudjoe said his words between sips at Noire's well.

Her shrieks announced the first wave of orgasm. Cudjoe entered her and she felt her insides grab hold of him and pump him dry. But this time it was she who was tired. She slumped against the wall and watched Cudjoe rinse off through half-closed eyes. He jumped out, wrapped a towel around his waist, and closed the bathroom door. Maybe now she'd get a few minutes alone.

"Well, I'll be—" Cudjoe eyeballed Innocent and didn't let him in the door. "We ordered lunch just now! Thought you were the deliveryman. Maybe you are."

Innocent kept the surprise out of his eyes and tried to match Cudjoe's defiance with his own. "Is Noire here?"

Cudjoe let the door close in Innocent's face. He made the three steps from the apartment's entryway slowly and leaned his lanky body against the archway that announced the main body of the living room.

Noire stepped out of the bathroom at long last, her body white with cocoa butter, and stared at the sneer pulled across Cudjoe's face. He was sexy, to be sure, but she definitely couldn't trust him. "What's up?"

"You seem to be popular among your ex-boyfriends." He flexed his body, the muscles of his chest squeezing and twitching in response.

"What?" Noire looked down and rubbed in the cocoa butter on her thighs. The front door slammed and she gasped. Her eyes caught Innocent's as he suddenly produced himself in the doorway. "Oh shit." Noire's voice was a miserable hiss that exited her like a clandestine fart that had made an unwelcome noise. Horror glued her to the floor, and the gaze of her former boyfriends and most recent sex partners upon her naked frame set her skin on fire. She clutched at herself. "*Why* are you here?"

"Which of us are you talking to, Noire?" Innocent saw the shame in Noire's eyes and lowered his gaze. He studied the fingers of her left hand, splayed across her crotch, and felt himself stir.

"You weren't invited in, mon." Cudjoe bit into Innocent's airspace.

"I doubt that you were, either."

Noire managed to rip her feet from the living room floor. She scurried into her bedroom and dug shorts and a sweatshirt out of Cudjoe's neat stack of their freshly laundered clothes. She picked out her Afro with her fingers. *Why is this happening to me? Why is Innocent here?* But her anger at his unannounced visit was only outweighed by her shame at Cudjoe's unplanned extended stay. She hadn't wanted Innocent to know. Not that it mattered how he felt about it. But still . . .

Not wanting to step aside for Cudjoe, Innocent stood firm as he brushed past him and opened the front door. Cudjoe paid the deliveryman and walked back into the room, busying himself with setting up Noire's two TV trays. They were silent, but Innocent heard all of the smug thoughts in Cudjoe's head. He tried to keep his own thoughts quiet.

Noire reemerged dressed in a shopworn sweatshirt and men's basketball shorts that Innocent did not recognize. He knew he shouldn't be there, but he wouldn't leave. He couldn't. "You look thinner," he looked at her body through the clothes that now covered it, and stood his ground. "Have you been ill?"

Noire flushed. Was he *ridiculing* her? "I should say the same to you."

"Our lunch is here, baby." Cudjoe's irritation was palpable as he tapped the empty space beside him on the love seat.

Noire's eyes followed the motion of Cudjoe's hand, but she still stood. "Innocent, we're about to eat." She allowed her own impatience and annoyance to shape her expression. She was a grown-ass woman. And Innocent was *not* her man.

Innocent nodded. "I was in the area—" He hesitated. "I was meeting with Reverend Anthony Trufant, the pastor at Emmanuel Baptist Church, right down the street."

Confusion scrunched her face.

He continued. "I'm helping to organize . . . there's going to be a memorial service for Alexander. At the church. He was a member there." He cleared his throat. "They found his wallet at the World Trade Center site a few days ago; his mother is trying to accept that he's really gone. I wanted to invite you."

"Oh." Noire choked on her own saliva and coughed. "Um, well . . . let me talk to you about that later, okay? I'll call you."

Innocent nodded his head and gave Noire the briefest of

smiles. He registered Cudjoe's disdain but was too deflated to return it. Just articulating the purpose of his visit had overwhelmed him.

Noire watched Innocent turn to go. He pulled the door closed
behind him. The last time she had seen his face was the day he
learned that his daughter had been born prematurely. Then, she
was in her deepest throes of shock and pain about Bonita's
death. Innocent had had the same expression on his face then as
he had now, an expression she couldn't read. She plopped down
beside Cudjoe and looked at the food before her as though she
didn't understand its purpose.

"Who the hell does he think he is dropping in on you like
that? Hasn't he heard of the goddamn phone?" Cudjoe's mouth
was full of his hamburger.

Noire had forgotten him, and his return to her consciousness
was unpleasant. "You did the same thing. Only you stayed!"
Noire's confusion morphed into a simmering anger that made
Cudjoe her target.

"I phoned you." He swallowed. "And you weren't complain-
ing when I was bowing between those thighs a minute ago!" He
licked his lips and challenged her with his eyes.

Noire felt her stomach ball up into a knot of disgust. "That
was rent, asshole. You *could* be homeless!"

His eyes became hard. "But you forget, Noire. You want me
here. I know how you are. You may want a man to 'make love'
to you, but if you can't get that, you'll take a good hard fuck. I
came along just at the right time." He reached out and grabbed
her breast through her sweatshirt. "I could slide inside right now,
girl! I know you're ready."

Noire sprang off of the love seat and knocked her food and
drink to the floor. "Cudjoe! Get the hell out of here."

"Aw, did Innocent get your punaani that out of joint?" He

snickered. "I can please you more with my little finger than he can with that Tootsie Roll he's got between his legs, Noire. You know it. If I couldn't, I wouldn't be here. Would I? You know mi a true, girl. I've known you a long goddamn time."

He rammed his hand down her shorts. Noire grabbed his wrist, twisted, and wrenched it out. "I hope you have a good memory, because this 'punaani' is officially closed! Get the fuck out of my house, Cudjoe. The gig is up!"

"Oh come on, girl. Let me nice it up—"

"The police come fast in this neighborhood, Cudjoe."

Noire propped open her front door with her umbrella stand and retrieved her baseball bat from the bedroom. She grabbed Cudjoe's duffel bag out of her hall closet and flung it at him. "You have ten minutes." She followed him around as he grabbed up his belongings and threw them into the bag. At nine minutes, he was finished. He stepped toward her and she jabbed the center of his chest with her bat. "Go."

And he was out the door.

⁂

"Girl, you look like shit for real," Jayna greeted Noire at the entrance of Sacred Sweat Hot Yoga Studio.

"Don't hold back, Jayna."

"And your teeth are looking jacked." She stepped closer and sniffed. "Are you still smoking?"

"Jayna, *please*."

"I'm a dentist, Noire. I can see yellow teeth in the dark!" She sucked her teeth for emphasis. "See, girl. Homeboys are pulling you down. Just say no, Noire."

"I have, dammit."

"Cudjoe may be black history, but it looks like you've got another bad habit to kick." Jayna picked up two yoga mats, towels, and a water bottle big enough to share and walked into the yoga studio.

Noire rolled her eyes. She peeled out of her layers of winter clothes, stripping down to a bathing suit top and boy shorts, and walked into the one-hundred-five-degree room toward Jayna.

"Maybe the class will send a little good karma your direction." Jayna's voice was a whisper in the dark, hot room. She rubbed her rented mat down with disinfectant before lying down. Noire ignored her and prepared for class by closing her eyes and resting in savasana.

"But what I don't get, Noire"—Jayna's face was just inches away from Noire's, her voice a terse whisper—"is why it took Innocent's unexpected visit to make you confront Cudjoe. I mean, if Negro had to go, then he had to go. Innocent's got nothing to do with it. Or does he?"

"Not now, Jay!" Noire hissed in return.

"That just doesn't make sense." She continued, undeterred. "You are a grown-ass woman and neither of them is paying your rent!"

Noire pushed up on one elbow, rearing Jayna out of her airspace. "What's that supposed to mean?"

Jayna was unflappable. "If you were really so unaffected, then you shouldn't give a shit about Innocent or Cudjoe. So what, they both saw you naked. They've seen it all before. You've already kicked Cudjoe to the curb. I say you forget Innocent's phone number."

"I told him I'd attend Alexander's memorial."

Jayna shook her head. "And that means something? Just don't show up!"

"That's not right, Jayna. Alexander was his boy. I want to show my respects."

"Innocent's got a baby mama back home that he managed

not to tell you about even after he fucked you like five times, Noire! *That's* not right!"

Noire watched Jayna lie back down and close her eyes. She followed suit, her lips mouthing words that Jayna didn't hear: "But I *want* to go."

∾

Noire blew her nose three times and wiped the tears that streamed out of her eyes. She was tired. This was the third memorial she had attended in four months. The third time she listened to friends sing the praises and mourn the loss of people who died too soon from tragic circumstances with dire consequences. The third time she had listened to people offer remembrances and invoke the name of God as though it were the magic elixir that would make everyone feel better. But she didn't feel any of it.

Innocent had read a poem by Aimé Césaire before recounting an anecdote from the time he and Alexander first started working together. And at Bonita's memorial, Nácio and others of her students managed to push themselves to their feet and share a memory of Bonita. Even at Dennis's memorial, held shortly after the 9/11 tragedy, Arikè offered a remembrance as a token of her love for Dennis. But Noire was silent. And though she wanted to say something to Innocent and go up and extend her condolences to Alexander's family now, she couldn't. As the others exited the sanctuary and went into the parlor for refreshments and more casual interaction, she left the church.

She began to walk home but, seeing the bus a block away, ran to get it as if by instinct just as it reached the bus stop. She arrived at Arikè's house ten minutes later and knocked on the door hesitantly.

"Sorry I haven't called" were her first words.

"Well, I'm here and I need some company." Arikè had thirteen-month-old Purpose balanced on her right hip. Her blouse was loose and her breasts visible. "Just pull the door shut. It'll lock." She led the way to the living room and sat in a pile of pillows. Opening her blouse to expose her left breast fully, she placed Purpose in the crook of her arm and his legs over her thigh. He latched on immediately.

"I've been thinking about weaning him. But it's the thing that Dennis most loved to see me do. I like to think that Dennis still enjoys watching me breast-feed. I don't want to take it away from him."

Noire stared at Arikè. Her breasts were rounded and beautiful. And Purpose looked peaceful, like he was made to be there. Maybe he was. She started to cry.

"Oh, I'm sorry, baby. You don't even know where all that is coming from. I shouldn't have laid it on you so quickly."

Noire riffled through the pockets of her skirt searching for a tissue that still could be used. She found none.

"There are tissues over there." She pointed toward a mound of diapers. "Baby wipes, actually."

Noire pulled a baby wipe out of the box and blew. The sickly sweet smell of the wipe assailed her nose. She coughed.

"I prefer the organic, unscented variety myself, but I can't very well reject folks' kindness."

Pulling herself together, Noire said finally. "Do you really think Dennis can see you?"

The faintest trace of a smile flitted across her face. "Yeah. I feel him sometimes. Watching me do stuff."

Noire was unconvinced.

"No one's energy ever really leaves. At least, I don't believe so."

She nodded and let that drop. She wasn't sure if she agreed. "So, how are you?"

"Alive. And today that's a good thing. Come, sit down next to us. So I can see you better."

Noire struggled down to the pillows, her skirt restricting her movements and her boots pinching her feet.

"Feel free to get comfortable, Noire. And don't worry about Purpose. He sees me naked all the time!"

Noire forced a laugh as she pulled off her boots. They were too tight. She bought them one morning as post-workout retail therapy and never considered that by late afternoon they would be too small. She unzipped the top of her skirt and pulled off the shrug she wore over a charcoal gray turtleneck.

"That's pretty." Arikè took Purpose off her left breast and positioned him on the right. She took a clean pad from a container and wiped her left nipple and areola carefully. Then she placed the pad back in its container.

"How does that feel?"

"Breast-feeding? Wow. I don't quite know how to describe it, Noire. It can feel very powerful, and awe-inspiring. I mean, that my body—women's bodies—can even do this, you know."

"But can you feel the milk? Can you feel him sucking the milk?"

"Yeah."

"And it doesn't hurt?"

"No. But when I first started, I'd feel really sore. And I did get an infection when he was about four months. But it's something I want to do and thankfully I made it through that hellish ordeal, so . . ."

Noire shook her head. She wanted to ask Arikè about other things. About how it feels to be a mother and a widow. About how often she thinks of Dennis and whether she feels happy anymore. But she didn't say anything. She couldn't.

"My mother has offered to come down and spend some time with me again. It's sweet of her, you know. But I think I just need some time. Just to be in this house and think. Dennis had a big insurance policy, which really helps, you know. But I know I need to go back to work soon. Once I can get Purpose into a good child-care situation. It's not easy to find."

Purpose had fallen asleep at Arikè's right breast. She removed him and ran a damp cloth along his gums and ten teeth before placing him into his playpen in the front parlor. "He'll be okay there for now." She wiped off her right breast as carefully as she had the other but left her blouse open. Her boy shorts rounded over a slight rise in her belly, making her body look like a more voluptuous incarnation of its former self. Noire remembered what it had been like to explore a new part of her sexuality, with Arikè as a willing participant. It had seemed so simple at the time. But now, as she looked at her friend's body, she had another kind of reverence for it. For what it had done and was doing for Purpose. For what she has endured.

"You're beautiful, Arikè."

"I don't hear that too much anymore. Thank you." She cried silently for several minutes, her left hand holding Noire's. Noire hugged her friend. It was all she could do. Finally, Arikè pulled away. "Sometimes that's the best thing. Crying alone can be so lonely. But crying with someone who loves you is comforting. But, so often, people won't let you. That's why I don't want my mother to come here. She's scared of my grief. She won't talk about Dennis because she doesn't want to make me sad. But she's not making me sad. It's the truth that makes me sad. Sometimes."

Noire looked at Arikè's face, wet and blotchy with emotion, and sighed. "I'm one of those people." She felt ashamed for every call she screened and every time she had thought about Arikè but chosen not to check in with her.

"Not anymore." She touched Noire's cheeks.

"I suck as a friend. I'm sorry."

"It's been a hard time for all of us. But sometimes we just need the space to admit it. It's okay to do that, you know."

Noire allowed herself a momentary reverie over the last year: her Pierre tryst, Dennis's death. Bonita's death, Innocent's fatherhood, her parents' upcoming wedding, Cudjoe's sliminess, and today, Alexander's memorial service. Half the time she didn't know how she felt about any of it. And the rest of the time she was too busy doing damage control for her own screwups to be able to regroup. "Yeah, if you looked up 'jacked up' in the dictionary"—she sanitized her language for Purpose—"there'd probably be a picture of me."

"That's not what I'm saying, Noire. You're no more jacked up than the rest of us."

"I'll let you believe that." She changed the subject. "How are *you* doing, Arikè?"

"You know, I'm hurting, Noire. I really am. I miss so many things about Dennis. I didn't realize how safe he made me feel, Noire. And I miss that." She cleared her throat. "But I feel blessed. I look at Purpose, you know. . . . God, his name says it all!" She adjusted herself, sinking further into the cushions and growing small by comparison. "When he turned six months old, Dennis insisted that we buy more life insurance. We each had $25,000 policies; I thought it was silly to spend so much money to get more because things were a little tight. I mean, Dennis was only thirty-six and we had other, more pressing expenses. But he said, 'Not everyone lives a long life. And if I don't, I want to know you and Purpose are taken care of.' He had a policy for $2.5 million."

Noire choked. She had no idea.

"I don't share that with people, Noire, because it can make them excited. It's a lot of money. But although it can offer financial security, it doesn't make me feel safe. And it won't last forever. Nothing does.

"The other day I met with my support group—"

"I didn't know you were in one."

Arikè nodded her head. "It's for widows and widowers under forty. This man said something that really got me. He said, 'We keep on talking about how our loved ones were robbed, robbed of the years they were still meant to live. But if we keep on talking about the years they lost rather than the years they had, then we're kind of discounting their actual lives. Maybe their lives were complete—at twenty-five and thirty-six and forty. I mean, for some reason they didn't get any more. So, even as we mourn their loss we have to celebrate the lives they lived and not always lament the lives they didn't live.' "

She clutched at her bare chest. "So I'm trying to celebrate the life Dennis lived, Noire. And be thankful that we had the son we had when we had him. Because there wasn't going to be another chance. Dennis had thirty-six years. That's all. And four of them were spent loving me." She pounded her chest as if trying to reach her heart inside. The skin of her breast turned red and spurts of milk came out with each blow.

"Don't do that, Arikè. Please." Noire pleaded with her. Unsuccessful, she stilled her hand with her own and there they stayed, feeling the pounding of her heart, shielding it from the pain that the world had inflicted upon it.

At last, Arikè calmed down and her breathing normalized. Her eyes were closed, her head leaned back against the wall. Noire watched a hint of a smile touch the corners of her lips. Arikè's eyes opened. "I love you, Noire."

"I love you, too, Arikè." She looked at her friend with fresh eyes. "You know, I've really missed you."

Arikè turned to look at Noire. "Life is too short to lose the people you love even while we're still here."

Noire nodded her assent. She sent Arikè upstairs for an indulgent soak in the bath and took a seat beside Purpose, asleep in his playpen. His face was a collage of happy expressions, his plump arms and legs sweeping through the air in what she imagined was a dream full of running and playing. Admiring his fearlessness, she wondered what she looked like while she slept.

❧

CHAPTER TWELVE

BODY BLOW

Innocent studied his morning erection in the available light of the loft. He touched himself, hoping to relieve his anxiety and fear. It was another day. Thirty-one days since he had last seen his daughter, Awura. Eleven days since Alexander's memorial service. Six days since he had left his apartment. Maybe seven.

His movements formulaic, he disassociated his actions from his mind and instead observed himself as if stealing a glance of a furtive act. This was the body of Innocent Kouakou DuCasse Pokou, laid bare on February 10, the morning of its thirty-sixth birthday. It was lean and fit, its nakedness quiet but assertive. Its penis lengthening out of a shock of hair, coaxed into a frenzy by an active hand pressing toward a goal. He watched the body clench, forcing its seed out like coconut milk from a shell smashed upon a stone. The release. The relief. The muscles slack. The skin sensitive. The body wanting to live in that moment. Only that moment.

"Happy birthday." Noire's hesitant voice exited the phone and burrowed into Innocent's ear.

"What time is it?"

"Ten-thirty."

"I overslept." He lied.

"I figured you were just celebrating."

"No."

"I almost didn't want to call you so early."

"Oh."

"So, how do you feel?"

Innocent sat up in bed. "I'm . . ." he heaved into the phone, ". . . lonely."

Noire was shocked; Innocent had never before admitted to loneliness. She thought he was immune to it, somehow. She listened to his breath, labored and unsteady. "Are you okay?"

Innocent was far from okay. He was far from all the things that were important.

"Do you— Can I, maybe, do something?"

"I doubt it." Innocent put the phone in the bed with him and lay back down. He was tired. It wasn't a good day. He would rest.

Noire tapped on Innocent's front door and waited. She tapped again, a little harder, and called his name. He opened the door and stood, his naked thighs streaked with dried semen. "Oh my God." Noire stepped into the loft. The air was thick with the smell of rotten food and Innocent's unwashed body. "Oh Jesus!" She whispered the shortest, most powerful prayer she knew and walked Innocent into the bathroom.

"I'm sorry." His voice was tissue paper.

"It's okay. It's okay."

Noire made him sit atop the toilet and ran a tubful of water. She ushered him into it and took his place on the toilet. With Innocent's back facing her, she grabbed his loofah and began to scrub it. She had always loved his back, the smooth dark skin wrapped tightly around little-known muscles that surprised her. His skin had lost some of its luster, but it was still beautiful. "Wash your face, you'll feel better," she instructed him. She watched him as he rubbed the washcloth over his face in ferocious movements, then scrubbed away the stubborn smells that clung to his underarms, and soaped his crotch.

Letting the water drain as he still sat in the bathtub, Noire went into the main room to investigate. She opened the windows to the February cold, stripped the bed, and emptied days-old coffee, spoiled sushi, and old cheese into a garbage bag. Making a quick trip to the incinerator, she returned to find Innocent's wet frame standing in the middle of the room.

"It's cool in here, Innocent. You need to put something on." She grabbed boxers, a sweatshirt, and sweatpants out of his dresser and handed them to him. "Oh, and here's your body oil."

She sat at his desk chair and watched him oil and dress. Finished, he lay down on his bare mattress. "No, Innocent. Don't lie down. Sit up and talk to me."

He pulled himself into a seated position, his shoulders rounded in submission to a force Noire couldn't see. She was scared. But she remained where she was.

"I can't stay here." Innocent looked at Noire's distraught face and wondered when would be the last time that he would see it. He loved everything about her face: its animation, the setting of her eyes, her sculpted nose and pouty lips that were pink on the inside and rimmed in crimson. She was a beautiful woman, a woman he would always love because she tried so hard to love him. And in a way she succeeded. But they had loved each other on terms that neither could accept. Not in the long run. He knew that they would not always share the same space. That his home wasn't her home. That he *had* to let his body finally rejoin his heart and stop denying that he needed his family to be closer than a day's travel and bigger than one sibling. He smiled and realized that he hadn't smiled since he returned from Côte d'Ivoire a month ago.

"I'm going home." He had decided it in the time it took him to utter the words, and yet his tone was decisive. It was the most certain thing he had said in a long time, and finally, it was the right thing.

"To Côte d'Ivoire?"

"I can't stay here."

"Why not?" Noire saw the faraway longing in his eyes, but she had to hear him answer her. For herself. Because she loved him. Because, despite all that she knew and didn't know, she tried to believe that there would always be a place for her in his life.

"*Un, deux, trois, quatre, cinq . . .*" His head bowed, Innocent slowed his breath to match his counting. By twenty-five he had affected some semblance of composure. He motioned for Noire to join him where he sat.

Noire weighed the offer. She wanted to be nearer to him, but only on her own terms. With her legs as propellers, she navigated the banker's chair to the foot of the bed and waited for Innocent to speak.

He nodded. "After you left my apartment when I found out about my daughter's birth, I tried booking a flight home. The soonest flight I could get left at eleven that evening. In the intervening sixteen hours, I packed and prayed. And vomited my shame that I had not been a witness to my own daughter's birth until all I could do was dry heave over the toilet bowl.

"Every minute of that nine-hour flight, I feared that I would arrive to the news that she had died only minutes before.

"I arrived at the hospital and knew that if I had been there with Chi-Chi, she would have given birth at PISAM, the country's best hospital, rather than an area community hospital that lacked the equipment to deal with a very premature baby's special needs. Thankfully they managed to keep her and Chi-Chi alive." He paused and looked at Noire's eyes. It was too late for him to try not to hurt her; he had done that so long ago. But he wondered if she was prepared to hear the whole truth.

Noire laced her fingers into each other and wound her legs around the base of her chair. Her face set into a frown, she prepared herself to hear more. "Go ahead."

Innocent painted a picture of his daughter's eventful life in vivid detail: her multiple health crises in the early weeks, Chi-Chi's recovery fraught with emotional setbacks. And he explained the significance of his daughter's namesake, Queen Awura, who began Innocent's father's bloodline in Côte d'Ivoire over two and a half centuries ago. He smiled unexpectedly. "She's legally blind, you know. From something called retinopathy of prematurity. But she can hear. She needs to hear her father beside her and feel my touch. Full-time." He shook his head in agreement with his own statement.

Noire's heart felt huge and weighted with every emotion it could hold.

"And when I returned to the U.S. last month after being home for two months, I was detained at the airport for fifteen hours because a man with my last name had been placed on an international 'don't fly' list. I was in a holding cell with other men from African and Arab countries. Even after nine years of being a taxpaying resident of this country, I cannot call it home, Noire, because it's *not* home. It's just where I live."

"And you wouldn't bring your daughter—Awura—here?" Noire was grasping at straws and she didn't know why.

"Then I would be doing to her what I did to myself: taking her away from her country and all the people who love her."

"Didn't you ever feel loved here, Innocent?" His words made her emotions a prickly pear.

"I did. And I do. You gave me more than I deserved. I wish I could say the same for myself." He offered his humility as an act of contrition.

She nodded her acceptance.

"Noire, some people can immigrate successfully. They can leave family and friends and create a life here in the U.S. that complements or even supplants what they left behind. But for me—for a *lot* of us, really—the conflict is too great. We have the trappings of a life—maybe a spouse and children, hopefully a job and at least a little money in the bank—but there's this disconnect. We live with the suspicion of our neighbors who may like our restaurants and festivals but who fear any customs or beliefs that don't square with their own understanding of Americanness. It's another kind of double consciousness. And of course we're always afraid of the call that will surely come—that a disaster has struck, a parent has died, our siblings are in trouble—and we can do nothing but send money if we have it and buy a plane ticket to arrive after the shit has already hit the fan.

"Home is only one place, Noire. If it's there and you're here, then it's like having a long-distance relationship with yourself. And if you make it *here,* then you've lost it there. You become a stranger to your family and grow unaccustomed to the tastes and sounds and smells you once knew.

"In my case, I told myself that this was home." He threw his hands wide, gesturing at the four walls of his loft. "I went to school here, made friends, bought the things I thought I wanted, and I met you." He smiled. "And I've offered my own intelligence, hard work, and charity in return. But the truth is that I was standing on sand at the shoreline, Noire. And every time a wave came in, it took just a little more sand out from under my feet."

Noire let his words sink in. She thought about herself, her own extended trips abroad. It had never occurred to her to make any of those places home for her. Perhaps it was because she didn't have a good enough reason. She hadn't fallen in love or secured a job she loved or had a child. But maybe that was by design. She thought about her earliest encounters with Cudjoe in Ghana when she was twenty-one and in love for the first time, and let her mind land at her most recent tryst with Pierre in Haiti. She had never thought of him as more than her enthusiastic lover and intellectual sparring partner. Perhaps she had just closed down the possibility of a lasting love because she wasn't willing to grapple with the choices it would invariably bring.

What was that about? Noire prided herself on being open to everyone, but in actuality, she rested comfortably inside her cocoon of American privilege that expected others to meet her within her own comfort zone and only to the extent that she allowed.

The unexpected blast of self-recognition dealt a sharp body blow that made her knees buckle. In an effort to escape her thoughts about herself, they ran aground again. Bonita. Just seeing her face in her mind's eye made her reservoir of grief overflow. Bonita had chosen New York over the Dominican Republic, her life as a neurotic professor and part-time misanthrope, for a life connected to her son and his family because she had been banished from home by her own grandmother when she was seventeen and a new mother. And her much belated trip to try and reconnect all the broken links killed her. It was too much for Noire to think about, too ugly to interrogate right then. She didn't know when she'd be ready, but she was sure it wasn't then, so she shifted the conversation to a place that was more comfortable, at least for her. "How are things after the coup?"

"Not good. The country is struggling with growing political and economic instability, which is unprecedented for a country that had been hailed by the West for having one of the most 'civilized' transitions from colonial rule to independence. Whatever that means." He shook his head. "But maybe I can do my part to stop the bleeding. After all, my own life's blood lives in Côte d'Ivoire. I have a daughter and elderly parents. And Chi-Chi."

"Who is Chi-Chi to you, Innocent?"

"The mother of my child. That makes her my family, too, I guess."

Noire watched Innocent's tears slide off his chin and make dark blue dots of wetness on her jeans. Then the dots started to connect like an inchworm with so many segments to its body.

She looked up at him. "Once upon a time I believed that if I loved long and hard enough, then that person would be mine forever."

"And I used to think that I was in control of *this*." He pounded the center of his chest with the heel of his hand. "We were both wrong."

CHAPTER THIRTEEN

31 N.D.

Noire counted balls of lint on her favorite sweater. Sixteen. She crossed her legs, first at the thigh, then, thinking it too difficult a position to hold for forty-five minutes, she uncrossed and recrossed them at the ankle. "So . . ." She smoothed her skirt out, fondling the edge between her thumb and pointer finger.

"Why are you here?"

Noire looked up abruptly, surprised to hear a sound come out of the therapist's mouth, though she had been waiting for her to say something.

"It's my birthday." Noire felt the words raise a lump in her throat. She looked for compassion in the therapist's stare but found none. "I'm thirty-one."

"What does that mean to you?" Dr. Branch took too long to say the wrong thing.

"Nothing. It's just . . . I'm just telling you."

"Why?"

"Isn't that the kind of stuff you want to know?" Noire was offended.

"I have your chart for that. Every day is someone's birthday."

Noire stared in disbelief. Wasn't she even going to say happy birthday?

"What does it mean to be you at thirty-one? Does it matter?"

Noire didn't like her question. She uncrossed and recrossed her ankles. "Doesn't everyone's birthday matter to someone?"

"We're not talking about everyone. We're talking about you. You told me that today is your birthday. I'd like to know why."

"Because in 1971, at the tender ages of twenty-six and twenty-two, Paul Demain and Flora Williamson became parents to a baby girl that they hadn't planned for. I was born in their adoptive borough of Queens, New York, at Jamaica Hospital.

"In the hospital pictures, my mother's Afro is a wild heap on her head and my dad's quasi-'fro is flattened in the back from the chair he had been sleeping in. There is a picture of each of them holding me, and one of the three of us together. They named me Noire because they always wanted me to know I was black."

"Do you have a middle name?"

"No. They liked that Noire, along with my last name, Demain, meant 'black tomorrow' in French. They didn't want to ruin that."

"How do you feel about being black?"

"I've been black my whole life. I'm fine about it."

"Not everyone is. Lots of women and men despise their blackness."

"I was raised to love it."

"How?"

Noire was stumped. She didn't even know if she was in fact raised to love being black as much as she was raised knowing that she was black. She thought about her hair and the fact that neither her mother nor father ever let her straighten it, even though Jayna had a perm and she pleaded for one in her final year of junior high school. She thought about the Kwanzaa celebration her father had every year in which she would read the description for Kujichagulia—Self-Determination—as he helped her light the appropriate candle in the kinara. She thought about trips to her mother's family home on Edisto Island in South Carolina and the explanation that they were enslaved Africans who came from unknown places along the West African coast. She remembered summers with her father's family where her fair-skinned cousins teased her about her black skin and kinky hair that looked nothing like theirs and her grandmother cursing softly in Louisiana French as she used the hot comb to "tame" Noire's "unruly naps" in time for church on Sunday and how she'd sweat it out by the time they returned from Mass.

"Maybe I was just raised to know I was black. Through the stuff we did, I did with my mother and father."

"Did you do things as a family?"

"We weren't a family."

"How so?"

"My parents split up when I was nine months old."

"Is sharing a household the only way to be a family?"

Noire was silent.

"Who are you, Noire Demain? What does it mean to be you?"

"It means I'm a broke graduate student who doesn't have prospects of a boyfriend and whose academic mentor is dead. Oh, and did I mention that the September Eleventh tragedy made my parents decide to get married?!" Noire was shaking now.

They sat in silence, Noire's defiant stare masking the hurt that lurked behind her eyes. She was sure she didn't like this therapist. She hoped her stare said that.

"Take off your glasses." Dr. Branch stared right back.

"Why?"

Dr. Branch hesitated until Noire did as she was told. "What do you see?"

"Very little." Noire discerned the top of Dr. Branch's head, and a moving hand. She imagined that she was writing down her response. It annoyed her. She put them back on just as she looked up.

"Not yet, Noire. For the next nine sessions, I'd like you to take off your glasses at the very beginning and keep them off until we finish. This session isn't about you looking at me; it's about you looking at yourself."

Noire felt offended once again. "I haven't decided that I'm coming back."

"Then make up your mind in the next couple of days. I've penciled you into this time slot, but if you don't want to continue, I'll remove your name."

Noire bit her tongue as she began to speak. Stopped by the pain, her silence was taken as agreement.

"Okay, for the balance of the session, I'd like you to tell me about the people in your life: family, friends, academic colleagues, romantic interests. Let me into your world."

Noire's nearsightedness made looking at anything beyond her own hands a strain on her eyes so she closed them. Her pose, stretched out on a lounge chair with an ottoman at her feet, felt indulgent and she realized she liked the feeling. When had anyone asked her about her with no motive of sleeping with her or sizing her up as a prospective friend or colleague? So she obliged Dr. Branch's request, giving her snapshots of her parents; her twenty-year friendship with Jayna; her half brother, Jabari, and his mother, Celine, in New Orleans; Arikè and Purpose; and Bonita Fuentes. She made no mention of Innocent or Cudjoe.

"Are you a lesbian?"

"No." Noire's eyes popped open, suspicious.

"Are you a virgin?"

"I have sex—relationships with men." Her tone was adamant.

"How long have you been celibate?"

"I'm not celibate."

"You didn't mention any boyfriends."

"That's because I don't have one."

"When was the last time you had sex, Noire?"

Noire turned her gaze toward Dr. Branch, her uncorrected eyesight barely able to make out her poker face.

"There's no one else in the room but the two of us, Noire, and *I'm* not judging you."

"Almost a month ago," she whispered, taken aback by her own timidity.

"Was that the first time you had had sex with this, *man*?"

She heard the question in the question and didn't like it. "He wasn't a *boy*." She answered the implied question first. "I've known him for ten years."

Dr. Branch didn't address the first part of her answer. "You've been in a relationship with him for ten years?"

"No. I—we were a couple when we first met. In Ghana. I was on a study-abroad program my junior year in college."

"He's Ghanaian?"

"Yes, and Jamaican. We've stayed—in touch over the years. He came to visit New York City in November and stayed with me. Until last month."

"Are you in love with him?"

"No."

"Were you ever?"

"I think so . . . yes. But *years* ago."

"What ended his stay?"

Noire thought about the scene in her apartment precipitated by Innocent's unexpected visit: her unplanned nakedness in front of him and Cudjoe, and the hellified argument with Cudjoe that followed. But she felt guilty somehow, talking about

Cudjoe when it was her complex web of feelings about Innocent that had driven her to therapy in the first place. Unsure of how much she wanted to share, she became cryptic. "We realized there wouldn't be a future for us."

Dr. Branch nodded and handed Noire her glasses, which had been sitting on a low table between the two of them. "Your time is over today, Noire. Please think about whether you will continue with me and call me by Wednesday. If you do, I'd ask that you be candid with me and truthful with yourself; that's the only way you'll make progress. Oh, and if you haven't been in a while, I suggest you make an appointment to visit your gynecologist. Lots of women schedule those kinds of things around their birthdays. Or when they change sex partners. Happy birthday." She swiveled to face her desk, leaving her unnaturally blond hair to cover her profile from view. Noire saw herself to the door.

∾

Innocent stood at the main entrance to the Howard University campus and flipped open his cell phone. He probably should have given Shema more forewarning of his trip to Washington, D.C., but he wasn't sure that he really wanted to see her. She had been a joy to meet during their quasi-date five months ago, but the way she had seen through him and what she had shown him of herself, mired with his own confusion, made him feel uneasy around her. He was nearly at her office on campus when he finally dialed her office number and then hoped she would be there.

"This is Shema." Her voice was rich and evocative, even when she was only saying her own name.

"*C'est* Innocent."

The silence made his heart pound louder.

"Shema?"

"I'm surprised you're calling me. Have you spoken with Mamadou?"

"I haven't been able to reach him. He's traveling for business, apparently."

"He is."

"Mmm. But I wanted to speak to you. To see you, actually."

"I think I've already shown you too much of me."

"I'm sorry, Shema. I should have been in touch. But I'm here."

"Here, now?"

"Yes. I'm on the campus. I can be to your office in two minutes."

"Innocent, I have to teach in a half hour."

"Then can you give me fifteen minutes?"

She gave a pregnant pause. "Fifteen minutes, okay."

Innocent stood in the doorway of her office and waited. He thought she would invite him inside and greet him, but instead she just looked up. He fidgeted and finally offered himself into the room and sat across from her at her desk.

"So, this is how you do it? You blow in and out of people's lives on a whim?"

He shook his head. "I haven't come to defend myself, Shema. My life has been crazy. That's all I can say. But I should have called you. To say thank you. To acknowledge that you shared something personal with me. And that I respect you. I do."

"I'm dating Mamadou, you know."

"Mireille told me that you met at his November gallery opening."

"He's a beautiful person. I finish my fellowship here in May and think Nakem and I will settle in Paris. I can't go back to Rwanda."

"Of course."

"So, you haven't spoken to him?"

"No, not at all."

"I didn't know if he knew about our meeting."

"He doesn't. Not from me, at least."

She looked relieved. "Well then, I'd prefer that he didn't. Not that there was anything wrong, Innocent. I'm not ashamed of having shared myself as I did. But, it's just simpler, I think, if he doesn't know that you've seen . . . me."

Innocent respected Shema's wishes. He understood that even a progressive man like Mamadou would feel threatened if he knew that Shema had shared with Innocent her physical scars that were meant to defile her body and bring shame upon her in the eyes of men and women, both. There was no need to infringe upon the relationship that they were building with extraneous information. "You deserve to be happy, Shema. I would never do anything that would jeopardize that."

She smiled her appreciation.

"Mamadou's like a brother to me. I guess he holds some of my secrets, too."

"I suppose he does."

"So it feels a little awkward."

She nodded. "The beauty about the past is that it's past. And things that happened more than ten years ago don't count at all."

"Oh, is that how it works?" Innocent chuckled.

"I think we all understand the need to respect where we are right now and not break confidences."

"Agreed."

"So, Mireille told me you are a father."

"I am."

"And that the baby came early. I am praying for her, Innocent. And for you and the mother, too."

"Thank you, Shema."

"Will you see her soon?"

"I'm going home. To live."

"That's a luxury some of us don't have. That's good, Innocent."

He nodded.

"When will you leave?"

"Less than a month from now. I'm hoping to move my travel up to March twentieth, or so. I have to put my loft on the market so I'll probably come back again later in the spring."

"Mmm. You're really doing it. Does Mireille know?"

"I'll tell her this evening."

They sat in silence looking at each other. At last, she spoke. "Innocent, you have a good heart. Don't let the struggles of this world destroy that."

"Maybe it already has."

"It hasn't."

Shema stood up and Innocent rapidly followed suit. They said their good-byes and Innocent watched as she picked up her pace after they exited the building. Shema was a good woman. He was hopeful for her and Mamadou, hopeful that they could find what had eluded him. Lasting love.

Innocent stood in front of The Original African, the restaurant Mireille had chosen herself, and watched his sister arrive hand in hand with a sandy-haired, blue-eyed lumberjack. He narrowed his eyes at the approaching couple. Mireille popped a kiss onto Innocent's cheek and kept her fingers entwined with the lumberjack's.

"This is Cedric van der Kloet. Cedric, my big brother, Innocent."

Cedric thrust his free hand forward and waited for Innocent's to meet his. And once it did, he wouldn't let go. "Good evening . . . sir." His French was faulty but his smile was ready.

Innocent didn't release his hand but Cedric dropped Mireille's.

"You're a student?"

"Here at Howard, yes."

"No need to respond in French, Cedric. I understand English.

Though I can't say I speak Afrikaans." He gave him a tight smile and let go of his hand at last. "So, why are *you* at Howard?" Innocent didn't see the need to be polite.

"The school is popular with Africans, um, as you know. And I wanted to be around my people."

Innocent looked askance at him.

"The way I figure it, I'm one of the faces of the new South Africa, too. And learning with so many future leaders of the African diaspora right here in the U.S. capital is the best of all worlds."

Innocent ignored Cedric. "How'd you meet him? In the African Student Union?" He was incredulous.

Mireille's eyes pleaded with him to be gracious. "Cedric was in my Francophone African literature class and we started studying together." She fumbled with her microbraids and shot a surreptitious grin at Cedric. He responded in kind.

Cedric's smile annoyed Innocent. "I guess English and Afrikaans just wasn't enough, huh, Cedric."

"I want to know about more than that. I'd like to be a South African diplomat and maybe work in West Africa as well as southern Africa. The region is just so culturally rich, you know."

"I know." His voice was flat.

Mireille's fingers were aflutter in her hair. "Uh, well, Cedric, I'll see you later, okay. Innocent and I are going to dinner."

"Okay, Mireille. And Innocent . . . sir, it was a pleasure to meet you." He offered his hand.

Innocent was slow to receive it.

"I have the utmost respect for Mireille and for black women. And black *people*."

"I'd expect nothing less." He squeezed Cedric's fingers before letting go.

"Bye, Mireille." He gave her an awkward peck on the cheek before turning to leave.

Innocent watched him walk out of earshot. "I hope that's your first kiss."

She let her hands fall from her hair back to her sides and cleared her throat. "Brother, I expect you to respect me and my choices."

"Mireille, just answer me this. How did you manage to find not just a white boyfriend, but an *Afrikaaner* boyfriend on a black campus in the black city of Washington, D.C.? It's just a little hard to believe."

"It's like I told you, Innocent. We met in class. And besides, lots of the other guys were just playing games, taking my number but never calling, trying to date me and all of my girlfriends at the same time. But Cedric said he wasn't interested in anyone else and he treats me well." She wound a braid around her finger.

"That's because every *black* African in D.C.—and there are a lot—would jack him up if he did anything else."

"Innocent, for godsakes. Cedric is not like that. He was eight when Mandela was released from prison and twelve when he became president. His father is one of the few *Afrikaaners* working in Mandela's government. I know that lots of Afrikaaners were oppressive to black South Africans. But Cedric's parents weren't like that. He wasn't raised like that. We talk about this stuff all the time."

"I'm not convinced."

"Well then, I won't be able to convince you. So you just trust me and take my word for it."

Innocent tried a different tactic. "And I guess I was under the mistaken impression that you spent your time studying rather than trying to rack up dates with coeds. Whatever happened to your boyfriend—" He searched his memory for the name of the twenty-three-year-old love of Mireille's eighteen-year-old life whom she had pledged her fidelity to when she started Howard two years ago.

"Abdul?"

"Right, Abdul! If memory serves, you were willing to give up Howard to stay in Côte d'Ivoire with him."

"Given how little you liked him in the first place, I would think you'd be happy to know that we broke up right before this school year started. He said that he didn't like having his girlfriend all the way in the U.S. and that he was afraid the country would corrupt me anyway."

"Has it?"

"Innocent, look. I am a twenty-year-old woman. Right now I'm trying to make the most of my time here at Howard and in the U.S. Cedric is a part of that right now. I'll worry about the rest later."

"Doesn't sound like much of a plan, Mireille. Weren't you the one who said you wanted to return to Côte d'Ivoire and not abandon it like I have?"

"Why are you making this personal, Innocent? That's not what I said. I never said anything against you or your choices."

"Sometimes it's what you don't say that speaks the loudest."

"Brother, I'm pretty good at saying what I mean. Even to *you*. That's how you and I are different."

Innocent recoiled, stung by her words. "Look, we're getting offtrack—"

"No, Innocent, we're right on track. If you are carrying around guilt over Chi-Chi and Awura, or Shema, or Noire, or even Lissette or some other women that I don't know about, that's your problem. So don't push it onto me. If you've done something wrong, then I hope to God you'll set it right. And if you're wondering, yes, I do feel that Awura deserves to have her father around like we had."

"No, like *you* had, Mireille. If Papa was around, I never knew it because I was at boarding school. And once Serge died, Papa wrote me off, too. I practically had to parent myself!" Lines of tension pulled his forehead down to his eyes, which were hard balls staring through Mireille and into his past. He hated this feeling, hated that he still felt anything at all. He had convinced himself that he had packed that away permanently, that feeling of needing his father and not having him. Serge's death had killed so many relationships: his with his father and with Maman and Charlotte as well. Only his relationship with Mireille survived because, at two years old, she was too young to blame Innocent. So he held on to her even as everything else slipped away.

Mireille grabbed Innocent's hands in hers. "I'm sorry about all of that, big brother." She kissed him on each cheek like he used to whenever she was sad. "But it's the *past*."

He nodded his head in acquiescence. He had to forgive Papa for his own sake. He smiled his gratitude at his baby sister who had grown wiser than him.

They rode a taxi back to the Akwaaba Inn in silence. Innocent rehearsed his announcement in his own mind. "Mireille?" As the cab pulled up to their intended destination, he finally spoke. "I didn't tell you my news, yet."

"What, Innocent?" She stepped out ahead of him and peered through the darkness at his somber face.

"I'm going back. Home, I mean." He slammed the door shut and stood in front of his sister.

"Really? What made you decide that? When did you decide?"

"My thirty-sixth birthday. Being alone. Missing Awura. Messing things up here. I don't know. I just need to try to get things right, you know."

"Have you told anyone?"

"Noire."

"Noire?" Her eyebrows asked another question.

"She's been a good friend to me. Through all this, Mireille. It was looking at her that made me know I had to leave."

Mireille frowned her confusion.

"It's just . . ." He thought about Noire bathing him, about making love to her because he was needy, about all the things he never told her about the demons in his head. "She deserves someone more present than I can be. And the more she did for me, the more I realized I couldn't do for her. That I had all this unfinished business to attend to."

"Well, I'm happy for you, brother. You're doing the right thing."

"That's all I've ever wanted to do."

❧

CHAPTER FOURTEEN

POKER FACE

S he looked through the smoke that engulfed her head and the haze of her rapidly darkening living room and out the window. It was snowing. Large flakes raced past her window faster than she could count them. It was March 1 and she received three pieces of mail: a belated birthday card from her mother, the invitation to her parents' wedding (wedding date: May 18), and her lease renewal with an accompanying letter from her landlord telling her what she already knew: that as of June 1, her rent would rise to twelve hundred dollars, from eight hundred twenty-five dollars.

Noire touched a new cigarette to the end of the old one and took a long drag. She was smoking generic cigarettes now; the clove cigarettes that Bonita had turned her on to were just too expensive for her growing habit. She had just reached a milestone: twenty-two a day. It had become bad, she knew. But today was too fucked up a day to stop. She had four more and it was not even six o'clock. She'd have to buy a new pack before the end of the evening.

Noire heard the phone ring. Once. Twice. Her answering machine picked up after the third ring.

"Hey, hon, it's Dad. It's kind of import—"

"What's up?"

"Were you sitting there listening to me?"

"I couldn't get to the phone right away." She lied.

"Why do you sound like that?"

"Like what?"

"That's what you're supposed to tell me. What's going on with you, Noire?"

"Nothing. Nothing at all."

"I don't believe you."

Noire didn't respond.

"So . . . did anything come in the mail?"

"I just threw it on the couch."

"Well, look at it."

"I'll do it later, okay."

"Before we get off the phone."

"Mmm."

"I'm calling with an invitation." He waited for a response.

Another one? "Oh?"

"We thought—your mom especially—that it would be nice to take a family vacation—"

"I'm thirty-one—"

"To New Orleans."

"Why are you going down there?"

"To see my mother, of course, and Jabari. Just to connect with everyone before the wedding."

"You mean that Mom wants me to help take some of the heat off her so that Grand-mère can ask me when I'm planning to straighten my hair and find a husband."

"Come on, Noire."

"I really don't have the time"—she blew smoke from the side of her mouth and lit a fresh cigarette, her third in twenty minutes—"or the money, Dad. I really don't."

"We wouldn't make it a financial hardship on you, Noire. It's just, our premarital counselor suggested we resolve things with you *before* the wedding."

"What's there to resolve, Dad? You and Mom are getting married and that's it. What has that got to do with me?"

"Noire, we talked about some of this—"

"You're right, Dad. We did. But Mom hasn't seen fit to so much as call me. And she sent me a belated birthday card. *Belated,* Dad. I've already been forgotten."

"You've got to realize how crazy you're sounding right now."

"Now I'm crazy."

"What the hell is *wrong* with you, Noire? You act like someone's done something to you."

"No, Dad. I'm acting like no one's done *anything* to me. Look, I appreciate you calling, but *you're* not the problem. And I don't need to fly all the way to New Orleans to talk to Mom. She knows my number and where I live, even if she *has* forgotten my birthday!"

"So, that's it, Noire?"

"I don't have anything else to tell you, Dad."

"Good-bye, Noire." And he was gone.

Noire walked over to the window and opened it. She tried to catch the snowflakes but they disappeared as soon as they landed on her hand. That's how she felt. Like she was melting. She lit another cigarette. Maybe it was better to burn.

∞

Black Man's Poker by Marcus Gordon screamed from the front window of Hue-Man Bookstore, Marcus's disembodied poker face adorning the oversized ace of spades on the book's cover.

Innocent looked past the poster, through the plate glass, to the real Marcus, smiling and autographing his latest book.

"Well, if it isn't the original big willy!" He gave Innocent the requisite black man's handshake with an extra pound.

"From the looks of things, that title suits you."

"I'm just a black man trying to make it—"

"And succeeding." Innocent gestured at the stack of hard-backs in front of Marcus and the crowd of his followers who still lingered at the bookstore.

"Doing my part for the cause." Marcus feigned modesty. "Man, you've been ghost. Thought you went off and married some white chick and moved to Montana or some shit. Nothing against white chicks or Montana of course." He chuckled.

"A lot's been going on." Innocent bobbed his head up and down.

"I wanna hear about it, black man. But look, Lydia made me promise I'd be home to put Nile to sleep and check in on Tunisia so that she could do some sort of home spa thing and his bed-time is ten minutes from now."

"Well, let me not hold you, then. Let's just connect at some point soon."

"I was going to invite you over. You can have some Brazilian cachaça or whatever you big dogs are drinking these days, while I get little man tucked in. Then we can catch up for a few and let you leave in time for your booty call." Marcus gave his poker face.

Home was the next thing on Innocent's agenda so he figured the detour would kill two birds with one stone. "Booty calls are out of style, so you got me all night."

Lydia had lost all of her plumpness, replacing it with hollow cheeks and the burden of loss. Innocent gave her a hug in greet-ing, feeling the grief that lived in her body. "Lydia, it's good to see you. I'm so sorry about your father's passing."

"Did Marcus tell you everything? He doesn't like to talk about it anymore. But that doesn't make it go away."

"Not everything." He lied. Marcus hadn't said much of anything.

Five-year-old Nile ran into the parlor and held his arms up to Marcus. He picked him up.

Lydia didn't miss a beat. "Dad died doing what he did best: cheating on Mom!"

"Lydia, why don't you do that home spa you told me about?" He rubbed her shoulder with his free hand. "I've got things under control out here. I'll come and look in on you later."

She sighed and walked out of the room without another word.

Marcus gave Innocent a helpless look.

"Man, do what you gotta do, okay. I'm here."

"Let me just get Nile to bed. And you haven't even met Tunisia?"

"No, not yet."

"She's asleep, but I'll let you peek at her in a bit."

"Sounds good."

Innocent sauntered around the cavernous family room looking first at the photos adorning the walls and then at the mound of old family pictures sitting loose on the coffee table. He thumbed through them one by one, studying the smiling people arrayed in hip-huggers, bell-bottoms, and the occasional leisure suit, with backdrops ranging from Disney World to l'Université Cheikh Anta Diop in Senegal. In each, Lydia's arms encircled her father, who stood at least a head shorter than her.

"Innocent," Marcus called from the steps. "Take off your shoes and come on up."

They walked into Tunisia's room where the two-year-old lay sprawled across her toddler bed, her thumb near her opened mouth.

"She's beautiful." Innocent felt full. Seeing her made him think of his own daughter; she was now twice the age she had been when he left Côte d'Ivoire. He could only imagine what Awura looked like now.

They returned to the family room and Marcus offered him scotch.

"That's a little strong for a Tuesday night."

"I thought the night was young for eligible bachelors like you. What's the hustle these days, Innocent? You look sleep deprived but not sex deprived!" He slapped his hands in anticipation of a story.

"What?"

"I know you single Africans are still in the fucking business. Least you could do is share a story, black man."

"Is that all I am to you?"

"Damn, man. No need to flip out and get self-righteous and shit. Things have just been tough. With Lydia and all. She's been . . . not well, you know. Mentally it's taking a toll."

"Look, I'm sorry to hear that. But a lot's been happening here, too."

"Fuckin'?" He pulled his face into a smirk and waited.

"I'm a father, dammit. I became a *father*."

"Oooooooh." Marcus was a popped balloon.

Innocent stood up and rammed his hands into his pockets.

"I just thought, you know, smooth African brotha such as yourself, and all—"

"Life is serious for *everybody*, Marcus. Not just you. I'm not just your fucking fix!"

Marcus picked up the scotch, poured it into a shot glass, and downed it in one gulp. "Hey, I'm sorry, all right. And I suppose I should say congratulations?"

"Of course you should." He stared down at him.

Marcus cleared his throat. "You know, life is some real bullshit. I mean, you plan for stuff and everything keeps on getting fucked up. My wife is a skinny ghost of a woman who can't sit down to eat a full meal and who cries when I touch her, and my kids are growing up in a world where folks fly airplanes into buildings and our own president treats national security as if he were a cowboy on a cattle ranch. It just makes a man feel, well, not like a man. I guess I was trying to live vicariously through you. My bad, all right."

Innocent nodded his acceptance of his apology. "We're all grown up. And not everything in the real world is what you thought it would be."

Marcus poured more scotch and raised his glass in salute. "So Innocent's a daddy. Who's the lucky lady? Is it Noire?" He looked suspicious.

Innocent had no intention of oversharing. "She's a family friend from back home. Our daughter, Awura, is four months old. But she was nearly three months premature."

"Oh wow. Damn."

"Yeah."

"But she's home with her mother. I'm moving back myself. In a couple of weeks."

Marcus stared at Innocent with new eyes, with the respect of an equal. "That's good, Innocent. That's real good. Pictures can't replace being there with your daughter."

"Don't I know it."

"So, let's toast to fatherhood, then!" He poured them both shots of scotch. "And to trying to do the right thing when everything is fucked up."

Innocent dozed in the backseat of the taxicab as it made its way downtown. The vibration on his hip nudged him back into wakefulness.

"Pokou—"

"I'm getting married!"

"Mamadou?"

"I proposed and Shema said yes. She said yes."

"*MALPT!*" He reined in his thoughts. "That's really quick, man. I barely knew you two were together."

"Yeah, well, we are."

"When'd you meet her exactly?" He knew the story but had never heard it from Mamadou.

"Four months, give or take. But look, I just can't wait. Abstinence is a bitch!" He chuckled.

"*Abstinence?!* Since when?"

The cabdriver threw a glance at him from the front of the car.

Puzzled by the cabdriver's consternation, Innocent noticed the mini Algerian flag dangling from the mirror. He understood French.

"Calm down, Innocent, okay. It's just that Shema is Catholic and a very private person; she doesn't want to share herself like that, you know, without being married."

Innocent was speechless. He pictured her body, scarred and sad and beautiful. Shema standing naked before him on the very night they met. Lowering his voice, he chose his words carefully. "But she's . . . a widow."

"Of course I know that. But she was raped, Innocent. I wouldn't want to force the issue and make her uncomfortable."

"So, you're saying she's been celibate all this time?"

"Goddammit, Innocent. When have I ever asked you about the sexual history of any woman you've been serious about? How can you even ask me that?"

Innocent digested his words. He was right, of course. He had no right to ask those kinds of personal questions. But he couldn't help knowing what he knew and seeing the image of her body in his mind. He noticed the cabdriver's eyes trained on him through the rearview mirror and decided he should cut the cab ride short. "This is fine, let me off here."

He screeched to the curb.

"Where are you, man?"

"Getting out of a cab. Let me just pay him." He jostled his wallet out of his pants pocket. "And where are you?"

"I'm at a hotel in Newark. I have meetings with folks at the Newark Museum tomorrow afternoon."

"Well, it's only ten, so why don't you come over and we can have coffee and talk."

Innocent poured Mamadou's triple espresso into a coffee mug and set it down in front of him.

"Are you trying to keep me up all night?" Mamadou narrowed his eyes at this friend.

Innocent poured a smaller version of the same for himself and sat down at the kitchen table.

"I should have asked you before. How's Awura doing?" He sipped the bitter brew.

"Good, by all accounts. It's hard to speak with Chi-Chi, though; I'm always calling at the wrong time, it seems. And her mother's not much better. She thinks I've made her daughter un-marriageable."

"Mmm. You know how things are at home. Even here. It's not easy for a single mother."

"I know."

"So, what's on your mind these days, Innocent?"

"Well, I'm going home. Permanently. Leaving on the twenty-first and I expect to come back to tie up loose ends by mid-May."

"You're selling this place?"

"Yeah. I have to. I can't give myself an out, you know."

Mamadou closed his eyes and frowned. "That's good, *mon reuf*. See, we knew that the right thing would come to you. And it has."

"Yes, it has." He gulped his espresso and looked at his friend. Their relationship spanning seventeen years, they were brothers and confidants. He knew that Mamadou was a good man in all of the ways that it really counted. He had integrity and empathy and passion and faith. And he was an optimist and an artist. Innocent admired his ability to create his own way in Paris from the time he was a teenager, and his willingness to pursue the things he loved rather than getting trapped by the things others expected of him. And that's what concerned him about Shema. He wondered how much he knew and whether he had expectations of fathering children she couldn't have or even if he knew about her scarring. He knew that Mamadou could handle it. But what if she hadn't told him? And why had she shown herself to Innocent so readily? What would it do to Mamadou to find out on their wedding night?

He didn't know the right place to begin so he picked any-place. "Would you say you know a lot about Shema?"

"Innocent, is this why you asked me over here? To quiz me on her? I don't think I need that from you, Innocent. What happened to unconditional support?"

"Mamadou." He let out an exasperated sigh. "You tell me that you're marrying a woman whom you met on a trip to Washington, D.C., four months ago and you expect me to just offer unconditional support?"

"Innocent, you impregnated a woman during a three-month trip back home and when you told me about it, I didn't pounce on you about her!"

"But you did question my choices. Around her and around Noire." He was defensive.

"That's because you said you didn't love Chi-Chi and she was the one carrying your child. And that you were sleeping with the ex-girlfriend whom you did love—" He paused long enough for Innocent to correct him but no correction came. "—but couldn't offer a real relationship. That's why I questioned your choices. Because they were fucked up, Innocent. You knew it yourself; that's why you called me."

Innocent squeezed his eyes shut and counted to ten. Slowly. He turned his gaze to the other side of the room. "You remember you told me that I was jerking Noire around because she wasn't operating on full information? Well, suppose you didn't have full information? I mean, do you know that you do?"

"Are you trying to tell me something, Innocent, because if you are, you're doing a very bad job of it."

"I'm not, man. I mean, Shema seems like a wonderful woman—you know I met her through Mireille in October—but I don't know. Maybe she's got a complicated history. She had to leave Rwanda, you know."

"I'm fully aware of that."

"So, it's just . . . there's so much to know about a person before you join your life to theirs on a permanent basis."

"I suppose you're learning that every day with Chi-Chi."

"Mamadou, please don't be defensive about this. Remember, I love you, too."

"Then be happy for me, Innocent. You know, the first time I saw Shema, I could see her story. It's in her eyes, Innocent. And since then I've grown to know her heart. She's a good woman. A *great* woman, Innocent. And I am willing to go on faith and to love this woman as my wife. I know that there are things I haven't learned about her or she about me. But at some point you have to believe that there's someone with whom you can make a life, even without complete knowledge. Because the truth is, we don't know everything there is to know about ourselves, either. We're growing in that knowledge every day that we live. But if we are honest, with ourselves and with those we love, then we've won more than half the battle."

Innocent was awed. Honesty. Innocent wished that he had never seen Shema. He wrestled with her words—"Look at my scars and respect my history"—and with the promise he made to her to keep their interaction private. But that was when he thought Mamadou knew more than him. Now that it seemed that he didn't—though he could not be sure—he felt that he was keeping something from his friend. And that Shema was, too, under false premises.

He changed his tactic. "Mamadou, you know that you can tell me anything. You know that. I guess I'm just surprised that you are willing to marry someone so quickly when there are so many things you haven't experienced about her. Especially since I know you to be a sexual man. Sexually active."

Mamadou shook his head. "You know what's funny about close friendships like ours that play out long-distance. It's that we think we know more about the day-to-day lives of the other person than we really do. And we used to. When we were horny university students who shared a dorm room. But that was four-teen years ago, Innocent. And we've become men with prefer-ences, habits, and issues, some of which we don't always share. And then you fall in love. And the stuff that you may not have shared with your close friend, you may share with her. Because you're going to build a life. Together. So I may know things about Shema, and she may know things about me, that I have not and will not share with you. That's my prerogative. I appre-ciate your concern, Innocent. I really do. But I appreciate your respect more. For me and for the woman I intend to marry."

They stared at each other for a long time, Innocent ingesting Mamadou's insights and reconciling it with his own fears. Mamadou had more faith in people than he did. He always had. If only Innocent could feel the same way . . .

Part Four

FAIT ACCOMPLI

❧

CHAPTER FIFTEEN

"I" STATEMENTS

Noire's glasses rested on Dr. Branch's coffee table. As did her mother's. They were facing each other but sat just far enough away to blur the features in the face she used to know better than her own.

"Okay, Noire. Now I want you to repeat what your mother says *exactly* as you hear it. No commentary, no spin. Just the words she says. You'll get your chance to do the same, later. Got it?"

"Yes."

"Flora." She nodded for her to begin.

"When you said that I didn't need to go through the trouble of being a bride dressed in white, I felt that you were saying I didn't deserve it."

"That's not what—"

"Noire, *repeat* what your mother said. Don't answer it."

Noire felt her blood pressure creeping up. "I heard you say

that you didn't like it when I said you didn't have to go through the trouble of wearing a white dress."

"Is that what you said, Flora?"

"I didn't say that I didn't like it. I said I felt that *you* felt I didn't deserve it."

"Okay, Noire. Repeat that part."

"You felt that *I* felt that you didn't deserve it."

Dr. Branch looked at Flora for her approval. "Okay. Continue."

"And when you acted disinterested at the dress fitting, it made me feel that you didn't care that this was a happy experience that I wanted to share with you."

"I heard you say that you felt like I didn't care about your happiness because I wasn't interested in the dress fitting."

"Not my happiness, in general, Noire, but that this—getting married—was a happy experience for me that I wanted to share with my daughter, who's also my maid of honor."

"Repeat." Dr. Branch nodded at Noire.

"You felt I didn't care about the happy experience of you getting married and sharing it with me, your daughter and your maid of honor."

"Is that what you said, Flora?"

"No! Noire, you're not even listening to me."

"What? I just repeated verbatim what you said—which happens to be dead wrong, but whatever—and I haven't been able to even defend myself! This is crazy. And now you're going to tell me I'm not listening. That's all I've been doing is listening to your wedding plans."

"Noire, you're getting ahead of things. I want you to trust the process. Just try to hear why what you repeated is not what your mother said."

"The *process*?! Maybe I feel like I'm not being heard, like she doesn't give a damn about the fact that it may not all be happy for me, that she chose to share her 'good news' the day after my mentor, and one of the people who was closest to me in my whole life, was killed in a plane crash, not unlike the goddamn plane crash that caused my parents to decide to get married. For godsakes, Mom. Didn't it occur to you that I could be dealing with my own stuff?!" Noire expelled air in a violent blast and crossed her arms over her chest. She couldn't see her mother well, but she could tell that she was holding her fingers at her temples.

"That's not fair, Noire."

"Flora and Noire, I just want us to get back to the mirroring technique. Just for a moment. And then we can unpack all that we've heard. So just calm down. We still have time."

Noire was unconvinced. "Just as long as *I* get to go."

"Yes, Noire, it's your turn now."

"When you told me about you and Dad getting married under the guise of checking in on me, I felt like you silenced my grief and discounted the importance of my relationship with Bonita as a friend, mentor, and second mother."

"Second mother!"

"Wait, Flora. Noire, that was too much. You need to break that down into at least two separate statements. Okay, Noire, try again."

She rolled her eyes. "When you came over under the pretense of checking in on me, I felt betrayed when you made the visit all about you and Dad getting married."

"Okay, good. Flora, repeat."

"When I came over to check in on you, you felt betrayed because I told you about Paul and me getting married."

"No, Mom. You didn't just tell me about the two of you. You talked about Bonita for like two minutes and then you just took over the conversation. It felt disingenuous."

"Shape that into something your mother can repeat."

"Fine. You were being disingenuous—"

"No, Noire. Don't use 'you' statements. Use 'I' statements.

You can't accuse Flora of doing something, you can only state how you felt about what she said or did."

"Oh, I can repeat that." Flora balanced at the edge of her seat. "You wanted me to just talk about your feelings and experiences and not share my own. But it doesn't work that way, Noire. Not anymore. You're a grown woman just like me."

"But you're my *mother*!"

"I'm more than your mother, Noire! I'm a full human being. And I'm not raising you anymore, Noire. I did that. And I did a good job.

"But one of the things I always hoped I would do one day is get married. And here I am, at damn near fifty-three years old. I'm getting married to the man I have always loved. Noire, I was really hurt when your father married Celine. But even that wasn't all about me. Because Paul was more than just my daughter's father. He was a man seeking his own way. I had to make my peace with that for you and for me. And Jabari, too. He's your father's son and your brother.

"Noire, I don't know why things happened this way. And I'm sorry that all of it hasn't felt good to you. But it's not just about you. Noire, I didn't know what Bonita meant to you; I guess we just never talked about it. Maybe it was my fault for not asking. Or maybe it was your fault for not sharing it with me. So when I told you about Paul and me getting married, I thought I was sharing something special, something happy, that you've always wanted. That's all."

Noire was crying now. "Mom, I guess that's part of it, too. When you told me that other people's lives moved you and Dad to act in a way that my own life never seemed to, it felt really fucked up, Mom. I'm sorry. But it did."

Flora pulled her chair closer to Noire. "Your life is the biggest reason that I am who I am, Noire." Their knees kissing, they held on to each other.

Coming home felt different from visiting home. Riding along the streets of Abidjan in his father's car, Innocent realized that he had never lived in Côte d'Ivoire as an adult. His adolescent and teenage years were spent between boarding school in Grand-Bassam and university at the Sorbonne in Paris, and his twenties between France and the French Caribbean until he moved to New York City at twenty-seven to begin Columbia Business School. Visits home meant a guaranteed bed at his parents' house, complete with their house rules and meal schedule, and no responsibilities beyond those he imposed upon himself.

By contrast, coming home meant he didn't actually have one, a home of his own choosing where he provided a place for himself and his family. He had managed to do this in New York City without questioning himself. But here it was different. Coming home involved crucial choices with bigger consequences. He felt humbled and hopeful, and a bit scared.

Innocent lifted Awura out of her bassinet in Chi-Chi's bedroom and inhaled. He filled his nostrils with her delicate baby scent that had drifted away from him in the months since he had seen her last. She had begun to get plump, and although her seven-pound, three-ounce body was far smaller than those of most of her four-month-old counterparts, she seemed huge and healthy.

"Ooh, look at you! Look at Papa's baby girl!" He placed tender kisses on her forehead and both cheeks, enjoying the warm softness of her new skin as he did so. "I love you so much . . . I missed you so much . . ." His words were a singsong that he repeated over and over, much to Awura's delight.

Remembering that Chi-Chi was in the room, he walked over

to her. "Thank you." He pressed his lips to her forehead, tasting salt on her skin.

She pulled away, a nervous chortle rattling in the back of her throat. "Okay, Innocent." She grinned. "I'm happy you've come back."

∞

"New York City sucks." Jayna rubbed old nail polish off her big toe and popped a tortilla chip in her mouth.

Noire looked at the polish remover sitting precariously atop her bed. "Don't let that spill, Jayna." She took a long drag on her cigarette and guided Jayna's removal of the bottle to the floor right in front of Noire's outstretched leg. She shook her head at Jayna's thoughtlessness and placed the bottle as far as she could away from her leg without toppling it over.

"Why are you still smoking that shit?" Jayna picked up the bottle of remover and saturated a cotton ball.

"Because New York City sucks." Two thousand two was not even four months old and already she was tired of it. All she and Jayna talked about was the dwindling population of eligible men and Jayna's wavering resolve to her newfound celibacy. Noire was celibate herself—strictly by circumstance—but nevertheless found it difficult to think about entertaining a relationship. Her emotions were still too raw, her body heavy with the lingering disappointment of her nonrelationship with Cudjoe.

"Let's order Thai!" Jayna's voice was an exclamation point. "Nothing like spicy food to perk us up!"

"True. But I'm kind of busted, Jayna. I've had a few extra expenses of late." She hadn't told her about her weekly sessions with Dr. Branch that, even with her student health plan, set her back twenty-five bucks a pop, so she kept things vague.

"How much is that tar costing you a day?"

Noire ignored her.

"Well, this is a high-rent neighborhood now, so I'm sure your friendly neighborhood Thai restaurant takes plastic."

"I think you're right about that. But only if it's your plastic, Jayna."

"Girl, you know I'm generous."

Noire dug up the menu and she called in an order for spring rolls and fried calamari for appetizers, shrimp pad Thai, and crispy duck for the entrees, two Thai iced teas, and deep-fried ice cream. "Oh, and I'm paying by credit card."

"What's the number?"

She recited Jayna's number into the phone and hung up.

"Thai food works every time."

"Is that what you're using in place of sex?"

"That's tired, Noire."

The phone rang.

"Hello?" Her voice was full of giggles.

"It's Thai Spot. The card did not go through."

"What?"

"I need another card, miss."

"Jayna, he needs another card. It didn't go through."

She grabbed the phone from Noire. "I'm so sorry, but we don't have another card. . . . I know you started making it. I'm sorry about that. . . . Uh-huh . . . uh-huh. . . . Okay. Okay. We won't!" She slammed down the phone.

"What happened?"

"He said not to call again unless we have cash."

"See, Jayna."

"Sorry 'bout that." She cleared her throat. "But, girl, you know with all the money I spent buying my new apartment and every-thing, it's just—I guess my credit card kinda blew up on me."

"Blew up?"

"It's maxed out, Noire. Damn."

"I know what it means, Jayna."

Noire walked to the kitchen and came back into the bedroom. "This is my credit card." She handed her a gallon-sized freezer bag with her frozen credit card suspended in a block of ice and the words USELESS UNTIL MAY 2007 written on it.

"Homegirl, whaat!"

"I'm not mad at you, Jay."

"Well, I guess you're not!" Jayna ran a finger over her toes. "What I need to do is go home and cook what's in *my* freezer."

"And maybe I'll fry this up!" She tapped the freezer bag and laughed. "Okay, I'll give you a call tomorrow morning."

"Make it the afternoon. I've got an appointment with my gyn, and the way she overbooks people on Saturdays, I know I'll be there for a minute."

"Will she be the first one inside that celibate vagina of yours or has someone else unbuckled the chastity belt." Noire giggled.

"You've got jokes, I see."

Jayna left, but not before sowing a seed of anxiety in Noire's mind about the three men with whom she had shared her own body in the past twelve months. Pierre had been good about using condoms except when she agreed to his request for sex *au naturel* as a thirty-eighth-birthday present of sorts. They had been together for nearly eight months at that point and—though she could hear Jayna's voice rattling off every safer sex campaign mantra she could remember while displaying her wide array of University Health Services condoms—Noire had barely hesitated to oblige his request after rationalizing that her birth control pills all but guaranteed that she wouldn't get pregnant.

Things had been different with Innocent. He had always made himself responsible for birth control, even before Noire was on the Pill and the heat of the moment had made her willing to throw caution to the wind. *But of course he did get his child's mother pregnant*, Noire thought with a grimace, and wondered if Innocent was only vigilant about protection with *her*. When they resumed their sexual relationship for a few months following September 11, Noire had found Innocent to be as responsible as ever, and she finished the last of the twelve pill packs she had taken with her to Haiti without refilling the prescription. And her recently resumed smoking habit further discouraged her from continuing to take the Pill. Her thinking was backward, she knew, but she rationalized that everyone was entitled to have a crutch for at least some part of their life, and right now, smoking was hers.

Cudjoe was another thing entirely. He was content never to broach the subject of birth control and only wore a condom when Noire had one protruding from between her lips. After her first late period three weeks into his stay, Noire got scared and dug out the diaphragm she had from college.

Noire had taken some unnecessary chances, though she would never admit it to Jayna or to anyone. It had been nearly a year and seven months since she had last visited a gyn and her own shame kept her from making an overdue appointment.

CHAPTER SIXTEEN

SMILE

Noire felt like she was having a baby in reverse. She drew in so many sharp breaths every time Dr. Sonria cranked the speculum open farther that she was sure she would soon be looking at her tonsils.

"Okay, Noire, now this will probably hurt some." Her gynecologist—a third-year resident at NYU Medical Center and one of a bevy of doctors milling around University Health Services looking a full five years younger than her—peeked her head above Noire's draped crotch just long enough to give the smile that her last name promised.

Because she had been holding her breath for five whole minutes—or so it seemed—Noire could not speak. She didn't want to imagine what could feel worse than this. And then it came. A blinding bolt of pain that felt like Dr. Sonria had clipped off the tiniest piece of her left pinky with a sharp pair of scissors. Shocked tears stood in her eyes, afraid to stream down. She yelped.

"Yeah, I know. I'm sorry." Her breath issued a warm puff of

air at the top of Noire's distended vagina. She came up again. "That's the part that hurts." The smile, still present, was more subdued.

Once her legs were released from the stirrups, Noire pulled herself into a fetal ball.

"We'll biopsy this and have results in a few days, a week tops. And we'll let you know. But you should know that I took the sample because I'm a bit concerned about the looks of your cervix. Also, your ovary has a cyst, but that's not serious." She pulled her gloves off and dropped them into the hazmat garbage can. "But we're catching everything early." She gave a perfunctory pat to Noire's paper-clad thigh.

"Aren't we supposed to talk . . . in your office?" Her words came out with great effort.

"Of course. If you want to. I'm happy to answer any questions you have." Her smile was bigger than the smileys that littered some people's e-mails. Noire hated it.

"But what do I have?"

"Didn't you say you wanted to talk in my office?"

"Please, just tell me."

"Well, we still have to run the lab work and do the biopsy, of course." She pointed to the slides recently swabbed with Noire's intimate fluids and the piece of her tissue that Dr. Sonria had just snatched out of her. "Your cervix looks a little suspect but it's probably nothing. All indications are that you have chlamydia—which is treatable—and your history suggests you caught it within the last few months to a year. Thankfully, you're here and we'll start treating you as of today. But if you had waited even a month longer, we may have been dealing with PID, pelvic inflammatory disease. And that can lead to infertility, among other things."

At that, Noire let her residual physical pain mix with her

emotional distress in the form of hot tears. "I'm so fucking stupid!" She thought about the many times the condom stayed in its wrapper even as she let Cudjoe inside of her and scolded herself between sniffles.

"You're not, Noire. Many women have chlamydia for months or sometimes years and don't know it. It often exhibits only mild symptoms and sometimes none at all. But you came and checked it out. You should alert your partner as well; he may also be infected."

"We're, um, not together anymore. It's been a couple of months already."

"Okay, well, you may still want to tell him or any other sex partners you've had within at least the last sixty days so if they have it they won't unwittingly pass it on to anyone else. And of course you need to abstain from sex for the duration of your treatment and for about four weeks afterward."

Noire nodded at the back of Dr. Sonria's head as she left her to get dressed. She was happy not to see her smile. There was nothing to smile about.

Noire sat on a bench in Washington Square Park, her back to the NYU Health Center, and pulled out a cigarette. She wished that it was raining, but the balmy April breezes and brilliant sunlight mocked her gloomy mood. She puffed violently, breathing in more tar and nicotine than even her habituated lungs could manage. She coughed just as violently, the hacking rattling her chest and rib cage and shaking her overstuffed minibackpack out of her lap and onto the ground. *I really must be an idiot,* Noire thought as she watched her new prescription for doxycycline roll farther away from her while she secured her burning cigarette in yellowed fingers and coughed sputum up into the back of her throat. Officially disgusted with herself, she threw the cigarette to the ground, crushed it underfoot, and retrieved the contents of her bag.

"Look, the lady littered." A child who looked to be a three-year-old doll baby pointed at Noire's left foot, which only partially covered the evidence of her exposed moral depravity.

"Oh, I'm picking it up now." Noire lifted the extinguished cigarette with the same two fingers that had protected it only moments before, and walked it over to the nearest trash can.

"Oh, miss, you didn't—" His expression was a mixture of apology and agreement.

"No, I did. I hate being a bad example." She gave a tight-lipped smile and sat back down.

Satisfied that the litter was now gone, the toddler smiled and waved at Noire. She smiled back. She was sure he was a boy, but his perfect baby 'fro and satiny milk chocolate complexion made him look like a doll come to life. Happy to have been forgiven, she waved and smiled in return. Turning her attention to the face of the apparent "daddy" several feet above that of the boy, Noire first sought to discern their shared features, and then realized that she had seen those features before.

Recognition overtook his face as well. He picked up the toddler and moved closer to her. "I'm sure I know you . . ."

She could see him searching for her name in his memory just as she latched onto his. "Dunbar! Right? I'm Noire."

"Of course, of course. I only had a momentary lapse on the name but immediate recognition of the burnished beauty."

Noire laughed aloud. He was true to her original encounter with him, on his first and last disastrous blind date with Jayna back in 1999. Their double date with her and Innocent had seemed like a safe and no-stress way for all to meet, but Jayna was thoroughly underwhelmed by his "loquacious poeticisms" as she later called them. Noire, however, had been more charitable in her assessment. And noting a bare ring finger, she realized him to be handsome as well. "You are still a poet."

"I'm a student of poetry, yes."

"And a father, it seems."

"Egypt's very proud godfather and uncle."

Noire nodded, glancing at his naked ring finger again. "But spoken for, I'm sure." She inquired just for the sake of it.

"Zero for two. I'm speaking for myself." He smiled easily.

She returned the smile. "I like his name."

"It's where he was conceived. My sister and brother-in-law's souvenir when we all went for a family vacation. They just had triplets two months ago."

"Wow!" She chuckled. "It must be great to have such an attentive uncle/godfather."

"I come in handy." He smiled again. That same easy smile.

Noire responded in kind, again. "Oh, so you did go to the Motherland after all." She referenced his broad understanding of Africa's boundaries that he had described as including the five boroughs of New York and anywhere that black people lived, as compared with his then very limited travel experience.

"That was my first trip to Africa. Egypt's dad is Somali, so he helped me to clear up some of my more fantastical notions."

"You did have a few, if I recall."

"Back in the day, yeah." He cleared his throat. "So, how about you? You were looking downright angry just a moment before. I didn't recognize you until you smiled at my nephew."

"I guess I was feeling pretty angry. But sometimes a child's unrehearsed smile is just what the doctor ordered." Egypt's smile was like Dunbar's.

"I feel that way every day."

"Yeah."

"Well, look, Noire, Egypt is about to turn into a pumpkin, so we've got to go. But it would be nice to talk more. Or to see you. Unless that would be uncomfortable or inappropriate."

"I think it could be both comfortable and appropriate to be seen by you, Dunbar!" She laughed again. "I suppose my contact info would facilitate that."

"It would, indeed." His pleasure was genuine.

"Then, here you go." Noire wrote on the back of the receipt for her final pack of cigarettes and put it in his hand.

"I remember you were a grad student here." He stuck his chin out at the NYU buildings that surrounded the park.

"Still am."

"I'm around here a lot myself, now."

"With your uncle's health food store?" Noire recalled the story he told Jayna about inheriting the store from his sick uncle.

"Oh, Uncle Africa's store?" He chuckled. "No, no. He's still alive, thank God, but we sold it to some cousins on my mom's side who decided to move up here from back home."

"Oh, where's home?" She tried to discern a southern accent or latent Caribbean ancestry.

"Philly." He produced a wide grin before continuing. "So anyway, I've been teaching for a couple of years and just finished my master's in middle-school special ed at Bank Street College last year. Now I'm kind of a 'principal-in-training' at a school on the Lower East Side. The ungentrified section." He gave her a knowing look.

Noire nodded her approval. She was duly impressed. "Well, all right then! Can't hate a black man for that."

"And with so many black boys tracked into special ed, some people could even love a black man for it."

Noire liked his style. A lot. "You know, some people really could."

"Hey, I'll contact you, Noire. And I'm not one of those

brothas who waits an excessive number of days before making contact so that you think they're not into you."

"That's good. Because I'm not one of those sistas who likes a man who sweats himself."

"I could tell."

Noire waved good-bye to Dunbar and Egypt and sat back down on the bench. But it felt different. Not because it had changed, because it hadn't. It was just her outlook that had changed. Egypt's admonition not to litter followed by his genuine smile and wave showed her something. She didn't have to remain burdened by her mistakes and judge herself because of them. Egypt let her know that she was okay with him, even if she had made a mistake.

Innocent was on a mission. He had a nonrefundable return ticket back to Côte d'Ivoire that gave him seven days to pack up his life in New York. All that stood between him and freedom was the closing on his loft on day two, shipping the few remaining items he thought he would keep and donating the rest on days three, four, and five, and selling his investment property to Noire on day six.

The short timeline had been intentional. He didn't want to be distracted by too many good-bye lunches with too many people who would spend the entire time trying to persuade him that he was making a mistake. He had made many mistakes before, but this decision was not one of them. In the nearly two months that he had been back, his professional and personal life had begun to fall into place. He had purchased a flat, which he had decorated and childproofed, in Koffi-Diabate's brand-new development in the Plateau neighborhood. And once he returned, he would assume partial custodial responsibility for Awura that would have her with him during the week while Chi-Chi started graduate school. The prospect both scared and delighted him, and though he knew that it would ultimately come as a relief to Chi-Chi, he had not expected her to agree as readily as she did. Technically, she didn't agree for several hours. But rather than spending that time making his case, he listened to her angst and to the professional and personal goals she had put on hold indefinitely when she found herself pregnant by Innocent and without the prospect of marriage with her former boyfriend.

She had been stuck. And Awura's prematurity and residual health issues compounded her guilt and frustration. She was sure she was a bad mother, certainly not the strong woman she had pretended she was. She was a fraud, and poor Awura suffered the brunt of her mother's insecurity and ineptitude.

Innocent protested her harsh assessment of herself until it became clear that she had to vent and didn't have a safe person in her mother, sister, or any of her friends who were long since married and raising more than one child. She felt like she didn't have the right to complain. And she really didn't want to. But she had to hear herself and she couldn't very well make Awura her sounding board. She didn't need one more burden resting upon her little shoulders.

So Innocent listened. So many of her arguments had been the same ones he made to himself.

❧

Noire watched her hair fall from her head in dark brown tufts with each snip of Rob's scissors. They were silent, he intent on his artistry and she reaffirming her resolve in her own head. With each snip she felt physically lighter, as if each strand of her hair had tethered her to too many regrets and too much pain. So, she was letting it go, returning it to the earth, or at least the floor of Renaissance Hairtopia.

"You have a great head for this look." Glen turned to size her up, but his hands remained active in his client's thicket of silky gray deadlocks. The lilt of his Trinidadian accent enhanced the compliment.

She produced a toothy grin.

"After everything that I've done for your hair, I wouldn't have even cut it for you, Noire, but your little smoking habit had ruined about four inches of growth." Rob tugged at several brittle hairs and let them break for effect.

"That hurt."

"It hurts me more than it hurts you." He gave her a look through the mirror that shamed her for her behavior.

"I was having a moment, Rob."

"Your 'moment' lasted five months."

"Yes, well, today I'm starting anew."

"It's your hair birthday." He snipped another clump and watched it fall.

It was. Noire had sported her free-form 'fro before it was the style and had worn it as a badge of black pride and a shield from the world of buppies who she assumed would consider her too left of center for their tastes and stay away. Her hair had become a weapon upon which she had grown overreliant. Not that her new brush cut would win over any new fans. But it wasn't about anyone other than herself. She needed a visual reminder that she was parting ways with her destructive thoughts and actions, including her "habit."

"I suggest you take a multivitamin, Noire. Your scalp is scaly."

"This really is a full-service salon!"

Rob spun her chair around to face him. "I'm serious, Noire."

"I know you are." She registered the caring behind his stern eyes and knew that Rob saw her as a younger sister more than just a client. "Thank you."

"I have too many clients whose hairdo is the only thing about them that's good. But I know you know better than that. And when you know better, you do better."

Noire nodded her head. There was nothing to say. She closed her eyes, signaling her surrender.

Rob snipped and snipped until only a small lumpy Afro remained. Then he oiled the clippers. "Okay, Noire, say good-bye."

She opened her eyes. "I already have."

Rob turned on the clippers and moved it in deliberate clockwise arcs that followed the direction of her hair growth. The hair that remained was too short to comb. She loved it. The nakedness. The slightest breeze awakened the nerves at each follicle. The hairs, free from their anchors, shimmied down her neck. "Mmmmm." She purred, enjoying the Noire that was emerging before her eyes.

Her hair gone, Rob turned off the clippers and stared. "You look hot, Noire. You should have no problem finding another man."

"This is not about a man!" She tensed her back.

"I know. Calm down." He laughed at her irritation. "I'm proud of you."

Noire let her body go slack and stared at this new picture of herself that she had never before seen. "It's really beautiful."

"It is." The pronouncement came in stereo: Rob, Glen, and the dreadlocked man still sitting in Glen's chair.

Noire looked at their serious faces and got nervous. Her eyes darted from Rob's wedding ring, to the naked fingers of Glen and the other man. She returned her gaze to Glen. "You *hate* it?!"

"Not at all. It's *very sexy*. Trust me." Glen had the manner of a government official delivering an edict.

His dreadlocked client, the group's elder, was more explanatory. "You look happy"—he smiled meaningfully—"and happiness is beautiful on a woman."

She smiled at the three of them, but mostly she smiled at herself. She *was* happy.

Noire's ears were cold. Her entire head was, without the natural insulation of her hair. She unwound her spring scarf from her head and neck and sat down in her living room. Then she got up and pushed her love seat into the middle of the floor. It seemed that everything needed a new place in the room; their old locations looked like the room of old Noire. She marched over to the windows and flung them open in an attempt to air out the smell of stagnant cigarette-tinged air that she hadn't noticed was hanging in every crevice of the room. The April air rushed in and made her head cold. Laughing, she grabbed her scarf and wound it back around her head, this time like a turban.

With her coat still buttoned up, she rearranged the room, her desk finding a new home right under the windows. And she stacked up every unread newspaper and discarded magazine that littered the floor. The exposed floorboards revealed candy wrappers, peach pits, and a few loose cigarettes. She pitched it all into the garbage and swept up errant strings, dust balls, and a forgotten sock of Cudjoe's. It all had to go. Noire made a pile of overdue library books by the door, tidied her own books on their respective shelves—each one dedicated to Spanish or Caribbean Creoles or novels or travel or erotica. Then she loaded all the refuse that she had collected into her shopping cart and wheeled it down to the trash cans in front of her building.

Now buoyant, she floated back upstairs, closed her windows, and lit some sage. The clean, sharp aroma of the white smoke displaced the stubborn smells of useless emotions and memories. The ritual was cleansing, almost spiritual, and Noire liked the feeling of humility it gave her. She was allowing herself to change, to be different, because she was accepting that not everything in her life had been good for her. She looked at the room, the furniture rearranged and the mess removed, and knew she hadn't done anything monumental. But her shift, though small, felt like a tiny piece of something very big.

❦

Noire walked into Dr. Branch's office and set her glasses down.

"No, please, put them back on."

She did.

"I'm not one of those therapists who tries to keep her patients indefinitely. My goal is your goal: to get to a place of greater clarity on your motivations, weaknesses, and childhood wounds. We've had ten sessions, and two with your mother. How do you think we've done?"

"Well, I— I don't know, Dr. Branch."

She nodded her head. "Do you remember how you looked on your birthday?"

"I guess."

She handed her a mirror. "Tell me what's different about what you see now."

Noire studied her reflection, her new hairdo set off by freshly waxed eyebrows, a shimmer of lipstick on her lips. "I'm better groomed."

"Okay, that's a good start. Now look at the next layer."

She scanned her face for pimples and only found one. "Less acne. Oh, and my skin kind of glows."

"Tell me about your eyes."

"They're—" She moved her eyebrows up and down. "They look happy."

"You're right. They do. Smile, Noire. What's going on there?"

"My teeth are whiter, cleaner." She admired them again. "I went to the dentist yesterday." She remembered Jayna's hookup of free after-hours teeth whitening to celebrate her new smoke-free mouth.

"What don't you see?"

"Tension, I guess."

"And less sarcasm, too, Noire. Your mouth says kinder things about yourself so you can be more generous in what you say about other people.

"Noire, during our sessions, you didn't have your glasses on. You couldn't see my face nor could you see your own. The only thing you could see was what was inside. But when you started to change what was going on in there, it changed your face. Do you see that?"

She did. And she was amazed. She finally looked like the woman she wanted others to believe she was. And she liked it.

"Noire, self-knowledge and self-actualization are continual processes because we are dynamic beings. We have to keep all aspects of that being limber or else we become stiff and sedentary. I encourage you to come back to me if you want to explore something new; changing life circumstances like a health or family challenge, serious relationship, or new professional consideration may require some focused work. But I want you to learn to do this work every day. Some people meditate or pray or do yoga in addition to their regular physical conditioning. I want you to find that thing that speaks to you and make it a daily practice. And every month, do a conscious check-in. Look at your face. If you are seeing things about it that you don't like, ask yourself why. I don't want you to get neurotic about little lines around your eyes or a few gray hairs; if you live a long life, you're sure to get plenty of both. But do look for sadness, and worry and hurt. And if you see it, make a plan to address it. You owe that to yourself."

"I'm speechless."

"No need to be, Noire. You've done very good work; you should be proud of yourself." She picked up an index card from her desk and handed it to Noire. "I like to give this to all my patients at their last session."

Feed your spirit and your body will always be full.

"I wish I could claim to be the author, but it's one of those anonymous sayings I came across when I was a stressed-out grad student. I think it does a nice job of helping us quiet all the noise in our brains."

"Mmm." Noire reread the phrase over and over before looking up at Dr. Branch. "Thank you . . . for 'feeding' me." Her face flushed in sincerity.

"Noire, you fed yourself."

Noire purchased two sheets of ochre linen paper, one sheet of her mother's favorite papyrus paper, one airmail and one regular envelope, and sufficient postage for each to arrive at their respective locations safely: Jamaica, Queens; and Port-au-Prince, Haiti. She stopped at the Better Bean and fished out enough change for a grande of the dark roast decaf and sat down on a shaggy red chair. The first letter, on the papyrus, would be an entreaty to renewed relationship, and the second would be an apology and her last and best good-bye. She wrote the shorter one first:

> Dear Mom,
> I love you and am so happy for you. It seemed important to say it "for the record" and minus my (former) therapist, so I figured that papyrus was the way to go!
> Mom, I want you to know that I recognize you to be a woman, a complex and beautiful black woman, whose concerns include me but don't stop with me,

and whose life extends beyond my own knowledge of you as my mother. And I love and respect *that* woman who has found lasting love with Dad. I realize that if we find a love that's redemptive—that's as humble as it is bold, and that supports us as our best selves living our best lives in partnership with another—then we have been blessed. And so, I can only be happy for you, for both you and Dad, for finding this in each other. And I'm happy for me, too, that you've chosen each other because I already love you both so much as my parents.

Mom, I'm so thankful that you have asked me to share in this special experience with you as your maid of honor *in addition to* being your daughter; it's a rare privilege. I don't know where my own journey in love will eventually lead, but I thank you for modeling redemptive love for me.

> I love you,
> Noire

The second was more nuanced:

Dear Pierre,

I write you with no expectation of a response. Indeed, I have not included a phone number or even the correct return address, so I can only hope that this reaches you in care of the newspaper. After all that transpired between us, and especially your generosity toward me during my auspicious return at the heels of 9/11, I realize that my actions may appear especially distancing. This is by design. It is also the way that I can be most generous in my thanks and my apology while also protecting my decision.

Pierre, you are a witty, sharp, interesting, and passionate man. I thoroughly enjoyed those aspects of your being during my time in Haiti. You are a big part of why I came to know the country as I did: to wrestle with its inconsistencies and my own place in the social strata as well as to love the pride, determination, and complexity of its people. Haiti is one of our most visceral connections to Africa, and I feel privileged to have lived there.

But there was more to who we were together, who I was with you, than the interesting repartee. There was our physical relationship. As you know, the sex that we shared was substantial and kept me awash in physical delight whenever I wished. It was also the reason I couldn't love you. I sought the sex we shared to fill the holes I let grow in my heart. But it was like plugging a leak with your finger; once it was removed, I was leaking again.

I think that you knew this, Pierre. You yourself mentioned that my tears were not because of you. And you were right. But somewhere in there, the sadness was okay with you, as long as my remedy for the pain was the same: sex with you. Understand that I don't blame you, Pierre; I can't. I'm responsible for making myself fit for a relationship and I hadn't put in the work. And now that I have, I understand why I wouldn't love you. It wasn't just my ambivalence about a long-distance relationship or even the prospect of uprooting myself from the home that I have always known. It was my own hunger, my own lack, and what we shared couldn't feed me. I had to learn to feed myself. And I'm learning.

Pierre, I hope that you find the love you seek with

a woman who expects more from you (and from herself) than I did, and that you won't let sex be a stand-
in for intimacy. Require that of yourself, and then
you'll be able to identify it in a woman.

With affection,

Noire

Noire finished her coffee and jogged the ten blocks to
Manhattan's main post office, the imposing edifice set adrift on
a sea of stairs. She took them two at a time.

∞

Félix Houphouët-Boigny International Airport's arrival terminal was bustling with activity. Six-month old Awura warmed the
center of her father's chest, secure in her place there and obliv-
ous to the sensory overload of her surroundings. Innocent
hoisted her diaper bag laden with formula, changing supplies,
an arsenal of ointments and salves, and two full changes of
clothes onto his left shoulder. Then he pushed his right hand
through the strap of his computer case, letting it hang from his
wrist. Wedging *Africa Week* magazine under his left arm, he
bought a cup of coffee and picked it up with his right. Then,
afraid he might spill it on his daughter if she were to fuss, he
threw it away. Struggling with her diaper bag again, he wondered
how a person so small could fill a bag to three times her weight.
Awura opened her mouth and arched her back in a full-body
yawn. She let out a few tentative whimpers before Innocent's re-
assuring hand on her back settled her down. He didn't have
enough hands to hold his cell phone as well so he stopped by a
plate-glass window near baggage claim and looked for Charlotte
while he called her.

"I can see you!" Charlotte's voice was pure jubilation.

"Well, where are you?"

"Just stay right there. We'll be there in a minute."

Innocent did as she suggested and waited.

"*Voilà!*" Charlotte approached them from behind and produced herself and two-and-a-half-year-old Bibi with a flourish.

They exchanged hugs. "Oh, Innocent. Look at how precious . . ." Charlotte marveled at her first niece whom she had not seen since she was in intensive care. "So tiny . . . but so perfect."

"Yeah." He nodded. "Even though she's six months, in terms of her development, she's like half that."

Her eyes moist with emotion, Charlotte hugged Innocent again. "I pray for her every day, Innocent."

Innocent's heart warmed. "I know you do. Thank you." Then he squatted down beside Bibi in her stroller, fresh from a nap. "*Salut.*" He whispered the greeting to his niece before introducing her to her first cousin.

Bibi stuck her arm out and touched Awura's head. "*Bébé!*"

"*Oui, c'est le bébé de l'oncle Innocent! Elle s'appelle Awura.*"

"Awura!" Bibi giggled her delight.

He kissed her forehead and stood up. "I'm surprised to see her." He nodded at Bibi.

"Michel and I are in counseling. A lot of bad things happened, but I think we're going to make it."

He wanted to ask more but figured that Bibi's ears didn't need to hear the rest. "Where's Dr. Olaji?" He looked around, recalling the features of the pediatric ophthalmologist from the small picture Charlotte had e-mailed him two weeks ago and trying to discern them in the faces of the men who walked about.

"In the men's room. He encouraged me to find you and said he would catch up in a minute." She smiled at her older brother. "Are you nervous?"

"Hopeful is more like it." He cradled Awura's head in his hand. "I'm just so anxious to help her." He offered a fleeting grin.

"Well, Fatima really raved about him. Her twin sons were born at twenty-nine weeks and Dr. Olaji has helped them a lot. He's helping to train several doctors at PISAM on some new techniques."

"This is just . . . *perfect* timing for us."

"Like I said, I've been praying for Awura every day."

∽

Noire pulled her mail out of the mailbox and a slim Amazon.com box fell at her feet. *Did I order something?* She picked it up and noticed that it had been opened and resealed and the original mailing address had been blacked out. *"What?"*

Jogging up the four flights of steps to her top-floor apartment was all she needed to heighten her curiosity. She ripped the box open and pulled out a CD. The cover was an orange piece of paper with a message:

> you, Kevin Webb, Ledisi, Tamar-kali, Lisala, M'Balia, Gordon Chambers, Nedelka, Duke, Angela Johnson, Fort Greene Collective, Marlon Saunders, Vernon Reid, Didá, Literati, Soulfège, and me

More confused, Noire opened the jewel case and found a continuation of the message.

> Brooklyn's own Blackstage Music Festival is *back* next Saturday, May 4th at 2 P.M. I'd be honored if you would reject your other suitors for that day and accompany me. If yes, please call me directly at 718–555–0410. If no, leave a message for my grand-

mother in Philly at 215–555-NOPE (her real number!)
and she'll be sure to give me the message.

—Dunbar

Noire laughed aloud, the fullest, loudest laugh she had uttered in a long time. It felt good. Great, actually. Reading the handmade label on the compilation CD he made with a song from each artist slated to perform at Blackstage, she nodded her head vigorously. "Creative. I'll give him that!" Her body buoyant with glee, she bounced over to her CD player to pop it in, but not before grabbing the phone and dialing the 718 number.

∞

Innocent held Awura still on the examining table as Dr. Olaji examined her eyes.

"Monsieur Pokou, as you know, Awura has stage three retinopathy of prematurity. That means she has significant abnormal blood vessel growth in both eyes. Because she was born prematurely, the blood vessels did not have an opportunity to grow along the surface of the retina and instead are growing toward the center of the eye. In addition, she has something called 'plus disease' which means that the blood vessels of the retina have become enlarged and twisted. This indicates that the disease has worsened a bit."

Innocent felt like an elephant was standing on his chest.

"But it also makes her a good candidate for treatment. Treating her at this point would greatly decrease the likelihood of retinal detachment. That would be stage four."

"What does treatment entail?"

"We have two very effective proven treatments for ROP: laser therapy or cryotherapy. Laser therapy literally 'burns away' the periphery of the retina, which has no normal blood vessels. And with cryotherapy, we use an instrument that generates freezing temperatures to briefly touch spots on the surface of the eye that overlie the periphery of the retina. Both laser treatment and cryotherapy destroy the peripheral areas of the retina, slowing or reversing the abnormal growth of blood vessels.

"As you may have imagined, these procedures do destroy some side vision. But this is done to save the most important part of our sight—the sharp, central vision we need for 'straight ahead' activities such as reading, sewing, and driving."

He studied Innocent's face to make sure he was still with him before continuing. "Because of the severity of the disease, and the existence of 'plus disease,' it makes it a good decision for her." He touched Innocent's elbow. "But it's your decision, Monsieur Pokou. Both are invasive surgeries and we haven't done this for long enough to know all of the long-term side effects of each. What I can tell you is that I've done both procedures thousands of times, and many have truly benefited. I can give you a list of parents whose babies had stage three and stage four ROP. Most did go ahead and have the procedure but a few did not. They can tell you about their own experiences with it and how their children are doing now."

Innocent swallowed as if to push the information into his brain. "It's a lot to take in."

"I know, Monsieur Pokou. I've been a pediatric ophthalmologist for eleven years and every case is different. But knowledge is power, and you've done the right thing to be aggressive in seeking it out. I will also give you a pamphlet and list of websites about the disease and its prognosis.

"You have a beautiful little daughter, and with you as a father, I know she's in good hands."

Innocent left the doctor's office in awe of his responsibility. This decision, as big as it was, was only one of many decisions he would be entrusted to make on behalf of a person who couldn't make any for herself. He had always known that, but now he *felt* it. Now that he had this little bundle strapped to his chest, he knew that life—his life and hers—was bigger than anything he could fathom. And it had only just begun.

∞

CHAPTER SEVENTEEN

SAY "YES"

Noire studied his face, concentrating on all the things she never looked at before—the nose that pointed slightly left, the shadow under his cheekbones—and made her peace with the fact that she still loved him, even the things she hadn't allowed herself to see. She watched hands a bit rougher than she remembered them grip his mug full of lukewarm green tea. "Why wasn't it me? I need to hear you say it."

His eyes drew together in a momentary frown, but for the first time there was no stiffness in his jaw. Things really had changed. He sat his mug down. "I could ask you the same thing, Noire."

"But you didn't, Innocent. I asked you."

He nodded his head. She had asked him a question that he didn't know the answer to until recently. He had convinced himself that their lives were not aligned enough for their relationship to last, but the hurt of their breakup had never allowed him to ask—even in the relative safety of his own mind—why *she* had rejected *him*. "It wasn't because I stopped loving you. I never stopped." He cleared his throat. "Even now."

Noire met the hint of his smile with her own.

"You know, most relationships end. They do. Even if there's love. Because although you need love for a relationship to work, not every love relationship was built for the long haul. But for me, it wasn't so much about you—your readiness or willingness. It was about me, Noire. I wasn't grounded enough to receive a permanent relationship. Without knowing it, I was drifting. Home was this big point of contention for me. I didn't really know where home was. But Awura"—his grin filled his face— "she helped me to learn something about myself. I am supposed to be in Côte d'Ivoire. At least at this point in my life. And I'm *supposed* to be Awura's father. And if love visits me again, I think I'll be able to nurture it. Because I love the man I'm trying to be, now." He felt the emotion of his words well up in his eyes and threaten to trickle onto his face. He smiled.

Noire closed her eyes and saw the inside of her thoughts. "Thank you. For saying that." She moved her face closer to his. "So many times I have second-guessed myself. And with good reason. Because I've often been wrong. I've often made decisions out of fear, or in order to preempt the punch below the belt that I felt was coming. During our entire relationship, Innocent, I was always afraid you would hurt me."

"Was I that threatening?"

"Your secrecy was frightening."

"I didn't think I was keeping secrets from you."

"It's the same stuff you kept from yourself, Innocent. The way you kept your emotions wrapped so tight."

He nodded in agreement.

"And I didn't trust myself to, like, to choose someone I could really grow with. Growing is scary. I didn't want to be found out, you know."

"Found out?"

"Yeah." Noire wasn't sure exactly what that meant but she knew what it felt like. It made her feel like a fraud. Because, in some areas at least, she wasn't nearly as evolved as she wanted to believe she was. But she was learning that that was okay. And she was trying. She looked at the time. "Innocent, it's getting late—"

"Which is why I want to get to the main reason why I wanted to meet with you." He laughed at her quizzical expression and pulled out some papers from his attaché on the seat beside him. "You know that I'm a businessman at heart, so I have a business proposition for you. It's an offer I'm sure you can't refuse."

"Innocent, what's going on?" She peered over at the papers and tried to read the headings upside down.

He covered them with his hand. "Just listen. And then look." His smile was unreserved. "You know that I sold my loft on Monday."

"Oh, so that went well?"

"Very well. Real estate in New York City is quite the investment and I cashed out at the right time. I sold it to a film production company for more than I ever would have gotten normally. Seven figures. Almost eight."

Noire's mouth fell into an O the size of a grapefruit.

"Yeah. It's a blessing." He smiled. "Well, I'm going to have a hell of a time dealing with the tax ramifications of that deal, so I figured I wouldn't further complicate things with trying to break the bank on the other condo I own."

"I didn't know you had another condo."

"I bought it from Lydia's great-aunt in an estate sale years ago. You remember, she's Marcus's wife?"

"How could I forget! She's the best thing about Marcus."

"Agreed. Well, I took it off her hands for very little money, but now I'd like to sell it to you."

"Innocent?" She was perplexed. "Why don't you just . . . rent it out? I'm sure you'd make a killing."

"I'm not trying to make a killing or be a landlord from five thousand miles away."

She furrowed her brow even more. "Look, cheap for you isn't cheap for me. I don't have any money to buy any property."

"You don't even know the price or where it is or anything."

"I don't need to. I've managed to keep that five-thousand-dollar investment that you helped my parents to set up for me, and since then I've saved all of one cent more."

"And that's the price!"

"What's the price?" She was incredulous.

"Five thousand dollars and one cent."

"Innocent, this is bananas. Please, don't do this."

"I'm not going to keep it, Noire. And I'd rather sell it to someone who I know would really get something out of it than to your neighborhood's newest influx of real estate flippers who would buy it, paint it and put in a new sink, and sell it within the year for double. I mean, of course you'll do with it what you want, but I really think you'd like it."

"My neighborhood? Where is this thing?" Noire could barely believe their conversation. The last thing she thought she'd be able to do is purchase property. But Innocent had created a possibility.

"It's on St. James Place between DeKalb and Willoughby. It's a real two-bedroom with a little nook that could be your study. And it's a duplex."

"Okay, stop it, Innocent. You could get *at least* a half million for that."

"And then give all of that money to the U.S. government. I bought it for pennies, Noire, really. So please stop counting it out. My loft had been a blessing to me and I want this apartment to be a blessing to you. Let me help to facilitate it."

"I don't know what to say."

"Say yes and then sign this offer letter. My lawyer will be in touch with you about the rest. Oh, and the common charges are four hundred dollars a month."

That was a third of her monthly rent. When her landlord sought to renew her lease, he raised it from eight hundred twenty-five dollars to a whopping twelve hundred. She signed a month-to-month lease instead of an annual one because she knew she'd never be able to afford it. And now four hundred dollars a month! She'd actually be able to start to build that rainy-day fund her father kept talking about and replace the money from her investment within three years. "Oh my God! Yes, Innocent! *Yes!*"

Noire popped out of her seat and hugged Innocent with all her might. She knew she didn't deserve this, but she was thankful nonetheless.

Innocent reached his arms around her body. He felt her energy flowing into him and thanked God that he had been able to love her, however imperfectly. She wasn't his future, but she'd always be a treasured part of his past. And it was beautiful.

∞

Noire held her mother's bouquet. She winked at Jabari, who fidgeted at their father's side as he held the wedding rings. He blushed, his twelve-year-old self-consciousness triggered at the least provocation. Noire chuckled to herself. She was happy. The early evening of that May day was filled with the promise of spring and the hope of her own parents' wedding.

She looked out and met the glassy eyes of Cassandra Bromfield. She had translated Mom's life into a wedding dress that was a visual representation of her history: Noire's baby booty sewn into the hem that grazed her ankles, the first love poem Paul had ever written her embroidered on the front apron, a hodgepodge of Big Mama's handmade buttons running down the back. Noire grinned her thanks—for Cassandra's sensitivity and for her mother's own life experience that had led her to this place today.

She turned her attention to her father. Paul gleamed like new money, from the silver strands of his curly hair to the gold threads that ran through his heavily brocaded Nigerian-style agbada. His teeth—whitened for the occasion—stayed on permanent display as he smiled his love to Flora and his eyes gleamed with both pride and humility.

"Dearest," Flora began, "few of us can claim to have witnessed their intended grow up as an adult, but indeed, I have. And you can say the same of me. We have been with each other through Afros and pregnant bellies, and more recently, graying hair and once again, rounded bellies. We have been lovers and we have not, but through it all, we have been friends. There is something to be said about a lifetime of friendship.

"We also became parents, to our darling baby girl, Noire, thirty-one years ago. I thank you for believing in me as a mother and always being a father even during those times when it was hard to be anything else. One thing I can say about you is that you've always been committed." She squeezed Paul's hand before reaching over and placing her hand atop Jabari's head. "And I'm thankful to have you, too. Thank you for being a brother to Noire, a son to Paul, and most important, a loving and resilient spirit who is blessing this world."

Jabari's cheeks flushed crimson and his eyes clamped shut in his biggest display of embarrassment Noire had ever witnessed.

"Today, I become your wife, Paul. Today, we take our relationship to a higher place in our life's journey. I make this commitment to you with love and with the knowledge that we will grow not just older, but wiser, happier, and better people, *together*."

"And Flora"—Paul smiled only at her, his eyes glistening with the essence of his heart—"I am so full of a lifetime of love, and awe, and respect for you. Thank you for loving me, being patient with me, forgiving me, and always knowing—as I now do, too—that beauty can grow out of difficulty, that the blessings are bigger than the pain, and that forgiveness is real. You are an amazing woman. Today I am your husband. I take your hand in marriage to continue this thirty-two-year walk as your lover, your advocate, your partner in parenting, and your friend. Thank you for being you and for sharing yourself with me."

Noire blotted happy tears from her eyes. Her parents were finally married. She thought of her childhood fantasy of having the proverbial normal family and knew that this was better than anything that her child's imagination could have dreamt up. They had come to each other in their own time and on their own terms.

Innocent washed strained carrots out of his crisp button-down before the stain set in. Freshly fed, Awura was a collage of carrots, yam, and mango. She wore her first twenty-three months of life with pride in a body that looked several months younger than its age but was no less vibrant. It was at these moments, when it was just Innocent and his daughter in their flat and the workday was yet to begin, when he could appreciate the miracle of her life begun nearly two years ago.

The stain persisted. Innocent sighed, took the shirt off, and contemplated a ready replacement before the baby nurse arrived in a few minutes. Now free of the constraints of business attire, Innocent took the opportunity to have one last moment with Awura.

"You see what you made Papa do!" He kissed the plump hands that had caused the wayward carrots to land on his shirt instead of in her mouth.

Awura squealed with delight, happy to have another opportunity to be in her father's arms, no matter the reason. Her smiling eyes magnified by miniature eyeglasses held to her head by a headband, she looked like a baby genius. Innocent often thought she was, her wizened demeanor seemingly aware that her legendary name connected her to an extraordinary ancestry even as she looked forward to a future that Innocent could not imagine.

With Chi-Chi in graduate school, Innocent had become Awura's primary custodial parent, and he approached his role with reverence and gratitude. Chi-Chi seemed as relieved as Innocent. She loved Awura, but oftentimes she was frustrated where Innocent would be patient. But she came to realize it was not Awura who burdened her. And when Innocent had proposed on Awura's first birthday, Chi-Chi demurred. She realized that she didn't want to marry him now, or maybe ever; doing so would have had her acting out of fear and others' expectations.

During Awura's first few months, Innocent had come to realize that he did love Chi-Chi. She had given Awura life, had braved the hardship of public ridicule and private hurt. He understood why she had been prepared to lie and claim her ex-boyfriend as Awura's father: saving face felt like her only option in an upwardly mobile Abidjan that had already passed over her as marriageable in favor of younger women considered more beautiful and less opinionated.

He had long since forgiven her for her shortcomings and he finally allowed himself to be forgiven for his as well. So when she rejected his proposal, he accepted it graciously, knowing that they would always be partners in loving their daughter. Awura's life made sense and that's all that seemed important.

The phone clattered into Innocent's thoughts. He picked up on the first ring.

"*Bonjour.*" Chi-Chi's voice was sluggish.

"*Ça va?*"

"Sorry I missed your call yesterday. Things got a little hectic; I was late handing in a paper and my professor wouldn't budge. How's my Bibi doing? I hope she doesn't think I've forgotten her."

"She would never think that."

"I got her a T-shirt from the university."

Innocent chuckled. "She'll follow in her maman's footsteps."

Chi-Chi returned the laughter. "It's probably big for her."

"I'm sure she'll wear it with pride!"

"How is she?"

"Wonderful, as far as I can tell. I can't believe how strong her eyes are getting."

"Yeah, those exercises seem to be helping her."

"It seems." Innocent shifted in the chair and listened to Chi-Chi's breathing on the other end. "School's good?"

"Ask me after I get this paper back." She cleared her throat. Innocent waited for her to say something else.

"So, Awura's feeling well? I mean, this morning."

"She's looking dandy. But let me let her tell you herself."

"Okay, great."

He held the phone to his daughter's ear and watched her face light up at the sounds on the other end. Her conversation was equally animated, if a little less intelligible. But looking at her joy, at her unqualified belief that she was enough just as she was, gave Innocent hope. He had given his whole heart and, finally, that was enough.